THE
DISAPPEARING DOCTOR

JACQUELINE BEARD

Vinci Books

vinci-books.com

Published by Vinci Books Ltd in 2024

1

Copyright © Jacqueline Beard 2023

The author has asserted their moral right to be identified as the author of this work in accordance with the Copyright, Designs and Patents Act 1988. This work is a work of fiction. Names, characters, places and incidents are the product of the author's imagination or are used fictitiously. Any resemblance to actual persons, living or dead, places and incidents is entirely coincidental.
All rights reserved. No part of this publication may be copied, reproduced, distributed, stored in any retrieval system, or transmitted in any form or by any means, including photocopying, recording, or other electronic or mechanical methods, nor used as a source for any form of machine learning including AI datasets, without the prior written permission of the publisher.
The publisher and the author have made every effort to obtain permissions for any third party material used in this book and to comply with copyright law. Any queries in this respect should be brought to the attention of the publisher and any omissions will be corrected in future editions.
A CIP catalogue record for this book is available from the British Library.
Paperback ISBN: 9781036701420

Printed and bound in Great Britain by Clays Ltd, Elcograf S.p.A.

By Jacqueline Beard

The Lawrence Harpham Murder Mysteries

The Fressingfield Witch
The Ripper Deception
The Scole Confession
The Felsham Affair
The Moving Stone
The Maleficent Maid
The Disappearing Doctor
The Camden Killer
Shadow Over Malvern

The Denman & Tallis Cotswold Crime Thrillers

The Girl in Flat Three
You'll Never Escape Me

The Constance Maxwell Dreamwalker Mysteries

The Cornish Widow
The Croydon Enigma
The Poisoned Partridge
The Cheltenham Torso

Dedicated to my loyal readers, without whom Lawrence and Violet would have ceased their adventures a long time ago.

Prologue

Richmond Park, April 1903

Trooper Frederick Smith, 1st Dragoon Guards

"I'm scared. Is there no other way?"

"No, Frederick." I hear a low whisper coming through the trees, fierce, insistent, yet curiously beguiling.

"I can't do it."

"You must, or ruin will surely follow."

"But Emma will understand."

"Undoubtedly, but would you humiliate your fiancée with your shame?"

"No. Of course not. Perhaps someone will offer a loan."

"You've tried that already, and the money did not materialise. And then there's the small matter of the medal."

My cheeks burn with shame as I recall a moment of madness, a rash act I cannot justify. In my mind's eye, I see Bernie's medal and signet ring gleaming on a blanket at the foot of his bed, there for the taking. He often left them unattended while performing his ablutions. And why wouldn't he? After all, he had no reason to distrust me. But instead of walking by as on so many other occasions, I reached out, and my hand closed over Bernie's hard-earned South Africa medal. Without a second thought, I scooped his pilfered possessions into my trouser pocket, where they stayed. And later, when he discovered the theft, I did not return them – even though I knew I would never pawn them as I'd initially intended. Some latent sense of honour still remained.

"I'm afraid."

"Don't be. Your problems will be over in a second. You won't feel a thing."

"But Emma will grieve my loss."

"Perhaps, for a while. But you will free her from the scandal that will surely follow. You can save her and give her a better life. Sacrifice yours for the greater good."

"I know, I know. But…"

My voice trails away as I contemplate Emma's visage, her deep brown eyes red with unshed tears, the look of hurt and disappointment on her face as the organ plays inside the church, and her bridegroom fails to appear.

My throat tightens. The words build in my head, but I can't get them out. Instead, I heave a stifled sob and brush my hand across my face to find it wet with tears.

"Be brave, soldier." The disembodied voice trembles with compassion, each word carefully chosen. Yes. I am a soldier, and bravery comes with the territory. I must harness every ounce of courage to commit to this terrible choice between love and honour.

"Shake my hand," I beg, appealing to the stranger. I have never cast eyes upon him, but I crave one more human touch before I go to my fate.

"You know I cannot."

"But how can it matter when we will never meet again?"

"Rules are rules. I have others to help, and the authorities do not understand. Would you have me let people down?"

"I would not. I am not a selfish man."

"I know. You are honourable and will do your duty as you must."

"Then say goodbye to Emma for me."

"That must come from you. Leave a note if you are so inclined."

"You promise it won't hurt."

"No more than a bullet on the battlefield."

"Then I will meet my maker now."

"Godspeed, Frederick. And know that you are doing the right thing."

My heart thumps as I replace my cap and make a move. The trees rustle behind me on the edge of Richmond Park, and I feel the whisperer's eyes boring into my back as I traverse the cemetery, passing the crosses, one of which will soon bear my name. I wonder if he is following me. I feel sure I am not entirely alone. But my musings stop when I reach the station, walking like an automaton to my fate. A woman passes, then a man, both nodding amiably. The gentleman doffs his hat in deference to my uniform. I return his smile, but it does not reach my eyes. My mind is too busy fighting visions of Emma waiting alone at the church, seeing my broken body, and then grieving at my graveside.

"Ticket, please."

I attempt to pass through the barrier, and a ruddy-faced conductor holds his hand aloft.

"I'm waiting for a friend," I say, my voice breaking under the strain of behaving normally. He does not notice.

"On you go," he says, waving me through.

I make my way towards the left luggage office, buying a few more minutes before heading to my final destination. I think of Emma and remember her excited chatter when we returned from the dress fitting barely an hour earlier. Emma was in high spirits, her dress ready and needing only a slight adjustment before tomorrow's ceremony. I had left her with my sister Flo, talking excitedly about flower girls and tomorrow's wedding breakfast. She waved me off, expecting me to go to the barracks to collect my helmet and sword in time for the ceremony and thence to Cannon Street station.

I had lied to Emma, saying I was taking delivery of a parcel at left luggage, but it wasn't true. And I never intended to return to the barracks in this lifetime. There was no need. I would never wear a full uniform again. Visiting Cannon Street would be fruitless for I had collected my parcel earlier that day, expecting to see a crisp five-pound note in the pocket of the jacket my friend had borrowed and returned. But he had let me down. His promised loan had not materialised, and the jacket had no monetary value. I was up to my ears in debt, owning nothing save the clothes on my back and a medal I could not bring myself to pawn.

I loiter by left luggage, considering the prospect of breaking into a locker to find cash or valuables to sell. But on checking my pockets I soon realise that I lack a tool to ease the lock open. A couple of futile tugs at the doors lead to nothing but disappointment. It is time to meet my destiny. I can leave it no longer.

My legs wobble as I walk onto the platform and turn sharp left. A conductor eyes me suspiciously as I cautiously proceed and sit on the farthest bench as his eyes bore into me. I pretend to drop my handkerchief and reach to pick it up, then linger, head bowed, until he moves into the waiting room on the other side.

I stride to the end of the station and jump off the platform into the rough, following the track for about half a mile until I know I am safely away from prying eyes. I pluck blades of grass and daisies as I wait, watching dusk settle over the sky. A raindrop trickles down my face, then another, as the April shower gently falls like tears from above. I want to cry too, but I don't, now that I am quietly resigned to what must be, and no longer saddened or afraid. An oncoming train whistles in the distance as wheels thunder farther down the track. I empty my pockets and place a white handkerchief on the floor, topped with a key ring, a medal, and a single halfpenny. Shuffling towards the line, I kneel, resting my head on the cold metal while clasping my hands to the side of my face in silent prayer. As the train draws closer, I think of my mother, dear Emma, and my comrades at the barracks. Discordant sounds echo around me, heavy vibrations, the piercing shriek of a whistle, a billow of warm steam, and then peaceful oblivion.

Chapter One

A TENUOUS CLUE

June 1904

"What in God's name is that?" Lawrence jumped back, startled, knocking his chair to the floor, and liberally spreading flecks of ink over his desk as his fountain pen ricocheted against a wooden tray.

"It looks like a frog, dear," said Violet, peering into Lawrence's top drawer.

"I know what it is, but what in the blazes is it doing there? Now, let me guess. Another one of Daisy's little tricks."

"Probably," said Violet. "She has a rather active imagination."

"She's a little minx and old enough to know better. I have a good mind to send her to school in London. It's done young Sidney the power of good."

"You're overlooking something."

"What?"

"The Merchant Taylor's school is for boys."

"Something similar, then."

"Absolutely not. Daisy's behaviour is perfectly normal for her age. She's learning her place in the world."

"Well, that shouldn't involve secreting amphibians in my desk."

"I'll have a word with her later."

"Make sure you do."

Violet placed her pen on the desk and stared pointedly towards Lawrence, her heavy brows set in a frown. "You could try discussing it yourself. She's your daughter too."

"I know, I know. Sorry. I'm preoccupied. Let's not argue over Daisy."

"Are you going to tell me what's wrong?"

"It's this thing with Michael."

"Don't feel bad. You've done everything possible to find Aurora. We both have."

"I know, but I'm in a quandary. Have you heard from Michael?"

"Of course not. He's on retreat, as you very well know. He won't contact us until he's completed his term."

"How much longer will that be?"

"At least a month, and then there's the travelling time."

"Why couldn't he find somewhere local?"

"I don't know. It's none of our business."

"But the Scottish Islands, Violet. He couldn't have gone much farther away."

"Don't take it personally. Michael is broken-hearted and needs a change of environment. And I don't blame him. Fate has not been kind to him with Aurora's disappearance and Francis' betrayal."

"Yes, well. But unfortunately, it leaves me with a problem."

"Which is?" Violet picked up her pen again, half-listening as she began adding columns of numbers.

"This," said Lawrence, brandishing a letter.

"What about it?"

"In short, it's a note from the assistant housekeeper to Aurora's former employer."

"Really?" Violet raised an eyebrow, giving Lawrence her full attention.

"Yes. But it's undoubtedly another false lead, and I don't know whether to bother."

"Tell me all about it."

"You remember the palaver with Frank Podmore at The Society for Psychical Research Headquarters?"

"Of course. He kept avoiding you and was always out when you called."

"Quite. So, I didn't get to ask him about The Sacred Order of The Crescent Moon."

"I know. Although I don't understand why you didn't speak to one of the other parapsychologists."

"I never got inside the place. I'm clearly *persona non grata.*"

"Perhaps I should try."

Lawrence pursed his lips and silently walked towards the window before leaning over the sill.

"Perhaps I could have tried harder, but I gave it up as a bad job and went to Knightsbridge to find Aurora's ex-employer instead. She was equally unhelpful."

"I remember. You made no significant progress."

Lawrence spun around and glared at Violet, examining her face for signs of gloating, and seeing none. "It wasn't entirely fruitless," he protested.

"But the lady of the house wasn't available."

"She was but chose not to see me, sending a message

through her housekeeper instead. Mrs, whatever her name was, seemed a little more obliging."

"Montgomery," said Violet.

"How do you know?"

"Because I pay attention, and it was only last year."

"I'd find it in my notebook if I cared to check. But that's by the by. The point is that Mrs Montgomery wanted to help but couldn't. Other than stating what we already knew, she had nothing further to add."

"Remind me what she told you?"

"I thought you already knew."

Violet sighed at his sarcasm. "What's wrong, Lawrence? You're in a horrible mood."

"Sorry. I don't mean to take it out on you." Lawrence walked behind Violet and kissed the top of her head.

"Mrs Montgomery said Aurora was a nice girl with a pathological loathing of cats."

"I'm sure she didn't."

"What?"

"Use those words. You're paraphrasing, Lawrence. What exactly did Mrs Montgomery say?"

"I can't remember precisely, but she told me that Aurora once saw a cat in the garden and locked herself inside until it went away. 'Mortally afraid' is an expression that comes to mind."

"Interesting. Just as Martha Brame remembered, I wonder why?"

"It's irrelevant, and I don't care. But Mrs Montgomery promised to contact me if anything turned up, and it has."

"What has?"

"Aurora's address book. She mentions it in the letter if you care to look."

Violet took the missive from Lawrence and hastily read.

"I see. But you sound unenthusiastic. Don't you think it's worthwhile?"

"I doubt it," said Lawrence. "And I don't want to offer Michael false hope after all he's suffered."

"Can't you ask Mrs Montgomery to post the book?"

"This letter is from Miss Farmer, the assistant housekeeper, presumably written on Mrs Montgomery's behalf. Regardless, there's little point in asking when she's already insisted we collect it."

"Well, there's no choice then. You must go to London, and the sooner, the better."

"It could be an enormous waste of time."

"What if you're wrong, and something in the book leads you to Aurora?"

"It's a long shot."

"I don't know about you, but I'd never forgive myself. Imagine what Michael would say."

Lawrence mulled the matter over for a moment. "Fine. Then why not come with me?"

"Come with you?"

"That's what I said. We could make a week of it – perhaps see Ann and young Sidney."

"He's not so young. Sidney's fourteen now."

"Impossible."

"I can assure you he is. Ann sent him back to school last month with a tuck box to share with the other boys to celebrate his birthday."

"How do you know?"

"Because he wrote and told me. I mentioned it at the time, Lawrence. Weren't you listening?"

Lawrence sighed. "Apparently not. I didn't realise you corresponded with Sidney."

"Well, I do. He's a nice boy, and I still remember our

time together fondly."

"I should have given you a son, Violet. You looked after Sidney very well."

Violet smiled, her plain face taking on an inner beauty at Lawrence's appreciation. "Don't be silly. I'm more than grateful for Daisy. And having Sidney in my life is a bonus. He's a dear nephew, and I adore him."

"A dear nephew you might want to visit?"

"Well, of course, if not for Daisy. But she's doing so well at school that I can hardly take her away."

"I understand. What a pity that Michael is so distant from us. Daisy would jump at the chance to spend a week with her favourite uncle."

"Yes. It's a shame. Michael would have enjoyed looking after her, and I would appreciate a trip to London. It's been ages since we set off on an adventure together."

"I'm not sure I'd call it an adventure, but it would have been nice to have company. A train ticket for one then, I suppose."

"When will you go?"

Lawrence glanced at the calendar. "Friday suits me best," he said. "I can pop in and see Ann over the weekend."

"If she's at home," said Violet.

"Where else would she be?"

"Working."

"Ann? Working? "She doesn't need an occupation. She can't be short of funds now that she's married to old Brocklehurst."

"She's doing it because she can," said Violet. "And Sir Mark isn't too stuffy and set in his ways that he'd try to stop her. Besides, it's not paid work. Ann is a volunteer."

"Doing what?"

"Visiting the frail and infirm at her local hospital."

Lawrence shuddered. "Ann has a stronger constitution than I do. The older I get, the less tolerant I am of medical establishments."

"Hardly surprising, given the time you've spent in them, Lawrence. I understand how you feel. But Ann is keen to give back in any way she can now that she's happy and free from her awful first husband."

"I'm sure her dedication is admirable, but rather her than me. I ought to look out Ann's address now that she's moved."

"Here. Have this." Violet reached into her handbag and retrieved a battered hard-backed notebook. "You'll find it somewhere in there. Take it with you."

"Thank you. We'd better press on if I must waste the end of the week in London."

Lawrence reached for a sheaf of papers and started reading them while Violet lowered her head and tallied numbers again. They continued in silence until the shrill sound of the newly installed telephone interrupted their progress. Lawrence lifted the receiver. "Bury five three?"

A few seconds passed. "Yes, operator. I will."

Silence fell again.

"Who is it?" asked Violet.

"I don't know. I've just agreed to take a call from an unidentified potential client, but it's taking an age to connect. What? Sorry? You heard that. Yes, I know it's not your fault. I don't believe... Fine, put her through."

Lawrence rolled his eyes as he spoke, and Violet watched, her lips curling with amusement.

"Hello. Can I help? Yes, we do. From where are you calling? Cheltenham. Yes, I know it. But I don't see how we can help from the other side of the country."

Lawrence put his hand over the mouthpiece and whispered, "Honestly, some people. She wants me to follow her husband. Not my favourite task at the best of times, but what a silly thing to ask from a distance. Fortunately, I can't be in two places at once."

"Be nice," whispered Violet as Lawrence returned to the call.

"Yes, I'm still here. But I can't visit Cheltenham until next month, assuming my workload allows it at all. No. It's not about the money. I need to be elsewhere."

Lawrence impatiently gestured as Violet looked on with affection, wondering why her husband was so easily frustrated. "Where am I going? London, actually. Your husband's in London! I thought you said he was in Cheltenham. Oh, you live in Cheltenham, but he's gone to the metropolis. Well, yes. I will be there on Friday, but I'm working on another case. Sorry, I can't do both. No, I don't know who you are; frankly, it doesn't matter. I only take cases that interest me nowadays."

Violet stopped what she was doing and glared at Lawrence, mouthing, "Too much. Too rude. We don't want to get a bad name."

"No, I don't recognise your voice," snapped Lawrence, now losing patience rapidly. "What do you mean I ought to? Are you royalty? No, I do not mean that sarcastically. It's a genuine question. Why are you laughing at me? Loveday? Loveday Melcham? Good Lord. I don't know what to say."

A burn of embarrassment coloured his cheeks as Lawrence held his hand over the mouthpiece once again. He stood, mouth open, staring at Violet like a floundering trout on the riverbank.

"It's Loveday," he said unnecessarily.

"Would you like me to speak to her?" Violet's voice was haughty and unusually cold.

"I don't know. What do you think?"

"Do you want to track her husband?"

"Of course not. Tom Melcham is one of my oldest friends. I can't imagine why she's asked me to do it."

"Perhaps it's her indirect way of telling you she's available."

"Really, Violet. That's a little far-fetched."

"You handle it, dear. I have work to do."

Lawrence cleared his throat. "Sorry, Mrs Melcham. The doorbell rang."

Violet raised her eyes heavenward and pursed her lips in faux concentration.

"I don't think using your married name is unnecessarily formal. I'm running a business, after all. Yes, I'm sure you mean well, but you must understand that I cannot and will not act against your husband's interests. It's not on. No, not even for you. I mean, not for anyone. A man must stick with his friends. Tom… disloyal? I didn't consider his marriage to you an act of disloyalty to me. Why would I? Anyway, it's ancient history. Regardless, the answer is no. Let's say no more about it. Goodbye, Mrs Melcham. No, I won't hold on. Nor will I change my mind. Goodbye."

Lawrence placed the handset firmly on the cradle. "Insufferable woman," he said.

"So, all is not running smoothly in the Melcham household?"

"Apparently not."

"What has happened?"

"I don't know. We didn't get that far, and we're not going to either. As if I would do such a thing to Tom."

"Do you think she will go elsewhere?"

"I hope so. But Loveday isn't well acquainted with the

word no. She has a distinct aversion to not getting her own way."

"Poor Tom. Do you think he's doing something he shouldn't?"

"No. It will be some silly idea in Loveday's head. Tom is an honourable man."

"You have a short memory, Lawrence. You were still engaged to Loveday when she threw you over for Tom, and I didn't hear of any reluctance on his part."

"Loveday's termination of our engagement suited me very well."

"But Tom didn't know that did he?"

"It's water under the bridge."

"Be that as it may, it shows a flawed character on his part. Colonel Melcham is not as straightforward as you think."

"I'm still not spying on him."

"Good. Neither should you. But don't put him on a pedestal, either."

"It sounds like you think Loveday's behaviour is reasonable."

"Not at all," said Violet, her voice rising in surprise. "I neither like nor trust the woman. And I wouldn't employ someone to follow you if I thought you were up to no good. There's no point in marriage if you can't trust each other."

"I'm glad to hear it," said Lawrence, mellowing. "I dread to think what she's hoping to achieve."

"You should have asked for more information, even if only for our entertainment." Violet's eyes sparkled wickedly.

Lawrence grinned. "You never stop surprising me. Now, back to work, woman. We have much to do."

Violet picked up her pencil and nibbled the end, gazing ahead deep in thought. "I know," she said suddenly.

"Know what?"

"Pass me the telephone."

Lawrence obliged.

"Operator. Swaffham one seven. Yes, I'll wait."

"What are you doing?" asked Lawrence.

"Shhh!," Violet raised her finger to her lips. "Thank you. Elsie, is that you? Yes, it's me, Violet. How clever of you to recognise me. Very well, dear. And you? I will visit, I promise. Yes, she is quite grown up now, and mature beyond her years. Of course, I'll bring her to see you. Now, is Norma there, by any chance? In her last letter, she said she was doing a few hours a week in the café. Wonderful. Might I have a word?"

Lawrence slipped into a reverie while sifting through the latest case notes on his desk. He'd already taken a cursory look but still hoped to find clues to the whereabouts of John Abbott, a butcher who had recently absconded from the parish with the ironmonger's nineteen-year-old daughter. Rumours of their whereabouts abounded, and with Tyler Goodrum, father of the absentee girl, ready to pay good money for her return, it was a lucrative case that Violet was keen to resolve. Lawrence circled a paragraph in a letter received in the previous day's post, suggesting they had taken a rental property in Framlingham and jotted it down on his list of things to do.

"Well, that's Daisy sorted," said Violet, beaming as she replaced the handset.

"Good. How?"

"Didn't you hear?"

"No. I was working. What have you arranged?"

"Norma Baker is coming to Bury to look after Daisy. I can join you, after all."

"Wonderful. Daisy will enjoy spending time with Norma. Shall I get Saunders to make up the guest room?"

"I'll do it. Norma can't get down until Saturday. I'll settle her in and join you as early as possible on Sunday morning."

"Capital," said Lawrence. "Now, how about a nice cup of tea?"

"Yes, please."

Lawrence strode towards the kitchen and returned moments later with a face like thunder. "What's that jelly-like substance in the sink?"

"Ah, that must be where Daisy put the frog spawn."

Lawrence sighed deeply. "Dear God. A trip to London can't come soon enough."

Chapter Two

BACK TO BATTERSEA

Saturday, June 11, 1904

As a man of means, Lawrence could have stayed in any of London's exclusive hotels but elected instead to return to the familiarity of the hotel in Battersea Park he had used while investigating the rat cake murders. He'd never enjoyed working away from home, but London without Violet was a lonely place, and he couldn't face trying a new establishment, however luxurious it may be. Lawrence checked into the Park Hotel, making his way to the reception desk as if he'd only left the previous week instead of many years before. The staff were all new but no less welcoming, and Lawrence unpacked and made his way to the smoking room for a quick cup of coffee before setting off for Lowndes Gardens.

The journey to London had been quick and trouble-free, and Lawrence was in reasonable spirits and ready to make the best of his time in the capital. Though his previous efforts to find Aurora had failed, he hoped to do more this time. He'd spent the train journey mulling over his prospects of success, battling fears of another wasted effort. But Violet had been right, Michael deserved any chance they had at their disposal to find his lost love, and acceptance of this notion had instilled fresh enthusiasm in Lawrence.

After enjoying a pleasant stroll through Battersea Park, Lawrence passed through Belgravia admiring the architecture before arriving in Lowndes Square, where he soon located the tall townhouse in which Aurora formerly worked. Ignoring the red-painted front door and polished knocker, he unlatched the iron-railed gate and descended to the basement level, tapping on the plain door of the tradesman's entrance, where a smartly dressed young man greeted him. On asking for Mrs Montgomery, Lawrence found himself on the receiving end of a blank stare. He tried again, this time producing the letter signed by Miss Farmer, and the young man nodded in recognition. "Enter," he said, beckoning Lawrence inside.

Moments later, an auburn-haired woman wearing a grey-striped housecoat strode down the corridor and greeted him with an outstretched hand.

"Eleanor Farmer," she said.

Lawrence returned the handshake, surprised at her firm grip and confident approach towards a man she might have deemed to have a superior social standing.

"I received your letter," said Lawrence.

"Good. Mrs Montgomery asked me to write to you when she was in better health. I am only sorry it has taken so long."

"Long? I've only just received your letter."

"Naturally. I only wrote it a few days ago. But I would

have sent it months earlier had events not overtaken this household."

"Events?"

"Would you care to step across the road, Mr Harpham? The gardens are pleasant at this time of year, and I'd rather not discuss our business in front of the staff." Eleanor Farmer looked pointedly down the corridor, where the young man leaned nonchalantly against a wall as if he weren't straining to hear her every word.

"Of course."

"Wait a moment." Eleanor disappeared into a side room and emerged moments later with a canvas bag slung over her shoulder.

Lawrence followed as Eleanor opened the door and led the way into the gardens before selecting a bench to sit on. He joined her, and she wasted no time explaining why she'd left the house. "Sorry. Too much interest from an idle young man who should be hard at work but finds every way to avoid it. This household has been at sixes and sevens for years now. I can't get the staff. Those who are useful don't stay, and those who remain are lazy, disloyal or both."

"It's the same everywhere," said Lawrence, his thoughts turning to Cynthia, the cleaner they'd employed for a few months and let go after several avoidable accidents. Cynthia had always been clumsy and lacking attention to detail, but her decision to place an empty kettle on a hot stove was the final straw. It had exploded, shooting molten metal across the back room, and igniting the curtain, which went up in flames. Fortunately, Lawrence had been hard at work in the other room, but with a pathological adversity to fire, could not contain his temper and sacked her on the spot. They had managed without a cleaner ever since.

"We haven't had a full complement of staff since Miss Sutherland left. And that was two years ago."

"Aurora? Did you know her?"

"A little. But she was a quiet girl. There wasn't much to know if you take my drift."

"I came here last year to find her."

"I know. Mrs Montgomery told me."

"Is Mrs Montgomery here?"

Eleanor Farmer bowed her head and gathered her thoughts. "In a manner of speaking."

"I don't understand."

"She suffered a stroke just after Easter. Mrs Montgomery is a shell of her former self."

"I'm sorry to hear that."

"Thank you. Fortunately, our employer is kinder than her tart demeanour belies. She has given Mrs Montgomery room, board and medical assistance here in the house. But her condition has declined, and she is in failing health. While Mrs Montgomery lives, I am her deputy and defer to her judgement."

"Can she speak?"

"Not now. But I have worked under her for many years, and I know how she likes the household managed, even if I wouldn't always choose that way myself."

"Commendable," said Lawrence.

Eleanor smiled weakly and reached for the canvas bag. She put it on her lap and rummaged inside before producing a small blue address book. "We cleared the servants' storage room just after Christmas and found this. It belongs to Miss Sutherland."

Lawrence took the fragile journal and opened the cover to reveal a handwritten inscription bearing Aurora's name. He turned several more pages to see occasional patchy entries. "She didn't know many people," he said, his heart sinking at the sparse information.

"So it would appear. Miss Sutherland was a solitary girl, from what I remember. She didn't go out much at all."

"Was Aurora here for long?"

"No. A year perhaps. She'd been employed elsewhere before coming to us."

"Aurora was an orphan. Did you know?"

Eleanor nodded. "So I heard."

Lawrence examined the tiny notebook with its scant entries. "Oh well," he said disappointedly.

"I'm sorry if it's not what you were hoping for."

"Don't be. It's not your fault."

"I would have posted it under any other circumstance."

"You've had your hands full with household matters and ill health."

"Oh no. That wasn't the reason I asked you to collect it. I would happily have sent the notebook to you, but I couldn't chance losing this."

Eleanor withdrew a small, scarlet, heart-shaped box from the bag and passed it to Lawrence. He stared at it, puzzled.

"Don't take this the wrong way, but even now, I'm in two minds about passing this on. If I could think of another reasonable choice, I would take it. But Miss Sutherland has no family and friends that I know of. You probably think I should write to the addresses in her book, but the entries are impersonal. There are no obvious relatives, aunts or uncles, and no mention of friends or contacts from a previous household. Only tradesmen and merchants. I tried phoning an entry in Miss Sutherland's book that appeared personal, but the operator put me through to a grocer's store in Putney. The box could have gone to someone unsuitable if

I'd continued contacting all and sundry without due care, so I stopped. But Mrs Montgomery gave me your card before she became too ill. I trust your profession and consider it honest. You are the best person to take custody of this potentially valuable item under the circumstances."

"What item?" asked Lawrence.

Eleanor said nothing, waiting patiently for Lawrence to open the box and find out for himself.

Lawrence eased the lid from the box, his damaged left hand trembling as he flexed his fingers and pushed aside a layer of tissue paper. A sparkling ruby-red brooch fashioned into a crescent moon lay inside. Picking it up gingerly, Lawrence held it aloft. "Are they real jewels?" he asked.

"I don't know."

"They look like the genuine article, but Aurora was practically penniless when we knew her. She could have sold this and lived comfortably."

"Quite. And that is the reason I didn't want to risk letting it go to a stranger."

"I wonder where it came from?"

"Look underneath."

Setting the brooch on his knee, Lawrence removed the tissue paper to find a velvet display insert with a tiny silk ribbon embroidered on the side. He lifted it, and the top came away, revealing a miniature card on the bottom. Carefully inked, in regular calligraphy strokes, was a message. "To Aurora, loveliest of the scarlet women. Your Felix."

Chapter Three

THE ORDER OF THE CRESCENT MOON

"I don't know what to make of it." Lawrence sat in the small room at Brown's Hotel in Albemarle Road, hoping that the helpful receptionist hadn't realised he wasn't a guest. London was light on public telephones, and having installed two devices, one at his home and the other in his office, Lawrence was becoming unwisely dependent upon the service. He'd used the telephone at Brown's once before, and as it was merely a twenty-minute stroll away from Belgravia, he thought it worth trying to gain access again. The receptionist hadn't questioned him, not even to check his room number. But his relaxed reclined posture and confidently crossed legs didn't make up for the furtive dart of his eyes whenever he heard a noise in the corridor.

"What does the brooch look like?" asked Violet across the crackly line.

"A small crescent moon."

"Then it matches the facts we already know. Aurora has connections to this order yet she's terrified of Netherwood's hidden room."

"And who is Felix? Have you ever heard this name before?"

"I don't know. It sounds vaguely familiar…"

"Are you still there?" Violet's words had tailed away at the other end of the call. Lawrence moved the handset away from his ear and peered anxiously at the mouthpiece as if Violet might suddenly appear.

"Yes, sorry. I was trying to remember. Perhaps it will come to me."

"Is Norma with you yet?"

"No. She must be running late."

"But you'll come to the hotel tomorrow?"

"I hope so."

"Hope so? I need you here. And something else, Violet. I've run into a snag with the room."

"What's the problem?"

"They've misunderstood my request and given me a single room. And I can't change it until another double comes available, which might not be for a few days."

"That's the trouble with small establishments. Especially at this time of year."

"We could change hotels when you arrive."

"Only if they haven't found space for me. Did they offer a second room?"

"Yes. But it's on another floor."

"Don't worry about that. I grew accustomed to separate rooms a long time ago. And I won't miss your snoring."

"Then you'll come quickly?"

"I'll catch the train as soon as I can. Don't worry. I'm looking forward to a few days in London with you."

"Excellent. Now, what should I do about finding Aurora?"

"Visit the order, I suppose. Do you know where they meet?"

"Yes. There's an entry in Aurora's book with the initials C & M next to an address in Blythe Road. It's probably shorthand for Crescent Moon."

"Good, but, Lawrence, do be careful. I worry about these organisations and their strange beliefs. Aurora was terrified the last time we saw her. There must be a reason for it."

"I know. I've considered approaching them at their offices and simply asking outright whether they know her, but I must be more subtle. So, I'll head over to Blythe Road now and try a different approach. It's a fair distance, and I can plan while on the move. See you at the hotel tomorrow and give my love to Daisy."

"I will. Take care."

Lawrence rang off and returned to the hotel foyer, raising his hand, and cheerily waving to the receptionist. Waylaying the uniformed porter, Lawrence asked for the quickest route to Blythe Road, thanked him and waited while the porter hailed a cab. Lawrence barely noticed the changing scenery as he considered a suitable plan and was still contemplating his best course of action when the cab stopped outside a magnificent red brick building with a white stone dressing. He paid the driver and stood for a moment, marvelling at the architecture before him. An engraved stone sign announced that the building contained the Headquarters of The Post Office Savings Bank, yet it seemed strangely empty, ghost-like and abandoned. Lawrence retrieved Aurora's address book and double-checked the entry, noting his destination as number thirty-six, then looked behind to find he was standing directly outside it.

The unprepossessing red brick building lacked the grandeur of the Post Office opposite, standing tired and unkempt with a shabby narrow door and arched window light near a lopsided tile bearing the number thirty-six. Lawrence watched a flake of paint beneath the door knocker float to the ground and contemplated the situation. He had hoped to find the building open to the public with a well-used reception area like the Headquarters of the Psychical Research Society. But the unwelcoming exterior of 36 Blythe Road implied secrets and a well-guarded existence away from outsiders' prying eyes. Discouraged, Lawrence pondered his next move.

Four long glass panes stood side by side in the window frame next to the door, all blocked with wooden shutters. Though the place appeared deserted, he couldn't be sure and ignored the temptation to duck down the nearby alleyway and break in from the rear. Such an action would be foolhardy and risk the wrath of the order. The only sensible course of action to discover more was by legitimate entry. Lawrence took the initiative, hammering on the door once, twice, then a final time, hoping that someone would hear him. He was on the verge of giving up and walking away when the door finally creaked open. A tall, high-cheeked man with dark hair silvering at the edges peered through the doorway.

"Can I help you?" he asked guardedly.

Lawrence mentally searched through the openings he had rehearsed and picked the most obscure. "I'm here about Felix," he said.

The man stood silently, eyes wide, while the colour drained from his face. Wiping the corner of his mouth with a trembling hand, he finally spoke.

"Has he sent you?"

Lawrence studied the man's demeanour, noting the tremor in his voice and a tiny tic beneath his pale blue eyes. This man was frightened, his face creased in fear and uncertainty, and Lawrence knew he must proceed carefully.

"No."

"Then what do you know of Felix Crossley?"

"Little. But I mean to know more. Can you help?"

"No."

"Is Crossley a member of your order?"

"Not now. Nor will he cross this threshold again."

"But he was?"

"Felix Crossley and his link to the order is not a matter for further discussion, and I suggest you stay away from him."

"Why?"

"Because he's disloyal and dangerous. Now go. I'm a busy man."

Lawrence acted quickly as the door swung closed, shoving his foot in the gap.

"How dare you?"

"Sorry, but I don't know what else to do. What will it take for you to tell me what I need to know?"

"Nothing, if Crossley is the subject of your visit. This society exists to further the study of occult matters. You are not welcome here unless you are interested in esoteric philosophy."

"I am interested. Crossley is merely a distraction."

"So you say. But are you truly intent on learning more about us?" The man's voice dripped with sarcasm.

"Very much so. Frank Podmore and others at the SPR can vouch for me." Even as Lawrence spoke, he knew he was on dangerous ground. Frank Podmore had once lived among men who had plotted his demise and was no friend to Lawrence. And though the danger from the SPR had long passed, they certainly wouldn't support his application if asked.

"Podmore, you say."

"Yes."

"His organisation is sceptical of ours. Don't make the mistake of thinking that a shared interest in esoteric matters implies cooperation."

"I don't. I am merely demonstrating my credentials, such as they are. And I briefly studied under Roslyn D'Onston." Lawrence was desperate now, blurting out names of people he would rather forget in his bid to convince the man standing sentry at the door of his regard for paranormal research. D'Onston's name hit the mark.

"Did you now? D'Onston attained the first order, but he is no longer part of our organisation."

"Then perhaps it's time to replace him?"

"We are strong in number, with members enlisted from every class of society. What makes you so special?"

"You could ask that of anyone. What are you looking for?"

"A strong interest in our aims, of course. And a willingness to study hard. Most of our initiates come to us through word of mouth."

"Then invite me."

"You are persistent. I will give you that. What is your name?"

"Alistair Blatworthy." Lawrence hadn't considered using his nom de plume up to now, but it emerged from his mouth unbidden.

The man sighed and offered his hand. "We'll soon find out if you are sincere. I'm Gregory Carmichael. Come inside."

"Welcome to the Nuit-Isis temple. I will show you around and if you are still interested, return in three days, and you may observe an initiate's meeting."

"Thank you," said Lawrence. "I will."

Carmichael opened a heavily painted white door to the left of the hallway leading to a darkened room. He pulled a gas mantle chain, and the room slowly brightened, revealing symbols Lawrence had last seen in the secret room at Netherwood. Several heavily bound books leaned against an altar at the far end, with a painted red crescent moon adorning the opposite wall.

"Impressive," said Lawrence, searching for something to say.

"Isn't it? Nuit-Isis is our most magnificent temple."

"Are there others?"

"Many. Follow me, and I'll show you our great and glorious history."

Carmichael left the room and proceeded upstairs, the creaking treads adding to Lawrence's discomfort. The building was unnaturally silent. They could be the only two people inside, and as determined as Lawrence had been to gain access, he had no reason to trust Carmichael. Visions of his last visit to the Society for Psychical Research stole into his mind, bringing unwelcome memories of his horrific discovery, hidden secrets, and a danger he hadn't seen coming. His heart raced in an adrenaline surge as he tried to ignore it, but fear infiltrated his thoughts as he recalled his brush with death, followed by a long spell in the hospital. Lawrence shuddered and finally dismissed the recollections.

They passed an open door on the left, and Lawrence regarded a large room with two solid desks that looked for all the world like a gentleman's study. His heartbeat slowed at the normality of it, and he followed Carmichael through the door ahead with less anxiety. It opened to reveal a sizeable wood-panelled room containing bookcases, cabinets of paraphernalia, and framed photographs over the wall.

"You wanted to know the location of our temples," said Carmichael. "Take a look."

He pointed to a large, penned illustration of a map of the United Kingdom and northern Europe, hand-coloured in inks with various symbols drawn around the outside.

"Here they are," he continued, pointing a slender finger towards Paris, Bristol, the Isle of Mull, Edinburgh, and London. "Five temples, five thriving repositories for our order. Not to mention three temples farther afield, including one in Mexico City."

"Can I attend any temple?"

"Slow down," said Carmichael coldly. "I have only invited you to observe a meeting. Don't take further accession for granted. You must study hard to become an Adept and we may yet find you unsuitable. But assuming you reach the first order, then yes. You may worship anywhere."

"What's that?" asked Lawrence, his sharp eyes drawn to a small crescent moon inked in the centre of the part of the map marked East Anglia. His eyes flitted over the drawing. Bold, red-inked crescents marked the more significant temples, but closer examination revealed half a dozen smaller un-coloured variations.

"Ah, an interesting question. Those symbols mark meeting places; lesser temples if you like. Some of our members cannot access the higher facilities if they live far away. I disapprove, as it happens." Carmichael pointed to a symbol close to the Scottish Highlands. "This, for example, was a designated meeting place, but we banished the owner from our order. We'd remove the others if it were up to me."

"What about this one?" Lawrence pointed to the Suffolk marker.

"What about it?"

"It's clearly in Suffolk, but the map is vague. Where is it?"

"Bury St Edmunds. And it's fallen out of use."

"Why?"

Carmichael's eyes narrowed. "Too many questions, Mr Blatworthy."

"Sorry. May I look around?"

"Indeed. That's why I brought you up here."

Lawrence moved through the room, picking up books here and there and asking carefully considered questions about the order as Carmichael followed like a shadow. He had almost circumnavigated the room, heading back towards the doorway, when Carmichael coughed and pointed to a photograph on the wall.

"You wanted to know about Crossley," he said. "And this is all I will tell you. Much as it aggrieves me, the other leaders insist on retaining our history, however unpalatable. Things have not always run smoothly here, and I will say no more on the subject except this. The man on the right-hand side of that picture is Felix Crossley."

Lawrence followed Carmichael's gaze to a photograph of three men standing below foreign skies. Having learned the art of photography some years before, Lawrence appreciated the sun-drenched lands even through the limitation of black and white prints.

"Where is it?" he asked.

"Mexico."

"Really." Lawrence stared, mesmerised by the young

man in the scene standing with his leg on a trunk, chest puffed out and wearing a curiously shaped pendant around his neck. Confident, arrogant eyes stared back at him in an intimidating gaze. But the photograph was unsettling, with a curious familiarity not immediately apparent. Lawrence recognised the man at the far end as Frank Podmore, but the face in between, with a visage just visible below a white fedora, was as familiar as his own once he realised to whom it belonged. The man in the middle was none other than his best man and former friend, Francis Farrow.

Chapter Four

PONSONBY & CREAM - PRIVATE INVESTIGATORS

Lawrence made his excuses and quickly left the Headquarters of the Crescent Moon after seeing the photograph. It was early afternoon, and his stomach growled, but he was too preoccupied with thoughts of old enemies to find somewhere to eat. He couldn't dislodge the image of Francis standing next to Felix Crossley under a blazing Mexican sun and needed to talk to someone who might understand the sick feeling of betrayal it had invoked. He could return to Brown's Hotel and phone Violet again. But she was involved too, and he would rather broach the subject in person. Ann Farrow, now Brocklehurst, would be sympathetic, and he would visit her the next day once he'd had time to come to terms with what he'd seen. But for now, Lawrence needed someone rational with no personal involvement and could think of no one more suitable for the task than Isabel Smith.

Lawrence hailed a cab and instructed the driver to head for the Municipal Building in Spring Gardens, then spent the rest of the journey strumming his fingers on the window as if that would make the travel time quicker. Speed was of the essence. Isabel might be out, and the sooner he got there, the more time he had to find her or wait for her return, whichever was the case. Travelling alone by cab made him nervous at the best of times, and he'd never forgotten his ordeal at the hands of Isabel's former departmental driver and his rat obsession. But that had been a long time ago, and Lawrence couldn't regret the experience despite the bad memories, without which he would never have met Isabel. Even as Lawrence travelled, he squirmed at his neglect of their friendship, not having taken the time or trouble to write and inform her of his impending visit to London. But Isabel would rise above the slight and welcome him, even though he didn't deserve it.

The cab stopped, and Lawrence alighted, paying the driver a larger tip than usual for not being a psychopathic murderer. Then, marching briskly towards the building, he went inside, following the familiar warren of corridors until he reached Isabel's department at children's services, where he approached the receptionist.

"Is Miss Smith in her office?" he asked.

"Yes. But she's not taking appointments today."

"She'll see me."

The girl looked doubtful.

"She will. Here's my card. Please deliver it to her office."

"Very well. Wait here."

The blonde-haired girl teetered up the corridor in hopelessly high heels, grasping Lawrence's card in her hands. She returned moments later, without it but sporting a cheery smile.

"Miss Smith will be delighted to see you."

Lawrence was unprepared for the wave of relief that followed.

"I'll show you to her office," the girl said.

"Don't trouble yourself. I'll find it. But thank you." Lawrence strode briskly to Isabel's room, knocking twice on the door.

"Come in, Lawrence." Isabel's familiar voice boomed through the door. She stood as he entered, took a step forward, and embraced him. He hugged her back in a rare display of affection.

"Thank goodness you're here," he said.

"Oh dear. Is everything all right?"

"Not really. May I sit?"

"Of course. Forgive me. I should have offered. Would you like a hot drink?"

"Yes, please."

Isabel approached the wall and rang a bell. Moments later, the receptionist appeared in the office. "Two teas, Miss Bright. Oh, and I'm expecting visitors shortly. Give me ten minutes with Mr Harpham and then show them in."

"Yes, ma'am."

Isabel waited for the girl to leave. "Now, tell me what's wrong, Lawrence. I can see from your face that you are not yourself."

"It's Francis," he said.

"Really? Has he returned?"

"No. He's in Mexico, as far as I know."

"Didn't I tell you that? I heard it from Frank Podmore."

"Probably. But I didn't know he was keeping company with Felix Crossley."

"Crossley?" Isabel's eyes widened. "Are you sure?"

"Certain."

"Well, you know more about it than I do."

"Are you acquainted with Crossley?"

"Only by reputation."

"Tell me everything you've heard."

"I will. But why are you so concerned?"

"He appears to have connections to Aurora."

"Are you sure?"

Lawrence removed the heart-shaped box from his pocket and passed it to Isabel.

She opened the lid and peered inside."

"Look underneath," said Lawrence.

Isabel frowned. "Oh dear," she said, peering at the card before turning it over and noting the blank reverse. "The name Felix is uncommon but not unique. It may not belong to Crossley."

"I'm afraid it does. Look at the shape of the brooch. And I've just come from the headquarters of The Order of The Crescent Moon, which is where I saw Francis in a photograph, standing between Frank Podmore and Felix Crossley."

"Too many coincidences for doubt," murmured Isabel as she returned the brooch to the box and passed it to Lawrence.

A rap on the door preceded the entry of the blonde-haired woman bearing a tea tray, which she placed on the desk.

"Thank you. That's all. I'll be mother," said Isabel as the door closed. She poured the tea and dropped a sugar cube into Lawrence's cup. "Help yourself to biscuits."

"So, Crossley. What do you know about him?" Lawrence sipped the hot tea and then balanced the cup on the saucer.

"He's only young, not yet thirty, I believe, but has already gained a sinister reputation. Felix Crossley is selfish, self-interested, and a law unto himself. And I mean that literally. Crossley lives his life by his personal doctrine – *Tuum est ius facere quod vis, quoties id facere vis*.

"Meaning?"

"Roughly translated; it is your right to do whatever you wish whenever you choose to do it. Crossley is unconventional and unwilling to follow the law, though more than happy to indulge in his own peculiar rules, of which there are many. I have heard him called the wickedest man in London. Fortunately, he has since moved to Scotland."

"How do you know so much about him?"

"He has come to my notice recently."

"Professionally?"

Isabel nodded. "I can't tell you too much; suffice it to say that when a man publicly boasts about his carnal activities and offends decency with his attacks on the church, the authorities inevitably take a closer look at his home life."

"Is he married?"

"Oh, yes."

"And if you're involved, he must have children?"

"Not yet. But Crossley's wife is with child and nearing full term. I couldn't tell you this were it not already a matter of public record. But Crossley has no sense of propriety and parades his wife and mistresses like trophies. We knew Ramona Crossley was pregnant almost as soon as she did from Crossley's writings in the Pall Mall Gazette."

"Who employed your services?"

"I can't tell you."

"Can you say why? Or what they feared?"

Isabel steepled her hands and sighed. "This may sound far-fetched to a sensible man like you, Lawrence. But Crossley has devoted himself to the dark side of the occult – questionable rituals, black magic and the like. He advocates the practice of blood sacrifice."

"For goodness' sake." Lawrence snorted, unable to contain his scepticism, but Isabel gently shook her head.

"As I said, it's irrational, but if a man truly believes in these things, then what lengths might he be prepared to go to prove them?"

"I hardly know how to respond. What could you do about it, anyway?"

"Very little. But while they lived in London, we closely observed Ramona. Crossley keeps mistresses and openly flaunts them in her presence. She pretends not to care, but it isn't true. And we know this because she has spoken of it to others. Felix Crossley cares nothing for anyone but himself, and fortunately, it is no longer my problem."

"Why? Is it because he moved away from London?"

"Precisely. He's now under the watchful eye of my equivalent in Edinburgh."

"That's a pity. Aurora is missing, and we know she's acquainted with Crossley."

"Then you must find her as soon as you can."

"How?"

"I'll telephone my Scottish counterpart. He may know if she is in the Crossley household. But I warn you, Lawrence. Don't be disappointed if you find she's there willingly."

"Why would she be?" Lawrence stifled a surge of anger at Isabel's implication.

"Because of the card in the jewellery box. Scarlet woman is a term of endearment Felix Crossley uses for his mistresses."

"Not Aurora? Surely. She was a frightened, broken soul. I can hardly believe it of her."

"Perhaps she broke away from his influence, but the gift from Crossley implies she was close to him at one time."

"I hope it isn't so. Michael will be heartbroken."

"Then don't tell him. Nothing is certain until you find Aurora. I presume you intend to keep looking?"

"I must. Fortunately, I secured an invitation to the next meeting of The Order of the Crescent Moon in a few days. They know Crossley, and if I speak to the right person, I may learn more about Aurora and her current location."

"Then be careful. And make sure Crossley doesn't come to hear of it. He still has connections within the organisation."

"I'm glad I sought you out, Isabel," said Lawrence. "It's always good to see old friends, but you've been a mine of information, and I can't thank you enough."

"It's my pleasure," said Isabel, stopping mid-breath as someone knocked on the door. "Ah," she continued." My next appointed visitors have arrived."

"Then I'll take my leave."

"Not yet. We spoke earlier of old friends, and I'm sure you would enjoy reacquainting yourself with these two.

"Come in," she shouted.

The door opened, and two women appeared.

"Well, I never," said the tall trouser-clad woman, reaching out her hand.

Lawrence stood and clasped it, grinning broadly. "Miss Ponsonby and Miss Cream. How delightful to see you again."

"Mr Harpham, you look so well." Coralie Cream gazed at Lawrence from under heavily mascara-coated eyelashes as if he were the most fascinating human being on earth.

Ignoring the uncomfortable flush creeping across his cheeks, Lawrence momentarily turned his head away as he offered her his seat.

"Why thank you," said Coralie, tucking her handbag

beneath the chair and patting her blonde curls. She arranged long, shapely legs to their maximum effect, and Lawrence tore his gaze away towards his host and fiddled with his collar.

Isabel Smith raised an eyebrow.

"Perhaps you would like to bring in a couple of chairs from outside," she said.

"Of course." Lawrence bolted from the room, relieved to be away from Coralie Cream. They had only met twice, but each time his body had reacted erratically to her presence with random hot flushes and an untameable heartbeat. Worse still, she knew the effect she had on men and had watched Lawrence sympathetically as he squirmed beneath her gaze, hoping that the physical manifestations of his arousal wouldn't get any worse.

Lawrence leaned against the wall, dug deep into his pockets for a handkerchief and wiped his sweating brow, inwardly thanking fate that Violet hadn't been there to witness his loss of control. He wondered what she would think and felt a jolt of disloyalty at his body's evident desire for Coralie Cream, which had nothing to do with rationality and reason. He waited for a moment until he was sure that his face had returned to its usual colour, then picked up a pair of chairs and backed into the room.

"Thank you," said Isabel.

Lawrence arranged the chairs around her desk and sat at one while Vera Ponsonby took the other, crossing her legs at the ankles in a mirror image of Lawrence.

"I was telling the ladies that you are in town for a few days," said Isabel.

"I am," muttered Lawrence. "And Violet will join me shortly."

"Jolly good," said Vera. "I would love to meet her. Perhaps you can bring her to our office."

"Here?"

"No. Not here," smiled Coralie.

"They've opened an establishment of their own." Isabel spoke with pride and a hint of sadness. "It was only ever a matter of time. My two best ladies have outgrown me."

"Have you started a rival typing pool?" asked Lawrence.

Vera snorted. "Nothing of the kind. We've taken a leaf out of your book."

"You're private detectives?"

"Exactly. You really must stop by and see us. We've rented premises near The Embankment, and it's going awfully well, thanks mostly to Miss Smith's recommendations."

Isabel laughed. "You really must stop calling me that. It's been six months since you last worked for me. Fortunately, Vera and Coralie still help when needed. So, as much as I miss them, things could be worse."

"Are you here on a case?" Lawrence let loose his curiosity, knowing they might not answer him if their current job required discretion.

Vera hesitated.

"It's fine," said Isabel. "I'd trust Lawrence with my life. You can talk freely in front of him."

Coralie licked her lips and reached into her handbag for a notebook, never losing eye contact with Lawrence. She flipped open the journal, smiled, and finally released her gaze.

"Subject lives with her husband and children in a rented house in East Sheen Avenue, near the junction with Vicarage Lane. She employs a daily servant and outwardly lives a respectable life with her husband, a certain Major

Henry Savage, who retired from the Indian army some years ago. The major is unemployed and depends upon his pension and occasional consultancy work. All things considered, they appear to be a perfectly normal family."

"But did you see the children?" Isabel leaned forward, placing her elbows on the desk and her chin on her hands.

"Yes. Two children, one boy and one girl left the house at…" Coralie peered closely at her notes, chewed her lip for a moment, and then continued. "Ah, yes, at three o'clock in the afternoon on Thursday, ninth of June, accompanied by the servant. They proceeded north along East Sheen Avenue and thence to Richmond Road, where they entered a grocery shop. I followed and observed them."

"Did they appear well?"

Coralie looked up. "I thought so, at first," she said, dropping the officious reporting style. "But when I looked closely, I saw red welts across the back of the boy's legs. Both children were subdued, waiting quietly in the corner for their guardian. I decided not to engage them in conversation but loitered nearby. Once the housekeeper was far enough away, they started whispering, the boy telling the girl not to be frightened and the girl confiding her fears about the spirit world. Mrs Savage, it appears, had fostered an environment of fear, controlling the children's behaviour with tales of malevolent spirits."

"Poor things," murmured Isabel. "But it is not enough. The report we received implied physical damage to the children."

Vera Ponsonby slapped her hand on the edge of the desk, making Lawrence jump. "But filling their heads with nonsense can be just as harmful."

"I cannot disagree," said Isabel. "But I am powerless to act on it."

"There's more," said Coralie. "Vera and I returned the next day to keep a close eye on the household. But there was little movement, and the children did not stir. Having noticed a pair of missionaries nearby on our way to the house, we approached it masquerading as the same. We rang the bell and waited outside, but nobody came. Major and Mrs Savage were too busy arguing to hear us. The parlour window was ajar, and we listened while they sniped at each other about the failure of their plan."

"What plan?" Isabel leaned forward, her eyes narrowed in concern.

"The ruin of a chap called Cameron Curzon," said Vera.

"Who is he?"

"We are trying to find out. But we have established that Mr Curzon is wealthy and interested in spiritualism. Major and Mrs Savage mean to exploit this."

"How do you know?" asked Lawrence, intrigued.

"The Savages are very loud," said Coralie. "And not terribly careful around open windows. We heard them declare it. Mr Curzon is to attend a seance at the house, which will take place on Monday evening."

"Good," said Isabel. "I hope you can attend. If you get inside, you might learn more about the children."

"We can't," said Vera. "I'm afraid we've blown our cover."

"How?"

"Major Savage lost his temper with his wife and strode through the front door before we had time to react. We reverted to the plan and pretended to be missionaries, so he yelled for his wife and stomped off up the road. We spent the next five minutes engaged in small talk with the lady of the house, who thankfully had no truck with religion. But they have seen our faces, and we can hardly coincidentally turn up to the seance."

"No, I don't suppose you can." Isabel frowned, her brown eyes distant and anxious.

"I'm not sure I understand," said Lawrence. "It's not unusual for a parent to physically discipline their child, and if living with a medium was a criminal offence, many more women would be in jail. And though they seem like a thoroughly unpleasant couple, the Savages are surely only minor con artists, assuming they successfully commit their intended fraud."

"If only it were that simple," murmured Coralie, looking at Isabel as if awaiting permission.

"There's more to it," said Isabel. "We're concerned about the children, who only appeared six months ago. Major and Mrs Savage are childless. We don't know where William and Millicent originated. They came to our notice from an intervention by a neighbour who claims to have heard threats of beatings. As Vera and Coralie attest, the Savages are not the quietest of people. They live in an affluent neighbourhood among gentlefolk unused to such displays of temper. And it's hardly surprising that someone has seen fit to intervene. There may be nothing in it, but I must find out where the children came from, and I can hardly knock on the door and ask without alerting the Savages to our concerns. Now, it seems that fraud may be involved, which complicates the situation. Thoughts, ladies?"

"It would have been useful to attend that seance," said Coralie.

"Why don't I do it?" Lawrence, who had been quietly musing, lifted his head.

"A single man interested in the spirit world?" Vera pursed her lips and shrugged.

"Why not? And anyway, Violet will be here by Monday."

Vera and Coralie exchanged glances.

"Wait," said Isabel. "Is this a public seance?"

"Yes. It's advertised in the grocery store. I saw it while I was waiting," said Coralie.

"Well, then. That's the perfect solution." Isabel smiled. "Are you sure you don't mind?"

Lawrence nodded. "Not at all. And this sort of job is right up Violet's street. If anything untoward is happening in East Sheen Avenue, we will get to the bottom of it."

"Take this," said Vera Ponsonby, handing Lawrence a white card. "Our address is on the reverse. Come and see us and tell us what you find out. We'll take it from there."

Chapter Five

AN UNWANTED VISITOR

Sunday, June 12, 1904

Lawrence woke feeling unusually chipper. He washed and dressed with the window wide open, enjoying the early morning sun, and trying to determine whether he had time to visit Ann Brocklehurst, given Violet's imminent arrival. His hotel room was a vast improvement on his last visit, with a window directly overlooking Battersea Park. And as Lawrence fastened his collar, he glanced outside to see a line of young children riding well-behaved ponies along the green. Smiling, he thought about Daisy and her love of animals. It was high time she learned to ride, and a slew of happy memories burgeoned in his mind when he thought of his sister, Louisa, and her excitement when riding with her big brother for the first time. Lawrence, six years her senior, had been happy to get involved, patiently leading Louisa's horse while their mother watched the little girl protectively. Louisa had grown into a fine horsewoman, eventually more proficient than Lawrence. But he hadn't minded. His summers in Bury had been carefree then, with a loving family and nothing to worry about except what to do when school finished.

Lawrence tore his gaze away from the window to stop his childhood memories from blending inevitably into his teenage years when everything changed. Today would be a good day. Violet was en route, and if he could work things out, he would soon see Ann. He glanced at the desk beneath the window and noticed a few sheets of blue notepaper embossed with the hotel address. Opening the drawer below, he soon discovered matching envelopes and sat down to compose a note to Violet. Finishing it with a flourish, a signature and a small x, Lawrence folded the paper and addressed the envelope. Then, taking his wallet and hat, he made his way downstairs.

The smell of grilled bacon wafted from the dining room, and Lawrence followed it, almost hypnotically, before remembering the letter. He quickly returned to reception and gave it to the girl behind the counter with instructions for her to hand it to Violet as soon as she arrived. That done, he marched to the table he'd dined at the previous night, smoothed a napkin over his lap, and waited for someone to appear. Within a few moments, a smartly dressed waitress arrived, bearing a notebook and pencil.

"Tea or coffee, sir."

"Tea, please."

"And what would you like to eat?"

"What have you got?"

The girl reeled off a long list of items, and Lawrence floundered for a moment, paralysed into indecision by the number of choices. Unperturbed by his silence, the waitress recommended bacon and eggs, and Lawrence concurred.

With matters concluded, she left for the kitchen, and Lawrence leaned back, watching the room.

He'd chosen a good time to eat. The sparsely occupied dining room suited him well, the only other incumbents sitting at the far end. Lawrence watched an elderly couple swap the contents of their plates, sharing two different breakfasts. They barely spoke, seemingly happy to be in each other's company, and he hoped he would still be as patient and loving to Violet in their twilight years as the elderly man was to his wife. Gazing away as his eyes grew misty, Lawrence fastened his attention on the only other occupied table in the room, watching as a mother and father lost the battle over food consumption with their young son. The boy fidgeted, his arms crossed and displaying a pouty bottom lip as his mother cajoled and his father threatened. His younger sister ate dutifully from her bowl, not intending to show her brother up but doing so all the same. Voices rose as the family argument became increasingly fractious.

"Eat up, Oliver," pleaded the mother.

"Shan't." The boy pushed his plate into the centre of the table, hitting the salt cellar and knocking it over the tablecloth.

"Why, you little…" The father raised his voice, his face beetroot red over his tight collar.

The boy cocked his head and grinned, and Lawrence realised he was smiling too. The young man might be misbehaving, his father enraged, but the boy was fearless, indicating his father's temper was benign. All bark and no bite, as it should be. Lawrence thought about little William and Millicent, subdued and compliant at the Savages' house. Cora's description implied subjugation, neither child secure enough to exert their own will. Lawrence would tell Violet as soon as he saw her and make plans to attend the seance, however ridiculous it sounded, to get to the bottom of the mystery. No child should be afraid, and if Lawrence could help, he would.

The family's table settled into silence as the boy shrugged his shoulders, leaned forward, and placed a forkful of food into his mouth. The father smiled, and Lawrence watched, intrigued, barely noticing a shadow loom beside him. He turned to receive his food from what he assumed to be the waitress. But she wasn't there. He looked a second time, barely comprehending the vision before him.

"What are you doing here?" he asked resignedly.

Loveday Melcham removed her bonnet and sat down opposite Lawrence.

"Over here," she called, beckoning to the waitress, heading towards them with Lawrence's order.

"Yes, ma'am." The girl placed a dish in front of Lawrence and a toast rack before regarding Loveday curiously.

"Take my coat, if you please," said Loveday. "And bring a cup of tea; Assam will do, and a small portion of kedgeree."

For a moment, Lawrence thought the waitress might refuse. But after a few seconds of contemplation, she scribbled on her pad, took the proffered jacket, and proceeded towards the kitchen.

Lawrence sighed and pushed his dish into the centre of the table.

"Oh, don't wait on my account," said Loveday. "Carry on. It will get cold and congeal." She wrinkled her nose at the sight of the rapidly cooling egg, and Lawrence brandished his eating irons and began. He'd only refused out of politeness but was starving and not about to waste a good meal because of the unwanted arrival of someone whose case he'd specifically turned down.

"How did you find me?" he asked, tucking into a sausage.

"I remembered you stayed here a few years ago when we were engaged," said Loveday. "And knowing that you are a creature of habit, I thought it worth taking a chance. So, I telephoned last night, and they confirmed your residence here."

"You should be in my job," said Lawrence.

"I daresay I would be good at it."

"Then why do you need me to keep track of your husband? Do it yourself."

"Don't be absurd. Tom would see me."

"He might anyway. It's risky coming to the capital when you know he's staying here."

"I'll be with my friends in Chelsea. You remember the Goodhalls, don't you?"

A feeling of déjà vu sent shivers through Lawrence for the second time in as many minutes. Being ambushed at the hotel by Loveday was bad enough, but memories of the affected, snobbish Goodhalls made him feel slightly queasy.

"Yes, I remember the Goodhalls," he said. "But surely they know Tom?"

"Thomas doesn't like them," said Loveday haughtily as if the concept of someone ambivalent to her friends was alien to her. "He's an impossible bore about them."

"Still has some taste," Lawrence muttered under his breath.

"I beg your pardon."

"This tastes delicious," he replied, forking another mouthful.

Loveday pulled a face. "If you say so. Anyway, Thomas won't think to look for me there, even if he notices that I'm not at home. The telephone hasn't rung once, nor has the butler delivered a single letter from my husband."

"Why not ask the Goodhalls to assist?"

"Don't be ridiculous, Lawrence. They don't engage in paid work."

"Well, I'm sorry, but I can't help. I will not act against my friend."

"Then make your assistant do it."

"Who?"

"Miss Smith."

"Violet? She's not my assistant." Lawrence placed his cutlery down a little too firmly, and it rattled on the plate.

"What is that?" asked Loveday, staring at Lawrence's ring finger with her mouth agape.

He smiled. "Haven't you heard?"

"Are you married?"

"Yes." Lawrence twisted the plain gold wedding band around his finger with a satisfied smile.

"To whom?"

"I can't believe you don't know."

"I didn't see an announcement in the newspaper."

"We didn't make one. Neither of us wanted a fuss, and in the end, we enjoyed a quiet ceremony. Just the two of us, with Daisy and Michael."

"Daisy? Your wife is called Daisy?"

"No. My wife is Violet, and Daisy is my daughter."

The waitress returned and placed a small bowl of kedgeree in front of Loveday.

"Take it away."

An expression of incredulity spread over the girl's face. "Sorry?"

"I mean it. Take it away at once. I'm not hungry, and it's making me feel sick. Not the tea, silly girl. Leave that here."

Lawrence glared at Loveday and got to his feet, following the waitress as she walked towards the kitchen.

"I'm so sorry," he said. "Mrs Melcham is upset, but there's no excuse for bad manners. Take this. I would have left you a tip anyway but have it now and please accept my apologies."

"It's not your fault. You've nothing to say sorry for," said the girl. She paused, then spoke again. "I know I'm talking out of turn, but you're too nice to be married to that harridan."

"Good lord. I'm not. I mean, I am married, but not to her. You'll meet my wife later. She's arriving today. She's much nicer, I promise."

Lawrence turned away and headed towards the table, Violet's imminent arrival now central in his thoughts. He resumed his seat and picked up his cutlery, intent on finishing breakfast as soon as possible.

Loveday was simultaneously sipping tea and scowling, her usually pretty face ugly with jealousy. "You chose Violet Smith over me?" she asked icily.

"Hardly. You terminated our engagement and married one of my best friends. I don't recall any input in that decision."

"You were awkward about London," countered Loveday.

"That's old history. You married Tom, and I married Violet. I hope you are as happy together as we are."

Loveday's scowl deepened. "Thomas is up to no good. I need help, Lawrence, and I won't take no for an answer."

"Sorry, old thing. But it's not happening."

"Come to dinner with me tonight. I can explain more. I know you'll help when you hear what's been going on."

"Sorry, Loveday. I'm not interested. Besides, Violet will have arrived by then."

"What, here, at the hotel?"

"Yes. She'll be along in the next few hours."

Loveday lowered her eyes and thought for a moment, lips pursed as if she was trying to contain herself. "You've demeaned both of us by marrying the hired help and adopting her child."

Lawrence shook his head, torn between telling Loveday some bitter home truths or laughing in her face. In the end, he answered calmly, having nothing to gain from losing his temper, especially now Loveday had displayed her envy for all to see. Nothing Lawrence did or said would make her look any more foolish than her own ill-advised words. "Violet and I are equal partners in the business, and Daisy is my child."

"How old is she?"

"Eight."

Loveday grimaced as she mentally performed the calculations that put Daisy's conception within weeks of their Liverpool entanglement. She stood, hurled her napkin to the table and stalked towards the coat stand. Then, placing the coat over her arm, Loveday stormed towards the door, returning to the table to collect her almost forgotten handbag. Flashing a look of unbridled loathing towards Lawrence, she flounced from the hotel.

Lawrence pulled apart a piece of toast and mopped egg from his plate, ruminating as he ate. He had never seen

Loveday so angry. It was as well that Violet's and Loveday's paths hadn't crossed. For a moment, he contemplated telling Violet about the conversation when he next saw her, but Loveday's remarks had been cruel and designed to hurt. Better to spare Violet's feelings, he decided as he drained his cup and left.

Chapter Six

OLD FRIENDS

"Oh, my dear friend." Ann Brocklehurst clasped Lawrence's hand while patting him on the arm in an extravagant show of enthusiasm. "It's so good to see you."

"And you too, Ann," murmured Lawrence. "It's been far too long."

"A year and a half, at least. I would have asked you to the wedding, but it was a quiet affair. Only a handful of people came. We've been married before, and Mark didn't want a fuss."

"Likewise," said Lawrence.

"Of course. You must have married Violet soon after."

"Indeed. Michael witnessed our marriage."

Ann laughed. "It amuses me to think of my little brother on the other side of the pulpit. I don't suppose you've heard from him?"

"Sorry, no. Michael is still on retreat but will write to us next month when he finishes."

"It can't come soon enough. I do so worry about him.

Anyway, come through, and I'll get Mrs Mahoney to fetch us some tea."

Lawrence followed Ann through the black and white tiled hallway and into a brightly lit breakfast room with views over Berkeley Square.

"Take one of the comfortable chairs by the window," said Ann.

"You have risen in the world," Lawrence replied, eyeing the spacious room and the silver dinner service set on a marquetry inlaid sideboard.

"I know. And I don't take any of it for granted," said Ann. "I have made a fortunate marriage, but I love Mark, and I couldn't be happier. When I think about my life with Gordon, abandoned and on my beam ends, I can't believe how luck has smiled on me."

"You deserve it."

"Thank you. But I could never have foreseen it, not with the taint of divorce in the background."

"Times are moving on, Ann. A broken marriage isn't the scandal it once was."

"But it so easily could have been a bar to my happiness. Fortunately, Mark is a modern-thinking man."

"Is he home?"

"Not today. Mark is in the city, visiting a friend. I wish I'd known you were coming. He could have put them off."

"Sorry. I should have written. Violet's always scolding me for my shocking communication. She tells me young Sidney is getting on well at school."

Ann smiled broadly. "Very well indeed, and with half an eye to university."

"Cambridge, I presume?"

"Sorry. Mark is an Oxford man."

"Gordon won't like it."

"He hasn't seen the children in five years. I almost wish he would get upset. Then, he might take an interest in them. But he's too busy living it up in India to bother."

"I'm sorry. I can't imagine not seeing my daughter."

"How is Daisy?"

"Unruly, naughty and utterly delightful. I'm missing her already."

"Ah, thank you, Mrs Mahoney."

A middle-aged woman with the sort of face that failed to leave a lasting impression walked into the room, pushing a carved oak trolley.

She silently took a tea tray and a loaded cake stand and placed them on the table before collecting silver tongs and a sugar bowl from the sideboard.

"Thank you, Mrs Mahoney."

"Ma'am."

Ann waited until the door closed, and they were alone. "I don't know what to do," she whispered to Lawrence.

"What's wrong?"

"I try so hard, but she won't talk to me. Just answers monosyllabically. I can't get a conversation out of her."

"You're in a different world now, Ann. Mark's a baronet. Did he bring Mrs Mahoney from his country pile?"

"I don't know, but probably."

"I expect she's been taught not to interact with her betters."

"That's not the way I want things to be. And Mark isn't like that. He enjoys a joke with Bellinger."

"Bellinger?"

"His butler and valet. Well, his everything, really. I don't know what Mark would do without Bellinger, and they have quite an informal relationship. Why can't I?"

"Are you lonely?"

"No. I still have friends in London, and they visit from time to time. Mark is very welcoming."

"But?"

"I didn't say, but."

"I know. You left it hanging in the air."

"Lawrence, you always were perceptive. I don't see my friends as often as I would like. They feel intimidated by my new surroundings. We've only been married for a year, and they are still getting used to the idea of coming to Mayfair."

"Do you visit them?"

"I try. But they're not always available."

"Jealous, perhaps?"

"I don't think so. Things will settle in time."

"What do you do with yourself when Mark is in the city? I assume he's still dabbling?"

"That's a good question. You were lucky to catch me in. I often visit the sick after church on Sunday, but Mark has the landau today. I'll go tomorrow instead."

"Ah, yes. Violet mentioned your charity work. Where do you do it?"

Ann opened the teapot, stirred the contents, and poured them through a silver strainer into their teacups. "Do help yourself to cake," she said.

Lawrence had already mentally selected a large choux pastry from the top layer of the cake stand and didn't need any prompting to take it. He bit into the bun, releasing a puff of sweet cream, and reached for a napkin. "Delicious," he said.

"Cook is French," replied Ann. "And jolly good too. My waistline has expanded horribly of late."

"You would never know," said Lawrence.

"Back to your question. I visit the sick at the Royal Free

Hospital on Gray's Inn Road. It's rewarding, though often sad."

"Free hospital? For the poor, you mean?"

"Yes. That's the intention, although it's not unknown for those who can pay to use the institution, but primarily, it's for the poor."

"Who do you visit?"

"Anyone who might need cheering up. I love seeing the children, but they don't need me as much. Those most in need of company live alone with no friends or relatives to lighten their stay. I report to the almoner. She gives me a list, and off I go."

"Almoner?"

"The almoner arranges convalescence and aftercare. But also deals with non-medical needs, raising spirits and the like."

"I see. And you enjoy the work?"

"I do, but one of my current ladies is proving difficult."

"Don't see her if she doesn't appreciate you."

"I don't mean that. Maria couldn't be more grateful. She's an unusual case; a sixty-year-old woman in much-reduced circumstances. She once lived well, but her husband died with debts, and she lost her home. Her son took her in for a while, but then he married, and his spoiled new wife lacked compassion. She forced him to expel his mother from the house, and Maria now relies on charity."

"Her son should be ashamed."

"Maria would forgive him, but he doesn't want to see her. She suffers from hip problems and walks with a stick. Yet she's the brightest, most positive woman I have ever met."

"Then why is she proving difficult?"

"Because she's leaving the hospital tomorrow. I feel I should do more for her."

"Can't you visit her at her lodgings?"

"I'm afraid it's frowned upon. The hospital governors have rules about conducting visits outside the hospital."

"Do they need to know?"

Ann sighed. "Probably not. But Mark says that if I allow myself to become too attached to one person, that one will become many. He thinks I mean to bring home every waif and stray I meet."

"Then give her a parting gift."

"I shall, even though that is also discouraged. Something practical, I think."

"You are kind, Ann. You and Michael put the rest of us to shame with your charitable works."

"I'm grateful for my life, and I like to give something back. And volunteering is rewarding. Especially now I've made friends with the doctors. Did you know that it's a teaching hospital for women? And they work on the wards as surgeons and anaesthetists. They're a pleasant bunch and always willing to chat."

"I'm glad."

"Have another cake."

Lawrence reached for an iced bun and then stopped, remembering the less pleasurable task he must now perform.

"Do take one. They'll only go to waste."

"I will, but I should tell you something first."

"What is it?"

"News of Francis."

Ann stiffened, and the colour rose in her cheeks. "Have you heard from him?"

"No. I doubt I ever will, and I've no desire to."

"Nor should you, after the abominable way he behaved. Our father would turn in his grave. I still can't thank you enough for keeping the scandal away from the press."

"Please don't thank me. His transgressions should not be yours."

"What did you want to tell me?"

"I saw a photograph of Francis yesterday."

"Where?"

"At the headquarters of a curious organisation known as The Order of the Crescent Moon. It's one of these half-baked esoteric societies."

"What were you doing there?"

"Looking for Aurora."

"Oh dear. I do wish you wouldn't."

Lawrence frowned. "Why?"

"She's made Michael so unhappy."

"Only because he can't find her."

"It's more than that. Michael told me about the hidden room at Netherwood. It wasn't there when I was a child. At least, I never saw it."

"We think Francis built it. You wouldn't have known."

"Michael implied Aurora had connections to these people. Clearly, you believe so too."

"Not only Aurora but Francis as well."

"Evidently. Poor Michael. It goes against all his beliefs."

"I know. And I'm sorry to have mentioned it."

"Don't be. I need to know. What was Francis doing in the photograph?"

"Nothing much. Just standing there. But the company he kept was surprising."

"Who was with him?"

"Felix Crossley."

Ann grimaced. "That animal."

"You've heard of him too?"

"Yes. Crossley exposed most of London society to his depravities – one half appalled, and the other thinking his views were fresh and exciting. Crossley is lucky to come from a wealthy background, where his proclivities are passed off as eccentricity."

"You don't approve?"

"Do you?"

"No. The more I hear about Crossley, the worse he sounds. And I fear Aurora may have fallen victim to him."

"Then you must look for her if that is what you wish, but I can't help feeling that Michael is better off without her."

"I understand."

"And as for Francis, he is lost to me. I'm glad you told me about the picture, and I prefer not to be kept in ignorance. But I won't willingly consort with my older brother again."

"Sorry to spoil my visit with this news."

"You haven't. Have another cup of tea, and let's talk of happier things."

Chapter Seven

THE LAVENDER BUSH

Monday, June 13, 1904

Lawrence had barely closed his eyes when daylight stole through thin curtains, waking him from a deep slumber. He'd slept well, albeit punctuated by dreams of mundane domestic chores with Violet and Daisy. He opened one eye and glanced at his watch to see that it was only a few minutes past six. Violet, who had missed the train the day before after a delay in her friend's arrival from Swaffham, wasn't due to arrive in London for another hour. And having nothing better to do, he rolled over for another short sleep. But Lawrence had forgotten to set his alarm and one hour rapidly turned into two.

A loud banging on the door woke him for the second time that morning. Clutching his watch and cursing loudly, Lawrence threw on a dressing gown, opened the door, and found Violet mid-knock and frowning.

"Oh dear. That's not the welcome I intended to give

you. Come in." Lawrence lunged for a kiss, but Violet turned her head.

"Did you forget me?"

"No. I overslept. Were you waiting long?"

Lawrence tried again and managed a quick peck on Violet's cheek as she sat on the edge of his bed.

"I didn't wait. I took an earlier train than I'd originally intended. You're not as late as you think."

"Then why did you ask if I'd forgotten you?"

"Because you're still in your nightwear, and my original train would have arrived at Liverpool Street station in ten minutes."

"Ah. I see. Well deduced. Yes, I overslept. But that's because I stayed with Ann longer than I intended. Mark came home and insisted I join them for dinner. He's a nice chap, Violet."

"So I hear."

"You must meet him."

"I'd love to. Perhaps over the next few days."

"If we get a chance," said Lawrence. "We might not have time."

"Why not?"

"I'll tell you in a moment. Will you wait while I freshen up? They've upgraded the hotel since we last stayed and built a bathroom down the corridor."

"I won't if you don't mind. I'd rather find my room and unpack. It's number six, apparently," Violet continued, holding up her keys. "Why don't I meet you in the dining room, and we can eat together?"

Lawrence thought of the previous day's attempt at breakfast, rudely punctuated by Loveday's unexpected appearance. Violet wouldn't benefit from knowing about the encounter and avoiding the dining room while the incident was fresh in the minds of the waiting staff seemed sensible. "There's a nice little café near the entrance to the park," said Lawrence. "Why don't we eat there instead? I'll meet you in the hotel foyer in half an hour."

Lawrence paced the lobby while glancing at his watch for the third time. Violet was five minutes late, out of keeping with her usual habitual punctuality, and he briefly considered going to her room. But after a further minute, Violet descended the stairs with the wary look of someone who could not believe the evidence of her own eyes.

"What's wrong, old girl?" asked Lawrence, worried at her expression.

"If this is your idea of a joke, it isn't funny," said Violet.

"What isn't?"

"The unwanted gift in my bedroom."

"I haven't left you one, though I probably should have now we've been apart for a few days. I can buy some flowers if you like?"

"Flowers? I'm not talking about flowers."

"Then what?"

"You really don't know?"

"Obviously not." Lawrence emphasised every syllable, his mood changing from concerned to irritated.

"I've just found six hedgehogs in a wicker basket in my room."

"Are you sure?"

"Stop it, Lawrence. I may be tired and hungry, but I haven't lost my sense of reason.

"Six hedgehogs?"

"Yes. Six. I counted them."

"Was there a note?"

"Are you being facetious?"

"No. I'm trying to get to the bottom of it."

"There's a better way." Violet marched towards the reception desk and rang the bell. A weary-looking young girl appeared from farther down the corridor.

"Can I help?"

"I hope so. There is a wicker basket in my room. Do you know how it got there?"

"Yes. Billy took it up."

"And who is Billy?"

"The odd job boy."

"Why did he take the basket to my room?"

"Because someone asked him to."

"Who?"

"The girl who made the phone call."

Violet shook her head impatiently, wishing she could hurry the conversation along. "Who made the phone call?"

"I don't know. The caller didn't give a name."

"Then what did they tell you?"

"To look out for a box from Leadenhall market and take it to room six when it arrived."

"And that was all?"

"As far as I know."

"Well, I'm afraid I don't want it."

"That's a shame. The caller was most insistent."

"You implied the caller was female."

"That's correct. Definitely a lady, and probably young."

Lawrence's stomach grumbled in anticipation of breakfast. Someone had clearly made a mistake with the hedgehog delivery arrangements, but it wasn't worth wasting any more precious time trying to find out who.

"Are you sure you don't know her name?" ventured Violet.

"Certain," said the receptionist.

"What about the hedgehogs?" asked Violet.

"Hedgehogs?"

"Yes. The hamper was full of hedgehogs."

"Whatever would you want with hedgehogs?" asked the girl.

"Nothing," said Violet curtly, struggling to keep her temper. "Please return them to the market."

The girl flashed Lawrence an uncertain look, and he removed a coin from his wallet.

"Ask Billy to deliver them to Leadenhall, please?" he coaxed.

"Right," said the girl. "Unless I can get our housekeeper to take them off your hands. She's always moaning about beetles in the basement."

"Ah, household insect infestations. That explains why they sell hedgehogs at the market," exclaimed Lawrence, pleased to have solved that part of the conundrum.

"Probably," said the girl disinterestedly. "But don't worry. I'll dispose of them. They'll be gone before you return."

"There. Problem solved. Now, how about a spot of food?" asked Lawrence.

"Do you mind if we eat somewhere else? I've ordered a book for Sidney, and I'm bound to forget if we're too embroiled in this thing with Aurora."

"Where's the bookshop?"

"Gray's Inn Road."

"That's interesting. Ann's hospital is there."

"Can we walk?"

"We could, but it would take an hour, and I'm not doing that on an empty stomach."

"Very well. We'll eat first. Let's find your café."

The Lavender Bush was a mere five minutes from the hotel, and Lawrence had only recently noticed it while walking over the weekend. He had yet to try it and hoped it would be a pleasant place to eat. Violet's face lit up as she spied the checked tablecloths and colourful linen napkins on the tables outside the front.

"Oh, this looks delightful," she said. "We can sit outdoors."

"Jolly good." Violet selected a seat in a sunny position, and Lawrence prepared to go inside to order when a plump woman arrived with a small, typed menu. They made their selections and waited, chatting while she prepared the light meal.

"Have you made any progress?" asked Violet.

"A little," said Lawrence. "Do you want to see the brooch?"

"Later. I'd prefer to know what you've found out."

Violet listened in silence as Lawrence described the Headquarters of the Order of the Crescent Moon and paled at the mention of Francis and his unexpected connection to Felix Crossley.

"Have you heard of Crossley?" Lawrence asked.

"No, though he sounds dangerous."

"I don't think so. But he's lacking a moral compass."

"That's my point. No good ever came from prioritising pleasure over the important things in life."

Breakfast arrived, and they chatted as they ate, Lawrence sharing his plans with Violet.

"A seance tonight?" she repeated, surprised at the arrangement.

"Yes. Will you help?"

"Of course, if young lives are at stake. But where and when?"

"East Sheen Avenue at seven o'clock."

"By train?"

Lawrence nodded. "I think that would be best."

"Then we'd better eat up and collect that book now. It's quite a lot of travelling to do in one day."

Chapter Eight

INCIDENT IN GRAY'S INN ROAD

The Barometer and Spyglass on Gray's Inn Road occupied a dusty, multi-paned, timbered building somehow clinging to life alongside its newer neighbours. Lawrence stood outside and stared appreciatively at the black and white timbered dwelling with its jettied second-floor frontage.

"Now that's what London ought to look like," he said. "They've destroyed far too many fine buildings in favour of, well, look at that." He swept an arm across the road at a partially built, red brick structure.

"What's wrong with it?"

"It's soulless, Violet. Just somewhere to live. No finer features at all."

"And probably cheaper because of it. People must have somewhere to call home."

"Doesn't it bother you?"

"What?"

"Losing our history?"

"We're not," said Violet, placing her arm through his with a gentle squeeze. "But we must move with the times.

London is full of people who can't afford a decent roof over their heads. We'd all love to see magnificently crafted properties going up, but it's neither practical nor cheap."

Lawrence sighed, momentarily wishing he could step back in time by half a century. Influenced by his university and a favourite uncle, he had long been a passionate advocate of well-designed architecture. The dull, flat-fronted building standing opposite the glorious Tudor specimen before him filled him with despair. Violet glanced at his face and recognised a glimmer of the black dog which once ran rampant through Lawrence's mind. She had taught him how to appreciate what he had, and his black moods were a thing of the past. And there they could remain. Taking Lawrence by the hand, Violet pulled him through the door and into the interior before he could become too introspective.

The door opened with a familiar jangle, like the bell in their premises. Violet marched towards the counter where a bespectacled middle-aged man compiled a list while thoughtfully chewing his pencil.

Violet smiled, but the man stared through her and clicked his fingers. "Ah, that's it," he said. "Sorry. I do apologise. I could not remember the author's name for the life of me, but now it is here in my head. Your arrival has triggered my synapses in a most felicitous manner." Lawrence's frown turned to a grin, delighted to hear the learned tones of the well-educated, well-spoken man.

"Now. What can I do to help? A scientific work, perhaps, or something medical?"

"My name is Violet Smith, and I ordered a book by telephone last week. I'm here to collect it."

The man opened a journal and scanned the page, scratching his silver beard as he read. "Indeed, you did," he said, snapping the book shut. He turned to a bookcase behind him, selected a brown paper package tied with string, and handed it to Violet.

"Wonderful," she said. "You don't mind if I open it before paying?"

"I would be more concerned if you did not," said the man.

Violet pulled the string, revealing the parcel contents, and turned the book upright. "Bertrand Russell: *The Principles of Mathematics*," she read. "Exactly as Sidney requested, and in excellent condition too. This will do nicely."

She moved to re-wrap it, but the bookseller reached over. "Allow me," he said.

Violet nodded, removed several coins, and passed them over the counter.

"Thank you," she replied, then turned to look for Lawrence, who had disappeared.

"Is there another floor?" she asked, perplexed.

"Through there, dear lady," said the bookseller, pointing to the far corner of the room. Violet followed his direction and found Lawrence on a mezzanine landing, poring through a red-bound book.

"Look," he said, brandishing it towards her.

"That looks very modern," she replied.

"Quite right, and no doubt the reason why I noticed it in the middle of a shop full of academic tomes. It stands out like a sore thumb.

Violet took it from him and turned to the flyleaf. "*Liber Occultorum*," she read.

"The book of secrets," said Lawrence.

"Is it all in Latin?"

"No. Only the title. Take a look inside."

Violet turned a few pages and stared at Lawrence. "It's about secret societies," she said.

"Exactly. Now, look at the author."

"Felix Crossley. Goodness. He's a writer too."

"Apparently so and published his book this year."

"I suppose we'd better take it with us."

"Wild horses wouldn't stop me. And it will give me something to discuss after the meeting tomorrow night."

Violet nodded, feeling sick with apprehension at the thought of Lawrence's involvement with yet another sinister secret organisation. She wished she were going with him and had broached the subject already, but Lawrence was having none of it and was determined to keep Violet safely away.

"I'll take this," said Lawrence, handing the volume to the bookseller. The man frowned and cautiously handled the book as if repelled. "If you must," he muttered.

"Don't you want to sell it?"

"I do, and the sooner, the better."

Lawrence waited, saying nothing, and hoping that if he remained silent, the man would embellish. His tactic worked.

"We specialise in scientific and academic paraphernalia," said the bookseller. "I have little time for esoteric matters, let alone modern, unprincipled ramblings like these."

"Then why sell it?"

"My young assistant took an order for it, and my reputation would have suffered had I not honoured the request. So, I purchased the foul thing, but nobody ever came to collect it."

"A good thing I'm here to take it off your hands, then," said Lawrence. "As a matter of interest, who asked for it?"

The bookseller re-opened his journal. "Major Henry Savage," he said.

"Well, that's a turn-up for the books," said Violet as they left the shop.

"Yes. Another coincidence, and you know how I feel about them."

"At least you can indulge in a little light reading tonight."

"I'll be burning the midnight oil. We have a seance to attend."

"Of course," said Violet. "I suppose we should go back to the hotel. Pity. There's a pretty-looking garden over there. I wouldn't mind taking a look."

Lawrence glanced at his watch. "We've got plenty of time. Hours, in fact. Let's do that, and you can tell me what Daisy's been doing for the last few days."

Lawrence reached for Violet's hand and held it briefly as they walked. But a narrowed glare from a top-hatted man sporting bushy white eyebrows, seemingly with a life of their own, quashed his public display of affection. He passed the parcel of books from one hand to another as an excuse to drop Violet's hand without hurting her feelings.

"I say, watch it." Lawrence spun around as he heard the thunder of running footsteps behind him. A young boy was hurtling pell-mell down the pavement, followed by a large, red-faced man who was gaining ground.

"Stop, thief!" yelled the man.

Lawrence prepared to act, but the boy lowered his head and charged through them. Lawrence jumped back, but Violet didn't move quickly enough and, finding herself unbalanced, tumbled to the ground.

"Are you alright, Violet?" asked Lawrence, breathlessly, crouching beside her.

"Yes. I think so."

He took Violet's hand and tried to lift her, but she flinched. "My wrist hurts," she said.

"Let's get you up." Clutching her other arm, Lawrence gently helped Violet to her feet. "Let me take a look."

Violet held out her hand, and Lawrence examined it, turning her wrist slowly.

"It's swelling up already. We'd better get someone to look at it. I think it needs a bandage."

"I wonder if they can help?" asked Violet, pointing to a nearby building.

Lawrence followed her gaze to a cream-coloured property at 228 Gray's Inn Road. A banner over the shop read *Medical Supply Association*, and the shop window contained walking aids and wheelchairs. "Sounds just the ticket," he said.

Chapter Nine

THE ROYAL FREE HOSPITAL

"Oh dear. Have you been in the wars?"

A pleasant young man of about thirty stepped forward as Lawrence and Violet entered the premises. He immediately noticed the unusual way Violet was holding her arm.

"My wife took a tumble," Lawrence explained. "Her wrist looks dreadfully swollen. We were rather hoping that you could sell us a bandage."

"Of course. Several hundred boxes if you are so inclined," he smiled. "We usually sell our wares in bulk. You know, to the hospitals."

"Just the one, if you don't mind," said Lawrence.

"Of course. Would you care to sit down?"

The young man gestured to a quartet of wooden chairs clustered around a low table.

"Violet?"

"Yes, please, Lawrence. I'm a little shaky still."

"Perhaps I could fetch your wife a glass of water?"

"That would be kind. I say, young man. Could you make that two?"

"Dickie," he replied. "My name is Dickie Connolly, and yes, of course. I'll be right back."

Lawrence sat down and wrinkled his nose. The shop smelled of an unsettling combination of liniment and mothballs. "That looks worse than it did five minutes ago," he said, glancing at Violet's wrist.

"I hope nothing's broken."

"Can you move it?"

"Yes."

"Then hopefully not. Ah, here's your water."

Dickie returned and placed two tumblers on the table, shrugging apologetically at the wet ring around the bases. "I'm sorry. I tripped up the stair. It's been there for years, and I should jolly well know better by now."

"Don't worry. It's kind of you to bother," said Lawrence, smiling benevolently.

"May I look at your wrist?" asked Dickie.

Violet raised her arm, steadying it with her left hand, and held it toward him. Dickie frowned. "It looks awfully swollen," he said. "Would you like a doctor to examine you?"

"Doctor?"

"My employer, Doctor Greville. He's a qualified medical man. I'm not sure a bandage will cut the mustard here."

"We'd appreciate that," said Lawrence. "Is he around?"

"Yes. Upstairs in the office. It's your lucky day. He travels between here and his practice in Kew and would normally be elsewhere. But we had a logistical problem, and he came to the office to sort it. I'll fetch him."

Dickie left, and Lawrence gulped his water.

"What a helpful young man," said Violet.

"Isn't he? We could do with a few more like him. How are you feeling, Violet?"

"Not too bad, but I could do with something to take the pain away. Ah. This gentleman must be Doctor Greville."

A middle-aged, monocled man strode ahead of Dickie Connolly and sat next to Violet on one of the spare chairs.

"May I?" he asked, reaching for her hand.

Violet offered it and watched as the doctor peered at her arm, slowly rotating it left and right. "Does this hurt?" he asked, placing a thumb over her wrist. Violet flinched, and he released his grip. "Clearly, it does," he said.

"Will a bandage help?" asked Lawrence.

"Yes, but this wrist is very swollen. If it's broken, it may need resetting first. You're only a few yards away from the Royal Free Hospital. Have you ever heard of an X-ray?"

Lawrence and Violet both nodded.

"Well, young Sydney Rowland has been touring the local hospitals. He's in St Barts, you know, but eager to promote radiography throughout London. I'm quite a fan of his enthusiastic approach. Anyway, Barts acquired a machine and gave it to the Royal Free. You ought to take advantage of it."

"I thought the Royal Free was for those unfortunate people who can't pay," said Lawrence.

"Indeed, but the hospital is more than happy to accept payment for services rendered. I can write you a note," said Doctor Greville. "Your wife seems quite pale to me. I daresay she needs pain relief."

"What do you think?" Lawrence regarded Violet solicitously.

"I daresay I should. But don't leave me alone there. I couldn't bear it."

"Of course not. No need for that."

"I'll leave you to it," said Doctor Greville as he stood and made for the inner door.

"Will you manage?" asked Dickie.

"I think so. Can you walk, Violet?"

Violet stood and leaned against Lawrence, her face pale. "I'm sure I can manage."

"No," said Dickie. "You don't look right. I know it's only a little way up the road, but please allow me to drive you. The car's outside."

"Are you sure?"

"Of course. Follow me."

Dickie opened the door and waited for Lawrence and Violet to pass before turning the open sign to closed. He stood by the car door and ushered Violet inside.

"Should only take a few minutes," he said.

"We're very grateful." Lawrence sat in the back with his arm around Violet as Dickie started the engine.

"My pleasure," said Dickie.

"Is this yours?" asked Lawrence, brandishing a copy of *The Principles of Psychology*.

"Yes. It's a fascinating subject, don't you think?"

"I know very little about it."

"Well, I recommend this book if you enjoy studying medicine."

"But can you really include psychology in a medical book? Isn't it considered a pseudo-science?"

Dickie turned towards Lawrence wearing an exaggerated frown and narrowly missing a pedestrian crossing the road. "It's a medicine of the mind," he said.

"I'd love to know more about it," said Violet, smiling through her pain.

Dickie laughed. "Ah, If I can turn you into a convert, my day has been fruitful."

A minute later, he pulled in front of the Royal Free Hospital. "We're here. I hope you get better soon."

"Thank you again," said Lawrence, tipping his hat.
"What a charming young man," said Violet.
"Never mind that. Let's get you inside."

Lawrence and Violet navigated through a maze of corridors, following directions until they arrived at a desk below a sign marked 'Accident and Emergency.'

They waited quietly until the nurse looked up from her notetaking, smiled, and asked if she could help.

"It's my wife. She's hurt her wrist. Doctor Greville sent this." Lawrence handed her the note.

"Take a seat," she said, glancing at the paper. "I won't keep you long. Doctor Campbell is on duty today, and she will want to see you before there's any talk of X-rays."

They took seats in the empty waiting area, resting for barely a moment before a young woman dressed in a white coat and carrying a clipboard bustled through. She glanced at her notes. "Mrs Harpham?" she asked.

Violet nodded.

"I'm Doctor Janet Campbell. Come with me."

They followed the doctor into a consulting room, where she examined Violet's wrist. "Could be a fracture, could be sprained," she said. "Dr Greville was right to suggest the X-ray machine. It's the only way we'll know. I won't be long."

She left and reappeared moments later, accompanied by the nurse. "Right," she said briskly. "Nurse Bryan will take you to the radiography department, and I will see you again when Dr Roberts has given his verdict."

"Thank you," said Violet. Lawrence stood, offered her his hand, and prepared to follow behind.

The Disappearing Doctor

"Not you, Mr Harpham," said Doctor Campbell.

Lawrence stopped in his tracks. "I'd like to support my wife."

"Sorry. Hospital policy doesn't allow it. You must wait here."

"Don't worry about me," said Violet, squeezing Lawrence's hand. "I'll manage perfectly well."

Lawrence left the doctor's office and returned to the waiting room before picking up a copy of *The Telegraph*. He was idly skimming the front page when another nurse appeared by his side and cleared her throat.

"Can I help you, sir?"

"Thank you, but no. I'm not unwell, just waiting for my wife."

"Is someone looking after her?"

"Yes. She's having an X-ray."

"Ah. Wonderful machines, aren't they? Both modern and useful. Science has come so far that it won't be long before they can rebuild human beings from scratch."

Lawrence nodded politely, but the nurse was in full flow. "You don't sound like a Londoner," she said confidently.

"Really?" Lawrence raised an eyebrow, genuinely puzzled at her assertion. Having experienced many manners of speaking, from the broadest cockney slang to the cut-glass tones of the rich, he knew there wasn't a standard London accent. And how would she know that he didn't occupy the vast range of options between them?

She continued as if reading his thoughts. "No, definitely not a Londoner. You'll be from the countryside."

Lawrence sighed, unamused with her game. Given his lack of Suffolk dialect, he doubted she could discern where he lived. He could have understood the remark had Violet been in the room. She had kept her warm Norfolk burr. But the nurse must be making a wild guess. The hospital was empty, and she was likely starved of conversation and making idle chatter.

"East Anglian, I'd say. Probably Suffolk."

Lawrence grinned, impressed despite himself. "Bury St Edmunds, actually. Do I really have an accent?"

"Not strong enough for anyone else to notice, but I'm an excellent mimic. My husband calls me his little myna bird. Says I ought to be on stage."

"Can you copy any accent?"

"Name one, regional or worldwide, and I'll give it a go." Lawrence reeled off several dialects, and the nurse duly obliged, supplying perfectly passable imitations of his every suggestion.

"Your husband is right. Your accents are entertaining. You should perform professionally."

"I tried taking paying entertainment once," said the nurse, sitting beside him. "But doing it for a living takes all the fun away. I couldn't wait to return to nursing. But hark at me prattling on when you'd rather be reading your newspaper."

"I'm not sure I would," said Lawrence, lowering the paper and returning it to the table. "It's full of bad news. Look at that. A young woman attacked in broad daylight." He pointed to an article on the front page.

"Where was that?" asked the nurse.

"Chatham," said Lawrence.

"Not Richmond, then?"

"No. Why Richmond?"

"Lots of bad things happen in Richmond."

"That's concerning. I'm heading there later."

"Then don't go through the park."

"I wasn't going to. My destination is on the outskirts, I believe."

"Are you seeing friends?" The nurse's capacity for gossip grated again.

"No. Not friends. I'm working."

"Oh. What do you do?"

"I'm a private investigator."

The flow of chatter stopped as she processed Lawrence's words then cocked her head and looked quizzically towards him. "A private detective, you say?"

"Yes."

"Can anyone employ you?"

"In theory. But I'm already working on a case, so not at the moment."

"What if it were urgent?"

"The same applies."

"But in a few weeks, perhaps?"

"Perhaps." Lawrence cast an exaggerated stare at his watch, hoping the nurse would take the hint. She was on the verge of outstaying her welcome, and her questions were becoming intrusive.

"Can I take your card?" she asked in a lower, more serious tone.

Lawrence reached into his pocket and extracted one from his silver card box. "Take this," he said.

"Where are you staying?"

Lawrence answered without intending to and inwardly cursed himself for the slip.

She reached out and quickly stowed the card in her apron. "It's not for me, but Ada will be glad of it," she whispered, her voice getting lower and more conspiratorial with each passing sentence.

"What's your name?" asked Lawrence, sensing an underlying problem.

"Nurse Atkins," she said. "Joyce Atkins. And you ought to know that something peculiar is happening around here."

Chapter Ten

A SINISTER SEANCE

"Off her rocker, I shouldn't wonder," said Lawrence as they journeyed by cab towards Richmond. "I would have told you earlier, but fixing your wrist took priority."

"I wouldn't worry," said Violet. "Plenty of people take our cards without ever getting in touch."

"Good. I'd prefer it if she didn't. Nurse Atkins was too familiar by half, and you know I don't mind talking to people, but that was a bit much. I was half expecting her to ask my collar size."

Violet laughed. "You hate conversation and are not terribly fond of people, either. I doubt anyone else would have minded."

"You weren't there, Violet. Even you would have found her intrusive."

"I'd rather that than spend the morning having my wrist strapped up."

"Good that you didn't break it though?"

"Yes. Doctor Campbell says it will mend in no time.

Such an intelligent and impressive woman. I was thrilled to be attended by a lady doctor. Quite a rarity these days."

"Not at the Royal Free," said Lawrence. "Ann says it specialises in training women."

"That's excellent news. What a shame we're dabbling in the kind of nonsense that gives women a bad name tonight."

"The seance? Yes, I suppose it does. But I can remember a time when you enjoyed seeing spiritualists."

Violet grimaced. "Communicating with the dead was fashionable for a while, but things have moved on. And if there's one thing I learned from Doctor Meyers, it's that mediums employ a great deal of trickery. And we've even more room to suspect it tonight."

Lawrence felt a momentary stab of jealousy at Violet's reference to the late Arthur Meyers, a man for whom she had harboured romantic inclinations before finding out his true character. He dismissed the feeling just as quickly. Meyers was long dead, and Violet was now Lawrence's wife, patient, loyal and, at times, long-suffering. She hadn't mentioned Meyers with any degree of affection, only to illustrate a point. And Lawrence had no right to judge after the exhibition he had made of himself in front of Cora Cream earlier.

"Why did Nurse Atkins take your card?" asked Violet, sliding towards the window as the carriage rumbled over a bump in the road.

"To give it to a friend."

"Did she say why?"

"Only that something odd was happening. She was uncomplimentary about Richmond and advised me to steer clear of the park. Like I said, not quite the full ticket."

"I'm sure she meant well."

The Disappearing Doctor

"I'm not. But never mind that. Are you happy with our plan?"

"Such as it is. As long as you appreciate that the opportunity to examine the house may not arise."

"I realise that, but if there's any chance, I will create an accident and ask to wash my hands, which should get me farther inside."

"Hopefully. But they'll likely direct you to the kitchen when we need to get upstairs for the best chance of seeing the children."

"I don't know how to do that short of barging up there. And it's essential that we stay undercover. Vera and Coralie have already come to the Savages' notice."

"If the worst comes to the worst, we will observe the seance, feign interest and hopefully join in another," Lawrence added.

"It depends on how regularly they have them."

Lawrence sighed. "I suppose it does. We can only do our best, but it would be nice to present something useful to Cora."

"And Vera," said Violet.

Lawrence squirmed in his seat. "Of course," he replied as the carriage slowed and then stopped.

"Ah. It looks like we're here."

Lawrence strode to the door, determined to make the right impression to gain entry. Though the seance was open to the public, he wasn't sure how many would attend. Rapping firmly on the door, he waited, rehearsing his story about his dead uncle Max and a missing will, which was factually incorrect. Although Max had been dead for some time,

Lawrence had significantly benefitted from his uncle's generous legacy, and no longer needed to work for a living. "I should be at home tending to my garden," he muttered as Violet caught up.

"I beg your pardon?"

"Nothing. I sometimes wonder why I bother taking on cases."

"Because you can't help yourself. You have an inquisitive nature."

Lawrence smiled and squeezed her hand, listening as footsteps echoed towards them. The door opened with a creak to reveal the sturdy form of a middle-aged woman, filling every inch of a plain black dress.

"Mrs Savage?" asked Lawrence.

"No, sir. Mrs Savage is in the drawing room. Come through."

They followed her along the hallway and into a spacious room already occupied by half a dozen people. A tall woman with an angular face and dark hair piled high on her head looked up as the door opened. "Ah. Welcome to my home. I am Jane Savage. You must be Mr and Mrs Harpham," she said, extending her hand.

Lawrence tried but failed to conceal his surprise.

"Your secretary called," she explained. "And quite right too. Tonight is an intimate gathering, but sometimes too many people turn up. There are limits to how many we can fit around the table, and we must turn them away. Dear Hepzibah won't brook too much company."

Lawrence exchanged knowing glances with Violet as they realised that either Cora or Vera had sufficient foresight to guarantee access to the seance by booking ahead.

"Hepzibah is my wife's spirit guide," said a white-moustached man, nodding towards Lawrence. "Now, first things first. My name is Major Savage, ex-Indian army. Have you served in the military?"

"Er, no," said Lawrence.

The major eyed him disapprovingly.

"Hmmm. I can usually tell, you see. Your bearing and demeanour indicate otherwise. What is your profession?"

"I don't have one," said Lawrence glibly.

"Ah, a man of means, which leads me to the rather shabby part of the evening. Hepzibah's services do not come free, and I act as my dear wife's accountant." The major waited, and Lawrence reached into his pocket, then thought for a moment. In the few minutes he had known the major, he had discerned a fondness for money and a disregard for civilians. If Lawrence were to impress the man, he must demonstrate his wealth. He felt for some banknotes in his emergency inner jacket pocket and retrieved them.

"Do you have change?" he asked guilelessly, handing over a five-pound note.

The major's eyes widened, and a flush settled over his face.

Sensing that Lawrence had overstepped the mark and embarrassed the man, Violet quickly opened her handbag and passed over seven shillings and sixpence in change.

"Thank you, dear lady," said the major. "Now, may I offer you a drink before we go in?"

"Brandy for me and a sherry for Mrs Harpham," said Lawrence.

"Very good." The major nodded towards the middle-aged woman standing discreetly by the door. "Baxter. Please oblige."

"Yes, sir," she said, heading towards a faded, inlaid mahogany drinks cabinet that had seen better days.

Moments later, she reappeared, bearing a silver tray with two glasses.

"Now, let me introduce you to Mr Cameron Curzon. You may have heard of him. He is a renowned explorer."

Lawrence had already noticed the younger man standing uncertainly in the centre of the room. With his slight build, thinning hair and a general air of malaise, he seemed too fragile to go outdoors, much less into unexplored territory.

"Pleased to meet you," said Lawrence, offering his hand.

Cameron Curzon returned the gesture with a limp shake. Then made an odd little bow to Violet.

"An explorer. How fascinating," she said. "Where was your last trip?"

"Up the Zambezi," he said, his face lighting up at the question. "And then on to Lake Rudolph. Good hunting there. Bagged a couple of tigers and an elephant."

Lawrence flashed an anxious look towards Violet, who had a horror of game hunting. But she impeccably masked her emotions, graciously smiling as if she approved. "It's a very different lifestyle here in Blighty," he said, trying to change the subject.

"Isn't it just? Too cold for me. I said that to Minnie the other day. Minnie is my fiancée, don't you know?"

"Does she travel with you?" asked Violet.

"I've asked her, but she says the African climate doesn't agree with her."

"Minnie is very frail, isn't she, dear?" said Mrs Savage, joining in the conversation. "Your mother often worries about her."

"Mother is too kind," said Curzon.

"Will she be joining us tonight?" asked Violet.

"In a manner of speaking," said Mrs Savage. "Now, my

dear. Were you hoping to hear something particular from the spirits?"

"Not really. But my husband wants to contact his uncle."

"I see." Jane Savage turned towards Lawrence and flashed a smile. "Were you recently bereaved?"

Lawrence marvelled at her indiscretion. He'd had little contact with spiritualists over the years but had expected some subtlety in collecting the facts needed for a convincing seance. Jane Savage exhibited no such restraint, but he was happy to go along with her questions to ingratiate himself into the household.

"Not recently. Some time ago, in fact. But my uncle's estate was unresolved."

"In what way?"

"Missing papers."

"I see. And you hope to speak with him?"

"I do. Any information could prove valuable."

"Excellent. Now finish your drink. We will begin shortly."

Lawrence waited until she turned her back, tipped over his glass and poured the remaining brandy onto his cuff.

"Blast it," he said. "Is there somewhere I can wash my hands?"

"Of course," said the major. "Baxter will show you."

Lawrence followed the hefty form of the housemaid farther up the corridor. She stopped and pointed to a door. "The water closet is in there, sir," she said.

On entering, Lawrence made for the washbasin and performed his ablutions. Ordinarily, he would be impressed with the modern plumbing that brought the facilities together in one room, but it allowed no opportunity to explore the house. Still, he could have a poke around before joining the others in the drawing room. The solid form of the housekeeper waiting outside in the corridor disabused him of that thought, and he wondered why she had felt it necessary to remain there. Under instruction, possibly, which implied that the Savages had something to hide.

He followed Baxter to the drawing room, but the occupants were already on the move. "My wife is ready," said the major. "You may go inside. But first, some house rules. Please only speak if spoken to. Do not, and I cannot stress this enough, leave the table until told to do so. Nor must you disturb the fabric of the room. Hepzibah will only appear under the right circumstances, and any deviation from these rules may disturb the spirits and place my wife in danger. Do you understand?"

Lawrence nodded. "We will observe your rules."

The major nodded. "Follow me. Curzon, you know what to do. Sit in your usual place."

Cameron Curzon smiled, his face alight with something akin to hope.

They entered the room, which must have ordinarily served as a dining room, as the centrepiece was an oblong mahogany table partially illuminated by gas lamps at either end. Lawrence peered through the gloom of the darkened room, noting the heavy velvet drapes drawn across the windows. Jane Savage sat at the far end of the table, her back against a wooden room divider, swathed in a black blanket. Cameron Curzon drew back a chair and sat to the right of Mrs Savage, her husband selecting a seat to the left. Baxter appeared and removed one of the remaining chairs, placing it near the door, leaving Lawrence and Violet with no choice but to sit at the farthermost end. They took their positions and waited.

Jane Savage drew a breath, then sat silently for a moment. "We will now sing a hymn," she said.

The major began singing loudly in a booming voice, unhindered by embarrassment. Cameron Curzon joined in enthusiastically, as did Mrs Savage. Violet bravely gave voice, but Lawrence, mortified by the public exhibition and too self-conscious to play along, mumbled the few words he knew, wishing he were anywhere else but there. After a few verses, even the major's enthusiasm waned, and their voices ground to a halt.

"We will now begin," said Jane Savage. "Hepzibah, are you there?"

A sudden sharp rap coming from somewhere in the room made Violet start.

"Will you join us tonight?"

Rap, rap, rap.

"Show yourself."

Lawrence waited to see what trickery Jane Savage would use to produce a physical manifestation, but nothing happened.

"Hepzibah?"

The table shuddered as if a train had passed, tipped slightly towards the left and righted itself. Lawrence glanced at Violet and reached for her hand.

"Hands on the table," snapped the major, and they duly obliged.

"Show yourself," repeated Jane Savage, as the farthermost gas lamp suddenly extinguished and the far end of the room fell darker still. A diaphanous mist appeared over Mrs Savage, masking her face, and drifting towards the floor. As it fell, a metal object appeared over her head, slowly following the tract of the mist until it settled on the table. She picked it up and caressed it. "The spirit trumpet," she breathed. "Hepzibah has answered and will speak through me tonight."

Raising the trumpet to her lips, she spoke again, this time with the voice of an old woman with a West Country dialect. "I have a message from Margaret," she said.

Cameron Curzon looked adoringly towards her. Lawrence could barely see his face, but a small amount of light reflecting from his cheekbones revealed a man in thrall. His gaze never wavered as she spoke.

"You must be careful," she said. "A woman, seemingly innocent, wishes you harm."

"Who?" he asked.

"I cannot say her name. You must work it out for yourself. Reach into your heart and understand who you can count as a friend and whose conduct troubles you."

"The Savages are my friends," said Curzon.

"Indeed, they are. You can trust them. But can you trust everyone? That is the question."

"What should I do?"

"Protect yourself. Protect your assets. Keep them safe, my son."

"How?"

"I will help you, but not now. My spirit grows weak. I must go."

"Mother. Do not leave me so soon."

"I must." The voice faded to a whisper, and Curzon put his face in his hands.

"Buck up," said the major. "Another spirit may soon appear.

Silence fell over the room, broken again by a series of raps. Lawrence closed his eyes and tried to concentrate, hoping for more sounds to assess the direction of travel. An explosion of tapping followed as the table rose several inches in the air. Violet gasped as their hands moved higher, but it did not distract Lawrence from his task. All hands were on the table apart from Jane Savage, who still clutched the silver-coloured trumpet. If human hands were responsible for the distant rapping, they did not emanate from anyone around the table. But farther up the room was a blanket-covered divider that might conceal something of which they were unaware. He wished he could see more.

"Silence," said Jane Savage. The raps ceased, and the table lowered.

"Hepzibah, may I continue?"

A single rap echoed in the silent room.

Jane raised the trumpet. "Ah. A stranger is among us. A man, elderly, I think. He is here for you, Mr Harpham. Your father, perhaps? No, a relative, but not direct. An uncle, I fancy."

"Uncle Max?" asked Lawrence, voluntarily leading the medium.

"Max. Yes, Maximillian. He wishes you well, Mr Harpham. And says he is sorry that he never met your wife."

Lawrence stared, momentarily caught out by the truthful statement. Uncle Max hadn't met Violet, having died long before their marriage, and Jane Savage had guessed well.

"Do you wish to ask him a question?"

Her voice vacillated between her normal tones and the West Country accent she had been affecting.

Lawrence cleared his throat. "It's a delicate matter, but I must ask. Your estate is unsettled. Did you mean it to end that way?"

"I did not." Jane's voice deepened by an octave.

"Then what did you intend?"

"That you should have my worldly goods."

"Then why not leave a will?"

"I did."

"Where?"

Violet flinched as the spirit trumpet clattered to the table, followed by Jane Savage, who slumped down with her head in her hands.

"Oh no. Are you unwell?" asked Curzon, reaching towards the stricken woman.

"Leave her," barked the major. "This is not unknown. It takes great energy to communicate with the dead. My wife is exhausted. Baxter, show our guests into the drawing room."

They filed behind the housekeeper and resumed their original positions. "Shall we sit?" asked Lawrence.

"No. My idea won't work as well."

"What won't?"

"Never mind. I hear voices. Mrs Savage has recovered."

Lawrence looked up to see the major and his wife entering the room. Jane Savage clutched her head but seemed otherwise in good health. She approached Lawrence.

"Your uncle is a powerful man," she said. "It took all my energy to keep the line of communication open."

"I thought Hepzibah did that."

"She does. But I am the conduit for their conversation. The dead cannot talk to each other, save through a living medium."

"I see. But I'm still none the wiser about my uncle's blasted will."

"Oh, but you are. Now you know there was one. You simply need to find it."

"Can you talk to him again?"

Cameron Curzon interrupted. "My dear mother speaks through Mrs Savage regularly. Their spirits are now so attuned that she doesn't always require the formality of a seance. Mother recommended an investment opportunity last month, which has proved highly lucrative. I can heartily recommend Mrs Savage's services."

"May we return for another attempt?" asked Lawrence, trying to disguise his disdain for the younger man's credulity.

"Certainly. When?"

"This week. Not tomorrow."

"Then the following day, perhaps?"

"Yes."

"How can I reach you?"

Lawrence faltered for a moment, almost reaching for his card, then thinking better of it. Instead, he gave her details of the hotel.

"I'll send confirmation," she said.

"I say, Violet. Are you all right?" Lawrence turned to Violet, who had suddenly swayed into his shoulder, clutching her head.

"I feel dizzy."

"Then take a seat." He took her hand and moved to guide her, but Violet fell to the floor in a faint.

"Violet. Violet." Lawrence crouched by his wife, his face pale with worry.

"Baxter. Fetch some smelling salts."

The housekeeper lumbered from the room, returning with a small vial she passed to Jane Savage.

"Here," she said, shoving the salts under Violet's nose.

Violet shuddered awake, clutching her throat.

"What happened?" she asked.

"You fainted clean away," said Lawrence, holding her hand. "It's been a long day, what with your wrist and everything. I should have come alone. Can you stand?"

Violet took his hand, and he pulled her to a seated position on the floor, but after staring at him through glazed eyes, her head lolled to the side again.

Jane Savage tutted under her breath and wafted the salts once again.

Violet's eyelids opened. "Oh dear," she said. "I feel terrible. Might I lie down somewhere?"

The Savages exchanged glances. "It's difficult."

"Surely you have a guest bedroom in a house this size?" said Lawrence.

"Naturally," spluttered the major. "Is it prepared, Baxter?"

"Yes, sir," she said.

"Can you walk if I support you?" asked Lawrence.

"I'll try."

"Show them upstairs, Baxter," said Jane Savage grimly.

Violet clutched the banister while leaning on Lawrence as they ascended the stairs. They arrived on a landing with a further set of stairs leading upwards.

"This way," said Baxter, showing Violet into a small room with a patchy counterpane smoothed over a pillow. Lawrence swept back the covers while Violet sat on the edge of the bed.

"Let me take your shoes," said Lawrence. "Now lie back. Can you fetch some water, please?"

Baxter eyed him, furrowing her dark brows as she considered the question. She hesitated.

"Now, please. My wife is suffering."

"Yes, sir."

Baxter retreated, and Lawrence turned to Violet. "What on earth are you doing?" he whispered. "You had me fooled for a moment."

"I couldn't think of any other way to get upstairs."

"But you went down with a bump. It was very convincing. Are you hurt?"

"Other than a sore wrist, no. But they won't know that."

"Baxter will return in a moment, and I bet she'll watch you like a hawk until we leave."

"I'm sure you're right. But I'm too ill to stand, so you'll need to leave without me."

Lawrence stared, aghast. "I'm not leaving you alone with these people. They are crooks and swindlers of the worst kind. That poor sap Curzon is firmly under their control. God only knows what they would do if they discovered your true profession."

"I'm more concerned about the children," said Violet quietly.

"Oh, but, Violet. Not at the risk of your safety."

"I'm staying here, and that's that. I'll wait until my hosts are asleep and look around the house."

"Absolutely not."

"Yes. Please don't argue."

Lawrence opened his mouth to disagree, but Baxter entered, bearing a glass of water.

Violet took it and managed a tiny sip. "I feel faint again," she said. "I must sleep."

Lawrence sighed and took his cue. "I should be elsewhere," he said.

"I know. Leave me here to sleep it off and come back tomorrow."

"Are you sure?"

"Yes, dear."

Lawrence kissed her cheek and exited the room. Baxter followed, remaining on the landing while Lawrence descended the stairs.

"How is your wife?" asked Jane Savage.

"Too ill to move, I'm afraid."

"Oh dear. I'm sorry to hear it."

"I trust she can remain here overnight?"

"Yes, she can," said the major, with more enthusiasm than his wife, whose face was a mask of resentment.

"Shall I call a doctor?" asked Mrs Savage.

"I don't think so. Violet needs rest. If she's no better tomorrow, I'll take her to the hospital."

"You'll come back first thing?" said Mrs Savage, in a tone that suggested a demand, not a question.

"By mid-morning at the latest," said Lawrence.

"Very well. We will see you then."

"Rest assured, we will take care of your dear wife," said the major.

Lawrence offered his hand and shook it with an insincere smile before leaving the house with a heavy heart.

Chapter Eleven

A PLEA FOR HELP

Tuesday, June 14, 1904

Lawrence woke the following day in the grip of the black dog. It had been years since he'd opened his eyes to an unwelcome crush of hopelessness, and he recognised it immediately. He'd left Violet, his stalwart companion and love of his life, alone in a strange house with its immoral occupants. And his melancholy came, at least in part, from guilt and worry. Lawrence checked his watch. The hand was barely past six o'clock, and the dining room closed, not that he felt remotely hungry. Violet had spent years watching his moods and keeping him buoyed in times of despair. Her loyalty never wavered, sanguine in the knowledge that he couldn't help himself. Something in Lawrence's makeup sent dark thoughts billowing through his mind for no apparent reason. She had pressed him to discuss the matter with his latest doctor, a young man barely into his thirties. Lawrence had resisted, having already succumbed to a breakdown under the care of Dr Mallory and refusing any further invasion of his medical privacy. But Violet had persisted, knowing that the black moods would not stay away forever. And eventually, Lawrence capitulated and discussed the matter with Dr Steel. His recommendation had been fresh air and exercise, ignoring Lawrence's preference to stay at home brooding. And a good slug of brandy would do no harm either. The doctor's words had seemed wise, and Lawrence would now follow them to the letter. He rose, washed, and dressed and made his way downstairs to the lounge, at the end of which stood a small, unmanned bar. But now was not the time to wait for the bar staff to arrive, and Lawrence helped himself to a double whisky in the absence of an open bottle of brandy. Tossing a few coins on the side in compensation, he knocked it back, and thus fortified, made his way to the foyer.

The young receptionist behind the desk stared into the distance as if fighting the urge to sleep. Lawrence tried to raise a smile as he passed, but it was an effort, and he doubted it reached his face.

"Oh, Mr Harpham. Wait a moment, please."

Lawrence stopped and then approached the desk.

"What is it?" His heart thumped momentarily, thoughts of Violet's safety uppermost in his mind.

"A letter," she replied. "Hand delivered this morning." She passed over the cream-covered envelope, and Lawrence's heart sank. He didn't recognise the writing, but he'd given the hotel address to the Savages only yesterday. Why were they writing? It could only be bad news.

"Thank you," he said, ripping the envelope open and snatching the sheets from inside. He stared for a moment at the neat cursive pen strokes, shuffling through three sheets of paper until he reached the name at the end. Amy Whittall. Who in God's name was she? He scanned the first page, quickly realising that the letter was a request for help and had nothing to do with Violet's condition. Sighing with relief, Lawrence shoved the letter into his pocket.

"Is everything alright, Mr Harpham?" asked the girl.

"I think so," he said, feeling his mood lift slightly. A good walk could only help, and he set off towards Battersea Park.

Lawrence circumnavigated the boating lake, already in use by a couple of rowing boats despite the early hour, and narrowly avoided a collision with a distracted cyclist. He passed the sub-tropical gardens and headed towards the pump house, where he settled on a bench. The fresh air had renewed his vigour and his curiosity. He withdrew the letter and settled down to read.

Dear Mr Harpham and Miss Smith

I hope you don't mind me approaching you, but my friend, Nurse Atkins, gave me your card, knowing that I have been deeply troubled for some time. Last summer, my dear friend, Sophia Hickman, left the Royal Free Hospital on Gray's Inn Road, never to return. Sophia's father alerted the police who began searching for her. You may have read about it in the newspapers. Their efforts proved fruitless, and we waited in vain for her to reappear. Two months later, we received news of the worst possible kind. Three young boys had discovered Sophia's decomposing remains in Richmond Park. We were devastated and assumed that Sophia had fallen victim to a criminal or lunatic, but following an inquest, the coroner recorded her death as suicide. I cannot adequately describe the terrible impact this has had on Sophia's friends and family. I had dined with Sophia, a lady doctor, only two days before she disappeared. She had recently started a new appointment at the Royal Free Hospital and was looking forward to it. Granted, she was anxious, as anyone might be in a new placement, but not to the degree that she would take her own life as the coroner suggested. I have known Sophia for twenty years, and there must be more to her death than the verdict implies. Her father feels the same and has sought to overturn the coroner's conclusion, with no success. I cannot provide any evidence or suggest an alternative means of demise. But only offer my firmly held belief that Sophia would never destroy herself when she had friends and family to support her. I have the funds to pay for your services, and I beg you to consider assisting in this matter.

I am, yours truly,

Ada Whittall, Putney 390.

Lawrence frowned as he read the letter, then returned it to the envelope and sat pondering his response. He had come to London to find Aurora and had already turned down Loveday's request for help. He had limited time, yet something about the earnestness of the writer appealed to his better nature. And with Ann volunteering at the Royal Free and his current embroilment with the fraudulent medium who lived on the outskirts of Richmond Park, he was well located to assist. Glancing at his watch, Lawrence noted that the dining room would now be open. He would take breakfast at the hotel, collect Violet, and show her the letter. If she was willing, he might investigate further.

Chapter Twelve

REUNITED WITH VIOLET

"How did you get on?" Lawrence whispered as he helped Violet into the cab, which had patiently waited for twenty minutes.

"We'll talk when our journey's underway," said Violet. "Jane Savage is watching from the window."

"I doubt she lip-reads."

"Nothing would surprise me."

Violet took her seat, wound down the window and waved to her hosts. Major Savage saluted while his wife tried to muster a smile which changed her natural frown into a more neutral position.

"You're looking well," said Lawrence. "Thank God. I barely slept worrying about you."

"I can see that from your appearance. You're very pale, Lawrence. The more pertinent question is, are you in good health?"

"Don't worry about me. Now, tell me all about your evening."

"Well, I spent four hours pretending to be asleep; not a simple task but one which fooled Jane Savage despite her instructions to Baxter to watch me from the landing. And a little before midnight, she relieved Baxter of her duties, and they all went to bed. I gave it another hour to be on the safe side before creeping around the house in my stockinged feet to keep the noise down."

"Poor you. You must be exhausted."

"Exhilarated, Lawrence. It's been a while since I've had a chance for some first-hand sleuthing. I'd forgotten how exciting it is."

"Do rein in the fearlessness, Violet. It might make you careless."

"Well, it didn't." Violet glanced sideways at her husband, trying to assess his mood, and deducing the rapid swing between concern and irritation.

"But was it worth it?"

"To a degree," said Violet. "My room faced a small staircase to the upper floor, and I naturally went upstairs for a look. But someone had locked the door, and I couldn't get any farther."

"Was it a door to a bedroom?"

"No. The whole top floor of the house."

"Perhaps they don't use it. The household furniture is pretty shabby, and the Savages appear to live beyond their means."

"No. But someone is living in the attic room, Lawrence. I heard children playing while I pretended to be asleep. And I waited by the upper door for some time, only to hear a little boy cry out in his sleep."

"In distress?"

"No, just a childish dream, I should think. But the

Savages have William and Millicent locked away in the attic."

"And yet, according to Cora, they go outside with the housekeeper or whatever function Baxter serves. Their presence in the house is no secret."

"Granted. Then why lock them away?"

"To stop them speaking with anyone else, I suppose."

"Precisely. And that's not normal."

"I know. But Isabel's department can't step in without good reason. Was that all you discovered?"

"No. After that, I took my search downstairs for fear of waking the Savages. I thought I saw the children in a family photograph in the living room, but they were younger than William and Millicent, so I can't be sure. The woman beside them looked like Jane. A sister, perhaps. And then I moved on. The major uses a small area about the size of a box room as a makeshift study. He keeps his desk unlocked, and I found a handful of unanswered letters in his top drawer, mostly relating to unpaid debts and one for an outstanding loan. He kept a journal in the other drawer containing details of his current finances, and he's added the sum of ten guineas to his records in the last week."

"That should resolve the worst of his problems," said Lawrence.

"It might if he didn't have the loan. But if he doesn't pay it off soon, he is still in a great deal of trouble."

"Did his records show where the money came from?"

"Yes. Cameron Curzon. At least, I assume so. The entry simply read, *Curzon*."

"The Savages are a nasty pair," said Lawrence. "Fleecing that simpleton because he cannot let the dead go."

"Spiritualism is still lucrative," said Violet. "Doubtless it will fade in time as more fraudulent mediums are exposed, but the bereaved need comfort and Jane Savage provides it."

"At a cool seven shillings and six for a measly half hour. It certainly beats working for a living. Anything else?"

"Yes. I made friends with Baxter."

"Is that wise?"

"Very, if we are going to continue with this matter."

"We will for a little while but searching for Aurora is paramount. And the more time we spend on this, the less we get to look for her. How long is Norma staying?"

"A week, perhaps a little more, if necessary. Though I don't want to leave Daisy for too long."

"How did you tame Baxter?"

"By being nice. The Savages seem indifferent to her. Baxter brought a tray of toast and marmalade to my bedroom this morning, probably on Jane Savage's instructions. No doubt she wanted to keep me confined to one part of the building. Baxter was about to sit outside on the landing, but I persuaded her to join me in my room, and we chatted."

"How riveting."

"It was, actually. Baxter has a friend who cooks for Doctor and Mrs Johnstone, who live a few streets away. Last year, they lost a house guest in dreadfully sad circumstances."

"Really." Lawrence feigned interest, but his attention was on the composition of the buildings they were currently driving past.

"Indeed. The poor woman rose in the dead of night, went downstairs to the doctor's study and drank from a bottle of *liquor arsenicalis.*"

"Suicide?"

"Oh, yes. No question about it. But Baxter's friend was dreadfully concerned about the events leading up to it. Mrs Locker had been so cheerful and had recovered from the loss of her child. The household was greatly relieved. Then suddenly, from nowhere, she destroyed herself. It's so sad, Lawrence."

"Hmmm." Lawrence was silent for a moment before reaching into his jacket pocket. "Read this, Violet," he said, passing over Amy Whittall's letter.

Violet lowered her head, murmuring aloud as she read. And when she finished, she returned the letter to Lawrence and frowned. "What a horrible coincidence."

"Isn't it?"

"You're not thinking of pursuing the matter, are you? We really don't have time."

"If it wasn't for Aurora, I might."

"But it's truly nothing more than a coincidence. No family ever wants to believe their loved ones would rather die than face the troubles of this world."

"You know what I think about coincidences."

"And anyway. This case wouldn't be good for you."

"Sorry?" Lawrence cocked his head to one side, baffled at Violet's remark.

She chewed her lip and considered her words. "You're inclined to melancholia, and keeping your spirits up is important. If you spend too much time dealing with people in despair of their lives, well. I don't think it's a good thing."

"You mean, you believe it will affect me?"

Violet nodded.

"I am not inclined to destroy myself."

"But hand on heart, can you say that on your blackest days?"

Lawrence stared out of the window as the carriage

slowed, gratefully recognising the signage of Ponsonby & Cream Private Investigators. The conversation had become uncomfortable and Violet's words, though well-intentioned, were deeply unsettling. He'd been dreading seeing Cora Cream in Violet's presence, but with the pall of gloom now settled between them, he was glad of the distraction.

Chapter Thirteen

REPORTING BACK

"Ah, welcome, Lawrence. And you must be Violet?"

Cora Cream reached out her hand and offered it, shaking Violet's with a firm, confident grip.

Violet smiled. "Miss Ponsonby or Miss Cream?"

"Sorry. I should have said. I'm Coralie Cream. Cora if you prefer, and my partner in crime is Vera Ponsonby."

Sitting behind her desk, pen in hand, Vera concentrated so deeply on her work that she barely registered their presence.

"Visitors, Vera," said Cora, smiling patiently.

"Oh, hello, Mr Harpham. Do you come bearing news?"

"Violet does."

"Good. Then I'll put on a pot of tea, and we can talk."

Lawrence idly watched as Vera Ponsonby strode to the back of the room, where a stove sat incongruously near a wooden filing cabinet. She opened a drawer and removed a tea tin.

"Penny for them?" asked Cora Cream.

"Sorry."

"Your thoughts. You seem deeply distracted."

"Nothing to worry about. Just an awful lot more to consider than I anticipated."

"With our case?"

"No. With London, in general. Whenever I visit the capital, I attract cases like a magnet."

"But we're not taking them, are we?" said Violet.

Lawrence licked his lips.

"What cases? Can we help?" asked Cora.

"I don't think so," said Lawrence.

"I don't see why not." Violet's response was a millisecond behind. Lawrence glowered.

"Tell me about it," said Cora Cream, gesturing to the two seats in front of her desk. And instead of sitting behind it, she leaned against the wall with her legs crossed at the ankle, giving Lawrence a glimpse of lacy black stockings beneath a hemline several inches higher than customary. He swallowed and looked away.

"Lawrence received a letter this morning from a young lady who asked him to investigate a missing doctor," said Violet.

Vera Ponsonby placed a tray of cups on the desk and returned moments later with a teapot. "I'll pour when it's steeped," she said. "Now, what's this about missing doctor?"

"She's not missing," snapped Lawrence.

"But she was," said Violet.

"You must mean poor Miss Hickman," said Vera, swishing her plain black dress out of the way as if annoyed by its presence. Lawrence tried not to stare. It was the first time he had seen Vera out of trousers, usually her customary day wear, despite public disapproval of garments considered male attire.

"Yes, that's right. The young lady was Sophia Hickman," said Violet.

"Then there's no case to answer." Cora's calm voice only made Lawrence's reluctance to discuss the matter firmer.

"Fine. We'll say no more about it," he countered.

"But why has someone written to you?" Vera Ponsonby's curiosity got the better of her.

"Miss Whittall isn't satisfied with the verdict," said Violet.

"That's unfortunate, but the coroner was in no doubt about it," said Cora. "I followed the case closely as it unwound. The young lady went missing in August, and they didn't discover her body until November when speculation reached fever point. The press made the most of it, advancing theories about kidnap, serial killers, and all manner of silly ideas. And in the end, it simply transpired that the poor girl could not face continuing with the stresses and strains of her life."

"What led the coroner to settle on suicide?" asked Lawrence.

"The autopsy results showed she died from an overdose of morphia sulphate, which she purchased herself from that place near the Royal Free on Gray's Inn Road. What's it called, Vera dear?"

"Do you mean the Medical Supply Association?"

"Yes. That's it."

"How bizarre. We've just been there to fix Violet's wrist," said Lawrence, his eyes alight with interest. "I wish I'd known."

"Why, when there's no crime to pursue?"

"Someone could have set upon her."

"I don't think so," said Cora politely. "Though not overweight, Miss Hickman was a young lady of ample proportions and not the kind to respond to an attack without resisting. But there were no signs of violence on her body."

"How could they know? Miss Whittall says her friend's body was in an advanced state of decomposition."

"I believe it was."

"Then they wouldn't have found any marks."

Cora sighed. "I'm sure they considered this during the inquest."

"Then it's not worth our time or yours," said Violet.

Cora looked at Vera, who shook her head.

"No. It's not," she said firmly.

"And yet Violet heard of another suicide in Richmond only this morning," Lawrence spoke through gritted teeth as if determined to hang on to the thread of suspicion.

"It's a vast place," said Violet.

"And Nurse Atkins implied there were more."

"I thought you didn't approve of Nurse Atkins."

"That's beside the point," said Lawrence tersely.

Vera Ponsonby poured four cups of tea and passed them around before pointedly looking at the clock. "We have an appointment in an hour," she said. "Now, how did you get on with the Savages?"

Violet dutifully recalled the events of the previous night.

"You didn't see the children, then?"

"No. But a family photograph tucked away at the back of the drawing room showed a boy and a girl standing with a woman not dissimilar to Jane Savage."

"A sister, perhaps?"

"I thought it likely," said Violet.

"That would be a good outcome," said Cora Cream. "We feared worse."

"But they're not well treated," said Violet. "The children live upstairs in the attic behind a locked door."

"How do you know?"

"I heard them."

"Were they distressed?" Vera Ponsonby clenched her jaw; undisguised concern etched over her face.

"Not that I could tell. The children didn't cry, but it makes no sense to lock them away."

"Unless it's to keep them away from house guests," said Lawrence. "Baxter is the only servant, as far as we can tell. If the children are boisterous, they might be difficult to control without a nursemaid. The Savages might want to ensure that they don't interrupt proceedings during their spiritualism charades."

"The children are allowed downstairs sometimes," said Cora. "I heard them talking about seances. They seemed fearful, yet knowledgeable, and must have witnessed a few to know how they work."

"Do we interfere or not?" asked Vera.

"Not," said Cora. "A locked door is insufficient evidence to proceed. What a shame. I'd hoped for something more."

"And you may yet get it," said Lawrence. "Jane Savage is expecting me back for another seance to help me find where Uncle Max has hidden his will."

Cora raised an elegant eyebrow, and Lawrence's face reddened. "It's not real," he muttered. "Uncle Max left me a generous legacy. And anyway, I need to step in and stop that young fool Curzon from giving the Savages any more money."

"Convincing him of their dubious intentions might help," said Vera.

"I'm not sure I can. Curzon believes every word they say."

"But sooner or later, he will start doubting them. And if the Savages have taken money under false pretences, he might be willing to talk to the police. There's a case to answer, and they would doubtless approach the major and his wife."

"How would that help the children?"

"The police are likely to summon them to the station, leaving the children at home with Baxter. We could arrange a visit to coincide."

"That's a tall order. Curzon hangs on their every word. He thinks Jane Savage is a conduit for his dead mother."

"Then convince him otherwise," said Vera.

"Or find another way to learn more about the children," said Cora. "Can you do that?"

Lawrence nodded. "I'll try."

"We both will," said Violet.

"Well, that's excellent and much appreciated."

Vera glanced at the clock again." Anything else?" she asked.

"Not for now."

"Then good day to you both."

"What is it, old girl?" asked Lawrence as they left the agency and found a hansom cab.

"I wish you wouldn't snap at me in front of other people."

"Did I?"

"Yes. I was only trying to help."

"In what way?"

"By spreading our caseload. You can't do everything, Lawrence."

"I know."

"And anyway, you can't help Sophia's poor father. It's too late."

"So it appears."

Violet glanced at her husband.

"Please don't."

"What?"

"You've got that look on your face. Promise me you won't get involved. There's too much going on, and I'm still unsettled about tonight's potential escapade."

"No potential about it. I'm attending the Crescent Moon meeting, whatever else happens. It's our best chance to find Aurora. What will you do?"

"I don't know. Wait at the hotel, I suppose. I wish I could do something more practical."

"Why not read through Crossley's book?"

"Do you think it will help?"

"It might."

"Then I will."

They travelled in silence for a while before Violet spoke again. "How well do you know Vera Ponsonby and Cora Cream?"

"I've met them a few times."

"Only she seems rather familiar."

"Which one?"

"Coralie Cream."

"That's fashion for you. Lots of women dress the same way."

"They don't, and that's not what I meant by familiar."

Lawrence turned a guilty eye towards the outside scenery. "Then what *do* you mean?"

"You don't seem very comfortable around her."

"She's difficult to talk to."

"I found her particularly friendly and extremely attractive."

"Well, I don't."

Violet raised an eyebrow.

"Alright. Cora is a handsome woman, but she doesn't interest me."

Violet pursed her lips.

"Don't look at me like that. I'm happily married to you."

"I know, and I'm not the jealous type. But I thought I'd mention it. It's important to talk about feelings, isn't it?"

Lawrence couldn't think of anything worse, and Violet's behaviour was baffling. Stoic and logical, it wasn't like her to harbour irrational thoughts of envy. She might claim otherwise, but Violet appeared threatened by the younger woman with no foundation for her concerns. Or was there? Lawrence inwardly groaned. His involuntary reaction to Coralie Cream, hot on the heels of Loveday's telephone call, might have discomfited Violet and reasonably so. He had acted unwisely in the past and only had himself to blame if she lacked faith in him now. Thank goodness he hadn't mentioned Loveday's appearance at the hotel. With a bit of luck, she'd be back in Cheltenham by now.

"How about something to eat?" asked Lawrence as the cab pulled up at the hotel.

Violet glanced at her watch. "It's three o'clock," she said. "The dining room will be closed."

"I expect you're right. But there's a nice chop house opposite the park. We'll dine there and discuss tactics for tonight."

Chapter Fourteen

DEGREES OF ENLIGHTENMENT

A torrential downpour beat upon the roof of the hansom cab as the horse picked its way down sodden streets. The heavens had opened, within moments of Lawrence's arrival at the hotel, dumping a week's worth of rain in a few hours. The roads were awash with rivulets of water, streaming towards gutters, backed up in part. Lawrence had collapsed his umbrella as he'd entered the cab, sympathetically nodding towards the driver, shrouded from head to foot in an outsized waterproof cape. The blinkered horse tossed its tail, hooves momentarily stilled by a sudden, ominous thunderclap.

Violet had waved him off from the comfort of the residents' lounge at the front of the hotel, her pale face visible through the window as she forced a smile. She clutched Crossley's book in her hand, hoping it would distract her from worrying about Lawrence's foray into the strange world of The Crescent Moon. Lawrence felt a momentary spasm of guilt at the thought of her worry-ridden eyes, regretting his shortness with her earlier in the day. Violet was loyal and long-suffering. She would quietly fear every moment he was away, remembering the night he fell foul of Frederick Meyers and the gang of men employed to dispose of him after the Ripper affair. They had worn masks that night, and Lawrence never discovered the identity of his attackers. But his lengthy hospitalisation while Violet drove the business forward was a constant reminder that he wasn't invincible. Though Violet tried to rationalise the unlikely chance of a repeat performance, Lawrence, out of sight, was a reason for her to worry. And she did. All of which streamed through his mind as the cab driver pulled into Blythe Road.

Lawrence grimaced at the thought of leaving the comfortable carriage to face the relentless rain and raised his coat collar as they halted in front of the building. He paid the cabman and darted towards the door, too lazy to open his umbrella, then knocked loudly and waited.

"Are you here for the meeting?" asked a man who had quietly sidled up nearby.

"Er, yes," he replied, detecting a note of familiarity in the voice. He turned to face the man and peered into his face.

"Good Lord. I know you. What's your name?" asked the man.

Lawrence stared open-mouthed at Dr Greville, who had ministered to Violet at the Medical Supply Association the previous day. His heart dropped as he realised their chance meeting was about to ruin his carefully prepared plans for attending the evening anonymously. Lawrence had given his nom-de-plume to Gregory Carmichael but had used his real name in front of the doctor. And it would be tricky to resolve. Lawrence searched for a suitable explanation, but the doctor smiled and clicked his fingers.

"Harpham, wasn't it?" he said. "And how is your good lady wife? I trust her wrist is better?"

"Much improved and no longer hurting," said Lawrence. "I say. Would you mind keeping my name to yourself? It's professionally awkward to use my real credentials. I'm sure you understand."

"I do indeed," said the doctor. "And excuse my poor judgement in addressing you personally. We only use our temple names inside Nuit Isis. Had I known yours, I would have addressed you so."

"I don't have one," said Lawrence. "Not yet. But I am very interested in learning more."

"Well, you've picked the right night to do it," said Doctor Greville. "It's been a good month for new initiates, and tonight's ceremony concentrates on the basics. Who we are, what we do, and our routes to spiritual development. I'm sure you will find it fascinating. Now, follow me."

Lawrence watched as Doctor Greville slowly rapped three times on the door, waited, and followed up with a rapid double knock. The door swung open, and a giant hulk of a man, clad in a scarlet robe with gold headwear reminiscent of an ancient pharaoh slowly nodded as he let them in.

"Peace be with you, Elder Bennu."

"And also with you, Brother Sed."

"Who is with you tonight?"

"A new initiate."

"Peace be with you, honoured guest." The robe-clad man stood aside and beckoned Lawrence into the first downstairs room. "Wait here," he said, briefly placing his palms together as he left.

"Good evening," said a voice nervously as Lawrence peered through the low-lit gloom to see a young woman smiling uncertainly. She sat beside a young red-haired man picking nervously at invisible hairs on his trousers, while another slouched uncouthly, legs akimbo while trying and failing to appear nonchalant.

"Are you an initiate too?" whispered the woman.

"Potentially," said Lawrence. "If I like what I see."

"I'm sure you will," said the girl, twirling a ringlet of hair around her index finger. She wore a plain red robe, like that of Elder Bennu but lacking the accoutrements that set him apart as a higher rank. Her alabaster skin glowed in the darkened room as if lit from the inside, and she chewed her bottom lip in anticipation of the evening's events.

"Have you been here before?" Lawrence asked as he lowered himself onto a nearby seat.

"Yes," she replied. "Only once, but it was a fascinating experience. Balm to the soul if you know what I mean."

"Was it really," Lawrence murmured, lost for something else to say.

"It's similar to freemasonry," said the red-haired man, crossing and re-crossing his legs.

"But with women," said the other in a tone that implied he disapproved.

"Alistair Blatworthy," said Lawrence, nodding to the group.

"Nebethetpet," said the young girl. "At least I will be after the initiation ceremony. Have you chosen your name yet?"

"It's too soon," said Lawrence.

"I rather fancy Mehen," said the red-haired man. "If someone hasn't already taken it. He's the serpent God, don't you know? Ra's protector."

"Must you all take names of Egyptian gods?"

"In this temple, yes," said the girl confidently. "But not necessarily in others."

"Why?"

"I'm not sure. There are reasons for everything."

"And you?" Lawrence addressed his question to the more casually dressed man.

"I'm in the same position as you," he said. "Uncertain whether I'll bother going any further with this. Still, it's worth a look and keeps me away from the other dens of iniquity."

The girl flashed him a look of pure contempt. "Don't be so disrespectful. Some of us want to expand our horizons and achieve heightened spiritual awareness. Your ignorant remarks denigrate our good intentions."

"Sorry I hurt your feelings," he replied unconvincingly. Lawrence waited until the man turned away, then watched surreptitiously and tried to assess his motives for being there. Something about the man's demeanour did not fit the environment, and Lawrence fleetingly wondered if he was a policeman.

"You may come through." Elder Bennu loomed in the doorway, his tall, broad frame silhouetted by the light, looking like an ancient god of old. His low, deep voice rumbled a further command. "Take a robe from the sideboard. Not you, Nebethetpet. And place it over your garments. In future, you must change first; we permit no other-world clothing in the temple chamber. "Hurry now. Follow me."

Lawrence reached for a robe, feeling coarse linen beneath his fingers. Nebethetpet, who had only attended once before, was clad in silk. The rougher robes must be for novices, the lowest of the low. Bennu guided them into the temple room, which Lawrence had glimpsed earlier that week. Wall sconces surrounded the crescent moon on the far wall, and the altar stood proudly surrounded by candles.

Bennu guided them to the rear of the room and waited while they placed the robes over their heads. Once they had stowed their clothes away, he led them farther into the temple towards a pew at the back of rows of chairs carefully arranged in a semi-circle around the altar. Lawrence waited patiently for something to happen, and in due course, two lines of people filed into the room, taking seats in front. Doctor Greville arrived and gave the merest flicker of a smile in recognition. Behind him, the more senior members appeared, clustering around the altar with their palms together in silent contemplation before Gregory Carmichael entered.

Carmichael strode into the temple, his feet echoing across the floor from metal tips inserted in his shoes, long robes flowing and covered in darkly sewn symbols. Around his neck, Carmichael wore a gold neck chain over a yellow collar, and, like Bennu, his headdress resembled a long-dead pharaoh. He stopped, clapped his hands together three times, and waited while the standing group chanted a string of names in a language Lawrence didn't understand.

Lawrence waited and watched, initially enthralled but soon bored by the heavily orchestrated ritual.

He had heard of ceremonial magic but had never anticipated how deadly dull it would be in practice, with every move unnaturally choreographed. The ceremony dragged on, but as Lawrence was on the verge of nodding off, Carmichael clapped his hands again, and silence reigned. He cleared his throat before inviting a man introduced as Imsety to address the group. Lawrence made a show of shifting in his seat to stifle a yawn and listened for another hour as Imsety described the various rituals required to become an initiate of the lower orders from the most basic circle to the sixth degree. His eyelids heavy, Lawrence fought to stay awake, the only moment of interest coming when Imsety described the long-held hope of achieving astral travel through meditation, which Lawrence found so ludicrous that he nearly choked on his snort of derision. After a further closing ceremony, under fully illuminated ceiling lamps, the crowd began to mingle.

"I trust you found this useful?" Gregory Carmichael approached Lawrence.

"Very informative."

"Will you come again?"

"I would like to think so. Will I need a sponsor?"

"No. But you should follow Bennu upstairs with the others now, where he will enlighten you on the path ahead. You must study before you can take the first step towards enlightenment. Your journey to the first degree begins when you've successfully navigated the Book of Mau."

"That sounds like a lot of reading."

"We offer Mau as a pamphlet. It will not take you long to read but a little longer to put into practice. Nevertheless, you must start somewhere. And the higher you progress, the more secrets there are to uncover. Hurry now. Bennu is on his way."

Lawrence strode towards the retreating form of Bennu, now looking less menacing in his robes than he did in a darkened room. He caught up with him on the stairs.

"Are you joining us?" asked Nebethetpet excitedly.

"Absolutely," murmured Lawrence, wondering what he was letting himself in for.

"Take these," said Bennu, passing over three manila

envelopes with a reverence Lawrence more commonly saw on the rare occasions he went to church.

Lawrence took the proffered envelope and peered inside to find the promised Book of Mau underneath a piece of black fabric.

Bennu pointed to his heavily embroidered cuff. "This is the single black band of the novice and should be attached to your robe, which you may purchase on your way out. You must wear appropriate attire for future events. Read the Book of Mau, feel it, and let it enter your consciousness. And if you can cite the first six-degree ranking requirements by next week, you may attend our Tuesday meeting. But I warn you. Learning this by rote requires work and concentration. You must devote yourself to studying. There is no shame in taking longer. Some initiates take weeks or even months to process the information. It depends on you and your commitment."

"I'll do it," said Nebethetpet. "I don't care if it takes up every minute of my time. I can't wait to progress." She clutched her manila envelope to her heart as if it were a love letter.

"Good. You may go." Elder Bennu crossed his arms, nodded, and left the room, soon followed by Nebethetpet and the red-haired man who trailed behind her like a shadow.

"Load of old nonsense," said the casually dressed man, shaking his head.

"Who are you?" asked Lawrence. "You're no more an initiate than I am."

"Lonni Carpenter. You?"

Lawrence took a gamble and gave his real name.

"So, why are you really here?"

"I'm looking for a missing person."

Lonni nodded. "I see."

"And you?"

"Seeking a story." He reached into his breast pocket and passed a dog-eared card to Lawrence.

"Lonni Carpenter, news reporter, *The Truth*," said Lawrence. "Forgive me, but I've never heard of it."

"It's a periodical," said Lonni. "We specialise in exposing fraud, criminality and places of dubious renown like this." He gestured around the room.

"Really," said Lawrence, his mind whirring at the potential possibilities of knowing a friendly reporter. Perhaps he could help find Aurora.

"Here's mine," said Lawrence, returning the gesture with a pristine business card, re-designed by Violet and only recently back from the printer.

"Private Investigator. Hmmm. Who are you looking for?"

"Not here," said Lawrence, casting his eyes towards the door. "I'll find you."

"Right you are." Lonnie tipped his forelock and left the room while Lawrence examined the photograph of Francis Farrow again.

This time he lifted the framed picture from the wall, feeling the familiar anguish at the sight of his former friend and best man. The pain of the betrayal had faded with time, but the sight of Farrow's face brought back all the old feelings of bitter resentment. He turned the picture over to find a label on the back. "Mexico City, 1900, Crossley, Farrow, Podmore."

"Damn you, Francis," he said under his breath.

"What's the matter?" Lawrence spun around to see the friendly face of Dr Greville coming towards him.

"Nothing," he said hastily, hooking the frame back on the wall.

"Ah. You've found the only remaining picture of Felix Crossley," said the doctor.

"Do you know him?"

"Oh, yes. I've been with the temple for a long time. I'm part of the second order, in fact. Crossley's not as bad as they say."

"I know little about him," said Lawrence.

"You've heard his name, though?"

Lawrence nodded. "Carmichael mentioned him."

"I'm surprised. They are bitter enemies. Carmichael would have consigned the photograph to the waste bin were it not for the other men pictured."

"Carmichael didn't seem particularly enamoured of Podmore."

"He isn't."

"Then what do you mean?"

Ernest Greville pointed to the face in the middle of the picture. "This man here. Francis Farrow. You won't have heard of him. But he's been instrumental in our hierarchy since meeting Crossley in '95. He had a temple built; all very secretive because of his place in society. Not that it matters now. Farrow is too entrenched in Templi Horus in Mexico City to travel back often. And anyway, I think he's crossed over to the dark side."

"Dark side?" Lawrence's heart rate quickened.

Greville placed his hands on his hips and regarded Lawrence. "Before I go any further, how interested are you in the order?" he asked.

"I'm fully invested and intend to return."

"Good man. I should warn you not to mention Crossley,

especially in front of Magister Templi Carmichael. They parted on bad terms."

"What happened?"

"Crossley tried to take Nuit Isis by force. An astral siege of epic proportions. He persuaded several of our members to join him, and they entered the temple brandishing knives. Carmichael had no choice but to call the police, bringing shame and ignominy upon the order. He banished Crossley who has since founded an order of his own. But it differs from ours. He practices dark magic."

"What has that to do with Farrow?" Lawrence tried to sound measured to disguise his interest, but the question exploded from his mouth, and Ernest Greville flashed an anxious glance towards the door.

"Keep it down," he said. "They don't like gossip."

"I'm sorry," said Lawrence. "Curiosity got the better of me. What were you implying about Farrow?"

"Theirs was an odd relationship," said Greville. "Farrow is much older than Crossley yet hangs upon his every word. If Crossley told him to jump off a cliff, I think he would do it. But then Crossley studies the human mind and has an innate ability to persuade. It's hard to explain if you've never known him. He and I occasionally met away from the temple, and he came to my office once or twice to collect items belonging to the order. But Crossley ran roughshod over poor Dickie and had him running errands all over town. I had to step in and stop him from taking advantage of the poor boy."

Lawrence clenched and unclenched his fists, trying to be patient with Greville, who was straying from the only point that mattered to him.

"And how does that relate to Farrow?"

"I was coming to that. We lost contact with Templi Horus for a while. They stopped corresponding, and we came close to sending someone to Mexico City, but Brother Khepri wrote a letter. He'd recently taken charge of the temple, not by agreement but because he had no choice. Anubis had vanished. Farrow, I mean. That was his temple name, a revered name inherited from a deceased founder member of The Crescent Moon. That's how it works. There are only so many names to go around, and we reuse them. But I digress. Farrow had gone. Brother Khepri visited his digs, but they were empty."

"Farrow has left Mexico?"

"We think so. And in hindsight, it's hardly surprising. Farrow had an unhealthy regard for Crossley and would inevitably follow him sooner or later. As far as we know, he's still abroad but where Crossley leads, Farrow will follow."

"And Crossley's current activities involve dark magic?"

"Yes, but that's nothing new. Felix Crossley was always a loose cannon. My life, my way, was one of his many guiding principles. He encouraged ritualistic selfishness. These principles have no place in The Crescent Moon, nor does his obsession with sex magic."

"You said he wasn't that bad." Lawrence shuddered at the thought of Farrow associating with the wickedness surrounding Felix Crossley.

"That's the odd thing. Crossley is a normal chap out of ceremonial garb, just a charismatic man with an uncanny ability for persuasion. He understands the way the human mind works like nobody else. You wouldn't look twice at him if you saw him in a social setting. But he would have you under his spell in no time, and you wouldn't know how you got there."

"What's the difference between esoteric study and black magic?"

"A good question. What you really want to know is how The Crescent Moon differs from Crossley's current temple?"

Lawrence nodded.

"Our intent, for one thing. And we promote fraternisation for the greater good."

"But what constitutes dark magic?"

Dr Greville sighed and eyed Lawrence like a teacher explaining a simple mathematics problem to a pupil. "For black magic, read blood magic."

"You mean like voodoo?"

"Greville nodded. "Animal sacrifice, blood rituals, sex magic. Take your choice."

"Absolutely revolting," said Lawrence. "It's hard to believe grown men participate in such filthy acts. Have they no sense of right and wrong?"

"None at all. They are no better than the rakes of old in the Hellfire clubs. You seem shocked, Mr Harpham. I am surprised that you haven't read about Crossley in the newspapers. He has gained much notoriety over the last few years."

"I prefer real news to gossip and scandal. Perhaps I should have paid more attention."

"Well, I'm sorry to have upset you. But I hope to see you here again. And do let me know if your wife needs any further medical assistance. Here. Take this. It's our second telephone line; much easier to get through to me directly."

"I will," said Lawrence, tucking the card into his pocket. They parted, and Lawrence left the building distracted by all he had heard. He'd already walked half a mile into an unfamiliar part of London before realising he had forgotten to hail a cab.

Chapter Fifteen

ASSISTING ANN

Wednesday, June 15, 1904

"I don't know what to say." Violet thoughtfully chewed a piece of toast as she mulled over Lawrence's news from the previous night. She had waited for his return, too tired to exchange more than a few words once he'd safely arrived back at the hotel, allaying her fears. Soon after, they both retired upstairs for some well-earned sleep.

"There's nothing to say," said Lawrence. "It's beyond comprehension that grown men dress up in silly robes, and practise peculiar rituals in a race to the top of their hierarchy. I can't see the attraction myself."

"That's a little rich coming from a former Freemason."

"You know Masonry was forced upon me. I had little time for it, unlike Francis."

"That's the first time in years that you've said his name without snarling."

"I had a lot of practice last night."

Violet reached across the table and took his hand. "It

must have been shocking to discover Francis was involved with the order. Do you think he believes any of the nonsense Crossley promotes?"

"What? The existence of the devil? That killing poultry does any more than create a pool of blood on the floor? No. Francis was an intellectual. So is Crossley, I hear. There must be nefarious reasons for these ceremonies and their participation in them... something I don't yet understand. The things Greville said about Crossley were alarming and not something I'm comfortable discussing in front of a lady. But curiously, Greville seems to admire the man, however reluctantly. They were friends at one time."

"So, you can't rely on Doctor Greville's judgement either?"

"Not entirely, though I'm inclined to. But Felix Crossley is the only clue we have to Aurora's whereabouts. We must find out more."

"Did you ask Greville about Aurora?"

"No. I may yet, but I don't know if I can trust him."

"And Frank Podmore was the third man in the picture?"

"Yes. He'd be worth talking to if only he'd see me. But he's avoided it like the plague so far. I'll just have to force my way into their headquarters."

"Don't be silly. I'll go instead."

"You? Absolutely not. Meyers' henchmen nearly killed me, and I'm not putting your life in danger."

"Nonsense. Frank knows me. I spent a lot of time conversing with him and other SPR members while you were lying ill in the hospital."

"Where they put me."

"Frank didn't."

"How do you know? My assailants wore masks."

"He wouldn't, and I feel sure he'd speak to me."

"What would that achieve if I agreed to it?"

Violet raised an eyebrow and stared wordlessly.

"I didn't mean it like that. You have every right to make your own decisions, but I can't bear to think of you entering that viper's nest without good reason."

"Finding Aurora is a good reason. You've learned a great deal, Lawrence. Except for Crossley's current location. If we want to find Aurora, we must locate him."

"And then what? March up to him and insist that he tells us what he's done with her? She could be anywhere with anyone."

"That's true. But it's still worth speaking to Frank."

Lawrence opened his mouth to continue his objections as a waiter appeared and handed him a small silver salver containing a folded note.

"This has just arrived for you, sir," he said.

Lawrence reached for the paper. "Thank you."

"Will there be a reply?"

"Bear with me a moment." Lawrence opened the note and quickly cast his eyes down the page.

"It's from Ann," he said.

"What does she want?" Violet craned her neck but couldn't read the scrawled writing upside down.

"To see us immediately. Ann will be at the hospital today and has asked if we can meet her there."

"Of course. Poor Ann. I hope she's well."

"I'll pen a quick reply." Lawrence flipped the note over and scribbled a response using the pencil the waiter had thoughtfully provided. "*Dear Ann*," he read aloud. "We'll be with you at about eleven thirty. Sincerely yours, Lawrence. Can someone deliver this?" he asked.

The waiter nodded. "Our errand boy will oblige."

"His name, please?"

"Billy," said the waiter.

"Kindly give this to Billy for his trouble," said Lawrence, passing over half a crown.

"Yes, sir."

"I wonder what Ann wants," Violet mused as she poured a second cup of tea.

"I don't know. But her writing was shocking. She seems upset."

"Wouldn't she stay at home if that were the case?"

"Ann has a very well-developed sense of duty. If she'd committed to the hospital, she'd be there come hell or high water."

"Well, let's plan for a long day out. We'll see Ann, and then I'll visit Frank Podmore at the Society for Psychical Research. Is it still in Buckingham Street?"

"As far as I know, but I'd rather join you."

"You won't get over the threshold. And anyway, you know where I'm going, and I'll be perfectly safe. Probably safer than if I stayed around here."

"What do you mean?"

"I wasn't going to mention it, but I took a quick walk last night at about eight o'clock to take my mind off your little escapade. It was still light, and I know this area reasonably well. Yet, I couldn't shake off the feeling that someone was following me."

"Good grief, Violet? Why would you think that?"

"Because it happened to me in Swaffham. I lost count of the number of times I heard footsteps or rustling leaves and assumed the worst before convincing myself that I'd imagined it. But of course, I hadn't. Francis was watching and following me the whole time."

"You don't think he's doing it again?"

"No, of course not. Francis wouldn't know or care about

me, even if he wasn't abroad. But I heard footsteps last night.

"Then you cannot visit Podmore alone."

"It's not the same thing. I'll be safe there in broad daylight. You can see me off if you're worried. Now, let's not dally. We have an appointment to keep with Ann."

"Now, that's a familiar-looking face," said Lawrence as he strolled through the main door of the Royal Free Hospital and into a brightly lit foyer. He stood for a moment, watching a young man standing behind a part-screened recess near a selection of walking devices propped up against a desk.

"It's Dickie Connolly," whispered Violet. "That nice young man from the Medical Supply Centre who drove us to the hospital. I must thank him again."

"He looks rather busy," said Lawrence, as Dickie held several walking canes of varying lengths towards a middle-aged man with a heavily bandaged leg.

"I'm not using that," the man snapped in a voice loud enough for Lawrence to hear.

"You'll be far more comfortable. And it's only for a short time," said Dickie, patiently.

"I have a perfectly good walking stick at home," the man retorted. "And it's a damn sight better looking than that."

"But is it the right size?"

"I don't care. I'm not carrying that utilitarian object. People will think I'm impoverished."

"You are fortunate to have alternatives, sir. Many patients cannot afford the luxury of choice. But please do not overlook the benefits of a properly sized cane during your recovery."

"Fortunate? With this leg?"

Dickie smiled warmly. "You have two, sir." He glanced across the hallway to an elderly uniformed man sitting upright in an invalid chair pushed by a nurse. The old soldier sat with his chest out and his shoulders back, the picture of dignity. But the checked blanket placed over his lap did not disguise the absence of his lower legs.

"Which stick might best suit me?" the middle-aged man humbly asked.

"This one, sir."

Dickie passed over the walking appliance, and the man removed his wallet and paid. Then, drawing himself to his full height, he walked smartly over to the far door in time to open it for the soldier.

It wasn't until the soldier passed through the door that the man winced in pain. Then he limped towards his wife, walking more easily with the cane than before.

Violet, seizing the moment, approached Dickie.

"Ah, hello, Mrs Harpham. How are you feeling?"

"Much better, thanks to your help yesterday. I really appreciated the use of your car, and I'd like to thank you again."

"You're welcome," said Dickie. "And I'm particularly grateful for your kind words today."

"Tricky customer?" asked Lawrence, lifting a stick from the display.

"Yes, but a good outcome, all the same."

"Quite remarkable how you turned the situation around," said Lawrence.

Dickie smiled. "It's nothing," he replied.

"Are you often at the hospital?" asked Violet.

"Once a week," said Dickie. "Medical canes cause more harm than good if they are the wrong size. You know, too much stooping or overbalancing. So, we bring a stock of them to the foyer where the patients can try them out. Invalid chairs, too, by request. Our stand is popular and a diversion from the boredom of the wards. Matron allows more mobile patients to visit unsupervised, and they often stop for a chat. Tea and biscuits, too, if I can get away with it."

"How kind," said Violet, remembering a particularly frustrating hospital spell where she felt more like a prisoner than a patient.

"I enjoy meeting new people," said Dickie. "And cheering them up."

"I'm sure you do. Well, it's nice to have seen you, and thanks once again for your help."

"Could you point us in the direction of the polio ward?" asked Lawrence.

"Of course. Go through the double doors, turn right, and then right again at the end."

"Thank you."

They left the foyer and walked down the corridor as instructed.

"Damn. I wish I'd asked young Dickie about Greville's friendship with Crossley."

"Would he have answered?"

"I see no reason for him to refuse. Dickie seems a helpful chap, and it would be useful to assess the friendship between Crossley and Greville from a different perspective. I don't know whether to trust Doctor Greville. He's too friendly by half."

Violet laughed. "You'd be suspicious whatever his

temperament. There's nothing wrong with being nice to people. You should try it."

Lawrence scowled. "I'm perfectly amiable, thank you," he said.

"Sometimes."

The door to the polio ward stood ajar and Lawrence quietly pushed it open and peered inside. At the far end, a masked woman with her head covered by a thick veil held the hand of a youthful occupant, lying prone and still on the bed. Violet squeezed past, holding her hand to her mouth as she watched in trepidation, fearing she was about to witness the last moments before death. But a sudden coughing spasm rocked the bed, and the covers fell away, revealing a young girl with pallid skin. The masked woman jumped up, took a cloth, and wiped her patient's forehead before tucking the blanket back around her. She looked up and saw Lawrence and Violet watching from a distance, waved her hand, held up five fingers, and motioned past the door.

"Must be Ann," said Lawrence. "We'd better go outside."

Violet nodded and peered through the window as Ann flitted solicitously around her patient until she became more comfortable again. When the girl settled, Ann filled a beaker with water, placed it on the bedside table and proceeded towards them.

"This way," she whispered, removing her mask, and walking towards a small room farther down the corridor. She opened the door, and glanced inside, ushering Lawrence and Violet through.

"Sit down," she said, pointing towards a wooden table. "We must hurry. The nurses use this room to eat their lunch and won't appreciate visitors. Thank goodness Matron is with Dr Roberts, or she'd have had your guts for garters. She's a stickler for the rules."

"Shouldn't we have come inside?" asked Violet.

"No. Polio is highly infectious. I'm only allowed to visit because I've already had it. It's my fault. I should have asked you not to enter, but I forgot to put it on the note. I wasn't thinking clearly."

"I'm not surprised. Your patient looks poorly."

"Felicity? Yes, I'm afraid she is, poor girl. Polio is a cruel disease, and there's so little we can do about it. Let me wash my hands. The nurse applied a poultice to her earlier. It's sticky and doesn't smell very nice."

Ann ran her hands under the tap at the far end of the room, searched unsuccessfully for a towel, and dried them on her skirts before returning to the table.

"I'm sorry. I can't offer you any hot drinks."

"We don't need them," said Violet. Will your patient recover?"

"Felicity? I don't know. Even if she survives, she may not walk again. Perhaps in the future, with callipers. Anyway. I have little time to spare, but I wanted to speak as soon as possible in case you can do anything about it."

"About what?" asked Lawrence.

"A very suspicious death."

"Death? What, here in the hospital?" asked Lawrence.

"No. A friend living in a seedy little dwelling in Holborn."

"Who died?"

Ann lowered her head for a moment, then looked up.

"Maria. The woman with the bad hip. We spoke about her when you visited."

"I remember," said Lawrence. "And I'm sorry for your loss. How did she die?"

"By suicide," said Ann.

"That's sad but not suspicious."

"It's not that simple."

Violet reached for Ann's hand. "How did Maria end her life?" she asked gently.

"On the end of a rope." Ann's voice wobbled as she spoke.

"How terribly sad."

"Were there any suspicious marks or bruises?" Lawrence left the table and helped himself to a glass of water.

"Not that I know of," said Ann. "I didn't see her body. It happened away from her house. I deeply regret not visiting Maria while she was still alive. But they only discharged her a few days earlier. Anyway, I took a bunch of lilies and laid them at her door as soon as I heard the news. Maria's next-door neighbour let me inside. The police had contacted her when they'd found poor Maria hanging from a tree in Richmond Park, and her neighbour was still suffering from the shock of it."

"You poor thing." Violet's face was ashen, almost as pale as Ann's. "Are you sure you want to talk about it?"

"Well, yes. I would like your opinion."

"It sounds like a sad case of melancholy," said Lawrence.

A flicker of irritation crossed Ann's face. "Maria left a note."

"A suicide note?"

"No. It was more like a shopping list. A length of rope, some cleaning rags, and scraps for her cat. Maria could hardly afford to eat herself, much less fritter money away on the means to end her life."

"Yet she did. It would help to know if the rope was new."

"It was. Brand new. The policeman made a point of mentioning it to Mrs Jewel, Maria's neighbour."

"I still don't see the problem."

"The problem is the six shillings on her kitchen table. And why she went all the way to Richmond to die."

"Then she wasn't hard up."

"Oh, but she was. The money was a gift."

"How do you know?"

"It came with a note. Here. Take a look."

"You kept it?"

"Yes. I didn't intend to. But I put the piece of paper in my pocket and forgot all about it."

Lawrence opened the single page and read, 'Use this to take the pain away.' He passed the note to Violet and continued musing.

"It's ambiguous, but probably a charitable act of kindness. Perhaps a small gift or a contribution to her medication."

"From whom?" asked Ann.

"A well-wisher?" suggested Violet. Lawrence flashed her a warning glance and she watched silently as he continued to lead the conversation.

"Doubtful. But what do you think, Ann?"

"I don't know. But not self-destruction. Maria had her problems, but she was always cheerful."

"Ann. She had a terrible life. Her son had put her out of his home. Who knows what anguish she suffered in private?"

"Not enough to do this to herself."

"Are you sure? I mean, truly sure. Isn't there the smallest doubt?" Lawrence tried to disguise his growing impatience.

"Not really. I mean, it's possible but improbable. You don't believe me, do you?"

"I believe you believe."

"You're just humouring me, Lawrence. Am I making something from nothing?"

"No. You care deeply for your friend and cannot comprehend how she could do such a thing with people like you to turn to."

"But the note?"

"It could mean anything. Look. I'll take it away and give the matter further thought. Will that do?"

"Yes. Thank you. And I'm sorry if I've wasted your time. I was so sure. I still am. But if you think otherwise, well. I'll leave it at that for now."

The door handle moved, and Ann spun around. "Oh dear. They'll want this room. Come along."

Lawrence strode through the door, barging past the nurses in the corridor, but Violet hung back. "Don't worry, Ann," she whispered as they left the room. "I'll speak to Lawrence later. Call it woman's intuition, but it doesn't sound right to me either."

Chapter Sixteen

LAWRENCE IN DISGUISE WITH GLASSES

Lawrence grasped the sweeping brush and ran it over the steps of 19 Buckingham Street for the umpteenth time. Violet had insisted on visiting Frank Podmore alone, and nothing Lawrence said would deter her. Lawrence was equally bent on preventing it, and the resulting dilemma required a nifty change of clothing and a false beard and moustache set, which had been out of commission for many years. Lawrence had persuaded Violet to return to the hotel before ordering a cab. This had taken some doing, as Violet hoped to leave directly from the hospital. But Lawrence had noticed Violet's favourite lamb stew on the lunch menu and successfully changed her mind. They'd arrived at the dining room in the nick of time. Any later, and they would have missed the sitting. But fortune had smiled, and Violet had left well-fed and in an excellent mood, giving Lawrence time to implement his plan.

First, he had located Billy and paid him to find a shabby suit, a hat, and a pair of glasses, which he'd brought to Lawrence's room. Then, he'd opened his trusty box with the

The Disappearing Doctor

spring and wired facial hair and fixed it to his face before applying a thin veneer of charcoal. A few years previously, Lawrence had fashioned a black tooth cap as yet untried, which he fitted over his front tooth before grinning with satisfaction at a job well done. Lawrence didn't look like a gentleman anymore, and his white, evenly-spaced teeth now sported a convincing gap. Looking like a hawker and failing to cover his disguise before coming downstairs, Lawrence had been chased from the hotel by the assistant manager without having arranged transport.

Fortunately, money talked. Clutching a fistful of notes, Lawrence attracted the attention of a not-too-fussy passing cab driver, who dropped him at the top of Buckingham Street shortly after Violet arrived at number nineteen. Someone had helpfully left a broom against the railings, and Lawrence grabbed it before masquerading as a street sweeper.

Unlike Lawrence, Violet had no trouble crossing the threshold of the SPR headquarters, and he spotted her through the uncurtained front window. He'd squinted through the misty glass but couldn't tell if she was with Podmore, with that part of the room obscured. But knowing he was nearby, and Violet was safe was all that mattered, and he continued brushing the street, feeling lighter at heart. Lawrence sneezed and automatically reached for a handkerchief, which he hadn't thought to bring, and wouldn't have been much help as both his pockets contained large holes. But the sneeze had attracted attention, and a sash window opened on the first floor before an unfamiliar face loomed above.

"Oi, clear off," snapped a red-faced, balding man.

Lawrence tipped his forelock deferentially and walked a short distance away before leaning against the wall. He'd give it five minutes and then sneak back. But the front door opened, and Violet emerged, followed by Podmore. Lawrence quickly turned away, facing towards the wall of the next-door property. They sailed past without giving him a second glance, and Lawrence waited for a heartbeat before following behind, listening as they talked.

"So good of you to join me," said Frank Podmore. "I enjoy my mid-afternoon walk and can't always manage it at the post office."

"I'm lucky to have caught you here," said Violet. "I hadn't realised you used the place so infrequently. But I couldn't visit the capital without looking you up after all the help you gave me when dear Lawrence lay ill in the hospital."

"Duty calls, my dear," said Podmore. "My time is limited these days. What brings you to London?"

"Several things," said Violet. "Not least my missing maid."

Lawrence stepped back into an alleyway as Podmore stopped and glanced at Violet.

"A missing maid. How interesting. Is her disappearance worthy of an investigation?"

Violet laughed. "Not of the supernatural kind you are implying, but yes, we cannot find her, and I am worried."

"She must be an excellent maid for you to bother. It will be like looking for a needle in a haystack if she wants to lie low. Did she run away?"

"I believe so."

"You are too kind to mistreat her. I must conclude that it was a failing on her part."

"I don't think so. As far as I can tell, she was an honest girl overcome with fright."

"What frightened her?"

The Disappearing Doctor

"Or who?" said Violet darkly.

"Oh dear. That sounds ominous."

"My maid was called Aurora," said Violet. "It's an unusual name, isn't it?"

"I don't believe I've come across another."

"Neither have I. Aurora left some effects behind, including a brooch. And a note written by someone called Felix."

Lawrence emitted an exasperated sigh, immediately regretting the sound and hoping it didn't give the game away. He had hoped for Violet's discretion, but she was saying too much too soon. He balled his hands around the broom, hoping he wouldn't need to turn and run, but Frank Podmore was too distracted by Violet's conversation to pay heed to the stranger behind him.

"Felix, you say," said Podmore. "Hmmm."

"Lawrence said it might be Felix Crossley," laughed Violet. "But I told him not to be so silly."

"Yes, it's an odd notion," said Frank. "Crossley thinks too highly of himself to dally with a servant."

"I thought that too. But then I read a little about Crossley in the newspaper and wondered if he might take advantage of her lowly status. He sounds unpleasant. Have you ever come across him?"

"Yes, once or twice. I admit Crossley is an acquired taste. I didn't much like him when we first met, and I've successfully avoided him since."

"You didn't get on?"

"Not really. He's an arrogant young pup. Full of self-importance, though charming, of course. And jolly difficult to refuse. But one gains proper insight into the man with the benefit of time."

"What do you mean?"

"I met Crossley in Mexico during a research trip with our American counterparts. My friend, Richard Hodgson, was there too. He's an eminent parapsychologist who knew Crossley from old. Crossley heard he was in the country and invited him to a ritual at The Crescent Moon temple. I knew little of Crossley in those days, but I admired Hodgson, and when he asked me to join them, I felt honoured. We arrived at the temple, sat through the ceremony, and I thought that was the end of it. But a few days later, Crossley turned up again and asked us to join him at a restaurant, so we went along. Crossley was as drunk as a lord by the time the entrée arrived, and I was uncomfortable with his behaviour. But Hodgson had seen it all before and didn't appear unsettled. For all Crossley's unpleasantness, he fascinated Richard Hodgson. And Hodgson was getting along famously with Farrow, Crossley's mismatched, older friend."

Violet inadvertently gasped at the sound of Farrow's name, and Lawrence felt a rush of blood to his head at the thought of Francis fraternising with Crossley as they had often done together in the past.

Podmore cast a concerned glance towards Violet. "Are we walking too fast?"

"Not at all. Do carry on."

"Where was I? Oh, yes. Crossley. Forgive me. I was about to tell you how badly he behaved. But that's an inappropriate subject for a gentlewoman's ears."

"Oh, please tell me what you know. I've become fascinated by Crossley since reading the newspaper article."

"Alright. But only the bare bones. Crossley is like a cobra; hypnotic, charming and deadly. And he is clever with people. If they are close, they remain in thrall to him. He has a gift, a way of convincing men into his service – men like Farrow. Well, my friend Hodgson is in the same line of work as I am. We are both accustomed to debunking frauds. Hodgson has brought down some of the most infamous mediums, yet he is certain that Crossley is the real thing."

"A medium?"

"No. That Crossley is as wicked a man as it is possible to meet on this earth. And that he will stop at nothing to maintain his reputation accordingly. The things that Crossley discussed that night were revolting. Human sacrifice, no less. And he said that his grand ambition was to extinguish a life begotten from a man of God. A human life. A child. Violet, my dear. I left the table, and I did not return."

"How utterly awful. Sickening. Did Crossley mean it?"

"I fear so. And worse still, he has returned to these shores. I have it on good authority that he intends to conduct a ritual by the end of the month. There's no suggestion of sacrifice, though I wouldn't put it past him. Interestingly, I think I know where this ritual will occur."

"Tell me?"

Lawrence listened with bated breath as Podmore hesitated. "I probably shouldn't say. And I may be wrong. But I rather think not. Still, it's not something I should gossip about."

"Oh, but it's so much more than idle chat. And I won't breathe a word you tell me."

"Please don't. We are a serious organisation, and all this nonsense about devil worship sits poorly with Sir Barrett."

"Who?"

"Of course, you won't know him. Sir Barrett is our esteemed leader and took over from Oliver Lodge. I don't much like him, truth to tell, but he's influential, and I'm not in any position to upset him."

Lawrence silently willed Violet to ask him why he

disliked the eminent Barrett, but she was more interested in pursuing the location of Crossley's ceremony.

"I understand Sir Barrett is dogmatic, but I promise I won't discuss anything you tell me."

"Very well. Crossley came across Barkworth recently. You remember him?"

"Yes, fondly. Thomas Barkworth is a pleasant man."

"Indeed. But unfortunately, easily flattered by Felix Crossley, who persuaded him to give too much information about one of our recent investigations. Crossley was intrigued when he mentioned that we'd experimented in a church where the devil purportedly lies beneath a stone."

"Really? Where?" asked Violet breathlessly.

"Akenham. In Suffolk."

"Oh, my goodness. I know it."

"Do you, my dear? I would give it a wide berth for the rest of the month. The pagan festival of Litha is fast approaching, and although it is one of the lesser sabbats, we have reason to think that Crossley intends to use it as a platform for more of his ritualistic nonsense."

"Why? Isn't midsummer a time for celebration?"

"Usually," said Frank Podmore, taking Violet's arm and guiding her over the road. "Let's take a turn around the park, and then I must return to the institute. Time is not my friend," he added, glancing at a silver fob watch he had removed from his pocket.

Lawrence darted across the road as they disappeared behind a high hedge. He slunk past, spying them only a few yards ahead, and lowered his broom while quietly sweeping a few paces behind them, still close enough to hear.

"Do you know much about the pagan festivals?" asked Podmore.

"Not really, but everyone knows something about the summer solstice."

"Indeed. But according to ancient lore, the battle for light and dark occurs over Litha. The Oak King, representing daylight, reigns from Yule to midsummer but then falls in battle to the Holly King, and the days get darker from Litha until Yule."

"It still seems an inappropriate time to perform what amounts to a black magic ceremony."

"That's the point. Crossley will subvert any occasion to suit his purposes. He intends to capitalise on his reputation for wickedness and is determined to act as he pleases, with no sense of public decency."

"Why?"

"To shock, thereby attracting more followers. He is a natural born leader and requires an audience."

"That in itself doesn't seem reason enough. If Crossley seduced my maid, the brooch he gave her wasn't a trinket and must have been valuable. Is he hoping to raise funds for his temple?"

"Money is incidental to Crossley. He desires knowledge. Knowledge and power. Money is only a means to an end."

"I still find it hard to believe that adult men would indulge in such practices. Of course, there are people like Crossley, but they must be scarce."

"My dear. Humans are irrational creatures, never more so than when they are unhappy. If life is too hard, or even too easy, they seek something to believe in, often with supernatural undertones."

"Do you speak from experience, Mr Podmore?"

Frank Podmore cleared his throat and hesitated. Lawrence stopped brushing and listened harder.

"No life is perfect," Podmore conceded after a long silence. Violet made no comment but walked on, and they perambulated without speaking for another few minutes.

"Surely your maid isn't embroiled with Crossley?" asked Podmore. "It's too much of a coincidence, not to mention poor judgement."

"I don't know. The man who gave her the brooch and signed himself as Felix referred to Aurora as his scarlet woman."

Lawrence watched as Podmore physically staggered backwards. "Good Lord. Then it is Crossley. You are on the right track. Felix Crossley always refers to his women that way. But I would not allow such a female in my household. The scarlet women are brazen, wanton creatures, lacking in morality. Your maid will be untrustworthy, bound to Crossley through cardinal sin. Let her stew in her disgrace. Leave her be, Miss Smith. Leave her be."

"But what if he forced her into it? She seemed so sweet and kind, yet pitifully afraid."

"Are you suggesting she reconsidered and escaped his clutches?"

"Yes. I am." Lawrence's heart ached at the forlorn tremble in Violet's voice.

"Even so, you should leave her well alone."

"But is Crossley dangerous? Will he harm her?"

"Felix Crossley is a despicable character, but as far as I know, he has never come to the attention of the authorities for anything other than offences against public decency. And if I hadn't heard how he spoke at the restaurant that night, I would assure you that the man is all show. But now I am not so sure. I cannot imagine he truly believes in the power of ceremonial magic, but he doubtless seeks to enforce fear in his disciples. Why else would he want to raise the devil from the ground?"

"The devil? Where has that notion come from?"

"Akenham, of course. Had Thomas Barkworth known the extent of Crossley's interest, he would never have revealed the results of our investigation, but as I told you, they met at a social gathering, and Barkworth said too much."

"About what?"

"Well, we'd long been interested in Akenham churchyard. The Reverend Ansell Jones is a friend of mine, and he took over from a rather controversial rector a few years ago. I won't bore you with the details, but his predecessor Reverend George Drury was embroiled in an unfortunate case about a non-conformist burial for a young child." Podmore hesitated for a moment as if trying to recall a long-lost memory. "Ah, yes, Joseph Ramsey was the little chap's name, and he sadly died during his second year. An ugly encounter ensued, and they lay the child in unconsecrated ground without a proper burial service. It was quite the scandal."

"But how is that of interest to your society?"

"There have been one or two recent sightings of apparitions. Not as many as we would normally prefer to make a study worth our time but given the personal connection and my fondness for Suffolk, I was happy to investigate, and Barkworth joined me. It wasn't until we arrived that we discovered the manifestations were not childlike but full-grown adults. And we wondered if they might represent Drury, who had died in 1895. We investigated to our normal high standards, and the results were inconclusive. But while we were there, the incumbent of nearby Rise Hall gave us the benefit of family stories passed down over the generations. According to legend, the devil sleeps below the church and will rise from a split gravestone for anyone choosing to walk thirteen times widdershins around the churchyard."

"Utter nonsense," spluttered Violet.

"Be that as it may, long-held beliefs are powerful things. You say you are familiar with Akenham, so you must know the splendid isolation of the silent churchyard with its endless vistas over the fields. But have you ever visited at night? Well, we conducted part of our research in the early hours of the morning. Just Barkworth and I alone in that building in the simplicity of the stark interior, listening out for every creak and groan. We have experimented in countless buildings, sat in many so-called haunted houses, and heard strange and inexplicable sounds. And you witnessed the peculiar occurrences at Chelmondiston, so you have some understanding of the powerful feelings evoked. But, Miss Smith, I have never before encountered a time in which a location's sheer stillness and remoteness conjured up such fear, such abject terror. It isn't the church or even the legend, but the situation and the scarcity of nearby human habitation that conjure an unholy dread. Crossley doesn't need ghosts and stories of Lucifer. He could read aloud from *The Young Ladies' Journal*, and the atmosphere would still be the same. Tension, fear, unnatural quiet and a sense of seclusion from the rest of the world. It is truly conducive to the image Crossley means to project."

"Do you really think he will go there?" asked Violet.

"He said as much to Barkworth," said Frank Podmore. "It is only a matter of time."

Chapter Seventeen

A SWIFT DRINK AT THE RAG

Podmore and Violet concluded their walk around the park so rapidly that they nearly caught Lawrence off-guard. They approached him head-on, and he doubled over in a coughing fit to conceal his face until they passed. Neither showed any signs of recognising him, and Lawrence trailed them from a distance, waiting at the end of the road to watch while Violet entered a cab, presumably summoned to the SPR. Satisfied that she was safe and had enjoyed a much better reception from Podmore than he would have done, Lawrence left Buckingham Street. He proceeded towards the Embankment, where he remembered seeing a spacious public facility where he could change and remove his disguise. Violet would be furious if she had the slightest notion that Lawrence had followed her, even for the best of reasons. After a few abortive attempts, he entered the building, braving an unpleasant smell of ammonia to remove the oversized shabby trousers and jacket that concealed his smarter clothes beneath. He popped off the tooth cap, removed the fake facial hair and washed away all traces of grime from his face before combing his hair and congratulating himself on a job well done. Violet wouldn't know a thing.

Leaving the old clothes in the water closet, Lawrence left the building and strolled up Cockspur Street, whistling contentedly. His black mood had lifted unusually quickly, and his relief at knowing Violet was out of harm's way made all his other problems seem trivial. And she had made good progress with Podmore, despite his initial reservations. It might even be worth visiting Crossley's dwelling if they could find the address. But failing that, a trip to Akenham on Midsummer's Eve might produce results or some further insight into Crossley's character. Now, all Lawrence needed to do was make an appearance at the Savages' seance, which, with the right outcome, might leave him free to investigate the missing doctor. He pondered the case while walking, trying to decide why he found Sophia Hickman's disappearance so fascinating. There could be no glad tidings. The girl was already dead, with little room for mystery. But his sense of fair play was on high alert, not to mention his innate ability to sniff out a case worth pursuing. He would telephone Amy Whittall as soon as he returned to the hotel.

Lawrence continued to muse as he strode through Pall Mall, failing to hear a man calling to him. Moments later, he felt a hand on his shoulder.

"I say, Harpham. Are you ignoring me?"

Lawrence spun around and found himself face-to-face with Colonel Tom Melcham. "Good Lord. What are you doing here?" he asked tactlessly.

"I could ask the same of you. I've been staying at the Army and Navy Club. Come inside and have a drink with me. It's only a short distance away."

Lawrence glanced at his watch. "Not sure I can, Tom. I'm supposed to be back at the hotel with Violet, and I'm already late."

"Where are you staying? Not that it matters, but does the place have a telephone?"

Lawrence nodded.

"Capital. I'll get Stephens to place a call when we get to the club. Let your lovely business partner know you are safe and well with me. How is Violet, by the way?"

"Well," said Lawrence. "And we're married. I should have told you, but it was a quiet ceremony, and you know how it is. We have a daughter too. Daisy. She's the apple of my eye."

"Well, well. Even more reason to join me to toast your nuptials and your lovely little family. What about it?"

"Alright. I'll join you. But only for an hour."

They entered the grand building on the corner of St James Square and proceeded towards an opulent bar.

"Not bad," said Lawrence, spying a shelf solely dedicated to different varieties of brandy.

"Choose your poison," said Tom. "Anything you like. I challenge you to ask for an alcoholic drink they don't stock. They cater well for us in The Rag."

"A large brandy of any kind will do nicely," said Lawrence.

Tom looked up as a tall, uniformed waiter glided towards them, returning moments later with their drinks and confirmation that the message was on its way to Violet.

"Now," said Melcham. "It's been a few years, hasn't it, my friend? I do hope we are still friends?"

"Why wouldn't we be?"

"That business with Loveday. I should have waited until your engagement was over, but I didn't know you were still an item when I first met her. She was rather reticent about the subject."

"It's water under the bridge," said Lawrence. "And we're both happily married now. No harm done."

"Are you, though?"

"Am I what?"

"Happily married?"

"Never more so. I took a few wrong turns along the way, but Violet has forgiven me, and yes, we are very content."

"Good, good." Tom Melcham lapsed into an uncharacteristic silence.

Lawrence sipped his brandy and hoped the stilted atmosphere would lift. He considered asking about Loveday for a moment, but after their recent awkward encounter, he felt too disloyal. And how could Lawrence explain her presence at his hotel? Strictly speaking, he ought to tell his old friend what she had asked of him. But no good ever came from interfering in matters between husband and wife, and Lawrence decided to keep his counsel.

"Marriage is a rum thing," said Tom unexpectedly.

"I suppose it is."

"You were married before and knew what you were getting yourself into, but I've always managed to avoid it. Plenty of girls, don't you know but none who wanted to tie me down. It takes a bit of getting used to."

"Sharing a home?"

"That, of course, and keeping a happy wife. Loveday always wants something. And it's usually expensive."

Lawrence groaned inwardly. The conversation was already entering dangerous territory, and he was only halfway through his first drink. He tried to change the subject.

"Still enjoying Cheltenham?"

"Always," said Tom. "Happy to spend a few days in the club, but I couldn't bear to live in London. Too cramped and stuffy. A pity my wife is so set on buying a home here."

"Well, split the difference and come to London for a few months once a year. That should keep her happy."

"She wants us to relocate. Permanently."

"Oh dear."

"Yes. I've been stalling for years, and Loveday accepted it at first, but now she insists."

"Buy a second home, Tom. Keep the peace and enjoy your lovely villa in Pittville. She'll come to understand."

"I doubt it. Loveday isn't the understanding kind. Didn't you say you had a daughter?"

"Yes, Daisy."

"Do you enjoy fatherhood?"

"Very much. I heartily recommend it."

"Loveday lost one. A baby, that is. She was in the family way, and then she wasn't."

"I'm sorry to hear that."

"Not that I would have known. She didn't, well, you know, I couldn't see a bump. And Loveday wasn't peaky or anything. She just said she was expecting a child and, three months later, told me not to bother getting someone in to paint the nursery. There would be no baby."

"What a terrible shame. Still, another child may yet arrive." Lawrence loosened his collar and shuffled uncomfortably in his seat. He had known Tom Melcham for many years without indulging in personal conversation. Tom had served in the Indian Army, and his upper lip was as stiff as it got, yet here he was, spilling the most indiscreet details, and Lawrence was running out of suitable replies.

"I don't think so. God alone knows how it happened the first time," said Tom, knocking back his whisky. He held up a finger, and the barman looked up. "Same again," mouthed Tom.

"Sorry, I can't. I really must get back."

"Nonsense. You can spare a little more time. The club has several automobiles at our disposal. I'll give Stephens the nod when you're ready to go, and our chauffeur will drive you back in style."

"I really can't," said Lawrence, but it was too late. The barman was back, balancing two large drinks on a silver salver.

"Cheers," said Tom, brandishing his whisky and chinking it against Lawrence's glass so firmly that the contents sloshed down the side.

"Sorry, old man," he said contritely. "Things on my mind."

"How is Freddie?" Lawrence was desperate to shift the conversation onto neutral ground.

"Same as ever. Did you know he lost his wife?"

"No, I didn't. Please pass on my sincere condolences."

"I will. It was a few years ago, though. Freddie's walking out with a young widow now. A pleasant girl. They seem very happy. I wouldn't be surprised if nuptials weren't in the offing." Tom swigged his drink again, eyes downcast and unhappy. And Lawrence couldn't help feeling disappointed in the change. Tom had always been ebullient, bubbling over with enthusiasm and enjoying life to its fullest. But the portly man before him seemed to have had all the joy sucked from him and was a husk of his former self.

"Of course, Loveday doesn't like her."

"Who?"

"Margot. Freddie's lady friend."

"Did she say why?"

"Only that she thinks Margot is selfish. I can't imagine

why and there's probably no foundation to it. I've asked Freddie to arrange an outing for them while I'm in London. It might keep Loveday happy while I am away. Perhaps I'll telephone her tomorrow and see how it went."

Lawrence swallowed and glanced in the other direction, feeling increasingly uncomfortable. He hoped Loveday had gone straight home and not to her London friends as she'd planned.

"Does Violet have foibles?"

"Doesn't everyone?"

"I'd like to think I'm a straightforward man with no quirks. What you see is what you get."

"I'm sure."

"Loveday has foibles by the bucket load. I can't even speak to another woman without a frosty atmosphere developing." Tom Melcham was slurring even though he hadn't yet finished his second whisky and had clearly been drinking earlier that day. It didn't bode well for the direction the conversation was taking.

"I bet Violet doesn't," Melcham continued.

"Oh, I don't know. She has her moments," murmured Lawrence, not mentioning that Violet's last display of pique resulted from Loveday's unexpected telephone call.

"A chap doesn't mind the odd moment or two. It's when things are more often tricky than not."

"I really must go," said Lawrence.

"And why wouldn't you? You have a lovely wife to return to. Do you know how long I needed to be in the metropolis?"

"No."

"One night only, two at the most. I don't even like London, but I've been here for a week because I can't face going home."

Lawrence sighed. Tom Melcham had just bared his soul, and Lawrence would have to engage with him and take it like a man.

"She sounds unhappy. Perhaps you should give her another child," he said.

"I can't be sure she had one in the first place."

"Melcham. That's a serious allegation. Why would Loveday lie?"

"Because we're rarely intimate. I don't think Loveday likes me. Not like she once did."

"Perhaps she doesn't trust you. Have you discussed the matter with her?"

"Of course not. She's my wife."

"Violet's my wife, and she knows everything about me, good and bad."

"I'll tell you what I think."

"Go on."

"I think she preferred you."

Lawrence raised his eyes to the ceiling.

"I mean it. I was always the second choice."

"You're wrong. There was little between us at the best of times."

"You were engaged."

"Without wishing to sound ungentlemanly, Loveday presented a *fait accompli*."

"You mean she manoeuvred you into it."

"More or less."

"Same here. I didn't argue."

"Well, there you are. She chose you over me. Never forget that. And I am blissfully happy with Violet."

"Are you really?"

"Truly."

"Well, thank you, Harpham. I feel a great deal better.

Glad we had this conversation. No need to speak of it again."

"Absolutely."

Lawrence drained his glass and waited another five minutes to make his exit seem less hasty. Then Colonel Tom Melcham called for the club car as promised, and Stephens gestured for Lawrence to follow him outside.

"Good to see you," repeated Melcham, offering his hand. Lawrence returned the gesture and stepped out into the night before entering the car with an overwhelming sense of relief.

Chapter Eighteen

A STRANGE AFFAIR

Thursday, June 16, 1904

Lawrence had arrived back the previous night to find three notes waiting for him in reception. One had been from Violet, announcing her intention to dine with Ann Brocklehurst as Lawrence would undoubtedly be late back. The second contained a transcript of a missed call from Ada Whittall, pleading with him to visit the late doctor's father, and the third was a message from Mrs Savage firming up their arrangement for a Thursday night seance. With Violet disappointingly absent from the hotel, Lawrence had returned Miss Whittall's telephone call, initially to put her off, but by the end of the conversation, having agreed to visit Sophia Hickman's father the following day. He then ate a late dinner and waited in vain for Violet in the lounge bar before slouching off to bed for an early night.

It was now a few minutes before breakfast, and Lawrence was pacing down the passageway to Violet's room, hoping she had returned safely the previous evening.

He knocked firmly on the door but received no reply and tried the handle, which did not budge. Trying not to think the worst, he strode downstairs and into the reception hall.

"Have you seen my wife?"

The young girl looked up, fixed her eyes on Lawrence, and then stared beyond him. "Isn't that her?" she asked. Lawrence spun around to see Violet emerging from a silver Bentley and heaved a sigh of relief.

"Thank you," he said, heading for the door.

"Good morning, Violet." Lawrence tried to keep his voice neutral.

She leaned over and pecked him on the cheek. "Sorry I didn't send word, but I made a last-minute decision to stay at Ann's late last night. Mark offered to get the chauffeur to run me home, but Ann suggested we make a night of it, and I thought you would be in bed by then.

"I was," said Lawrence. "I spent barely any time with Melcham and could easily have joined you there."

Violet thanked the chauffeur and made for the hotel lobby.

"I assumed you'd dine with him."

"No. And I would have told you if that was the case."

"Never mind. Ann was feeling low, but she's much better now. We had a good chat. Mark is such a nice man and gave us plenty of time alone. But he joined us for dinner and was wonderful company."

"Jolly good," said Lawrence moodily, thinking of his lonely dinner for one with only the newspaper for company.

"You don't mind, do you?"

"No, of course not. Have you eaten? I'm famished."

"Well, yes. But I'm happy to join you for a cup of tea and some toast."

"Right, to business," said Lawrence once they had settled.

"Yes. We have little time left to find Aurora. What have you planned?"

"I'm seeing the Savages tonight. You needn't come if you don't want to."

"But I do. You haven't asked how I got on with Frank Podmore?"

"Oh, yes. What did you learn?"

Lawrence half-heartedly listened while Violet recounted the conversation, he had already overheard the previous day.

"Crossley is a truly unpleasant character," said Lawrence when Violet finished.

"Indeed. But there's more. Frank left the SPR headquarters while I waited for a cab, and I chatted with Thomas Barkworth."

"Oh yes. How is he?"

"As pleasant as ever. Free with his opinions and even freer with personal information. Not his, of course. Crossley's. Look what I have here."

Violet produced a ruled card with a name and address written in pencil. "Felix Crossley, Duncryne House, Strathclyde."

"Good grief. That's a fair distance away."

"Correct. It's on the banks of Loch Lomond. A pity, it's too far to travel."

"But Crossley is our only lead to Aurora."

"I know. But there's nothing we can do about it until Michael returns. A great shame. If Crossley were here in London, or even somewhere vaguely south of Hadrian's wall, we could do something about it. At least we can think about returning to Daisy now."

"I wasn't planning on leaving London this soon."

"I didn't mean immediately. We promised Vera and Coralie our help. We'll see that through, of course."

"I spoke to Ada Whittall last night."

"Remind me?"

"The friend of the doctor. You know, the lady who vanished."

"I thought we'd decided not to get involved."

"We're here for a few more days, Violet. It can't do any harm to look into it. I said I'd visit the girl's father today, time allowing."

"I'm not sure it does."

"What would you prefer to do?"

"See Michael," said Violet, visions of their friend looming large in her mind.

"Are you missing him?"

"Yes. Ann spoke so fondly of Michael last night that I dreamed about him. He was kind to me and my only connection to my old life for a long time."

"I'm sorry I wasn't there when I should have been."

"Oh, I didn't mean to drag up old history, but seeing Ann reminded me of my fondness for Michael. I wish he hadn't holed up in the middle of nowhere."

"He's hiding," said Lawrence. "Punishing himself. He's had a rough few years."

"I wonder if we ought to tell him about Crossley?"

"I thought that myself. But I'm reluctant to put it in writing. I mean all that stuff about the scarlet women. He would hate to hear it."

"Michael will want to find Aurora, no matter what. He understands human frailty like nobody else."

"But we can't reach him until he breaks his retreat."

"Didn't Isobel say she had a Scottish contact?"

"Yes. But how does that help?"

"They might be able to send word to Michael. Then he can decide whether to proceed."

"But what can he reasonably hope to do? We'll be breaking his retreat for no good reason."

"That's right. But Michael should know what we've discovered so far. Then he gets to decide, and we don't need to worry about Scotland or Akenham."

"It's fair enough about Scotland, but I can't ignore Crossley's possible visit to Akenham when it's so close. Litha is less than a week away and perfectly timed. We'll be on our way back by then."

"Before then," said Violet.

Lawrence opened his mouth to reply as the waiter appeared. "Message for you, ma'am," he said.

Violet took the proffered note and read it aloud. "Please call Belgravia 311 immediately. Ask for David."

Violet wrinkled her nose. "Who is David?" she asked. "And how does he know how to reach me."

"I was about to ask the same thing." Lawrence peered quizzically at the note.

"Well, there's only one way to find out. Excuse me for a moment."

Lawrence rose as Violet left the table and resumed the attack on his scrambled eggs. Minutes later, she reappeared, looking baffled.

"Who was David then?" asked Lawrence, dabbing his lips with a napkin.

"I don't know, neither do I appreciate his misguided sense of humour," said Violet coldly.

"Sorry?"

"I telephoned, the operator connected me, and I heard an open line, but nobody answered. Then, from nowhere, somebody sounded a horn into the receiver. It quite shook me, Lawrence. And I'm not of a nervous disposition."

"I know, old girl. What a horrid thing to happen."

"Especially as he asked for me by name. I've rather had enough of London."

"Ignore it, Violet. Some silly prankster, no doubt."

"You say that, but when taken with the unwanted hedgehogs and a distinct feeling of being followed, I'm finding things unnerving."

Lawrence squeezed Violet's hand across the table. "I'm sorry. But please don't worry. I won't let you out of my sight."

"That's kind, but I won't become a victim. And wouldn't you hate going to the seance alone?"

"I don't want to go at all. But I don't need you there if you'd prefer to do something else. As long as you keep to public areas and stay safe."

"I'll think about it. But if you insist on speaking to Miss Hickman's father tomorrow, I'll visit Isabel. She can send word to Michael through her contact. I'll rest easier once he's in the know."

"Good plan," said Lawrence. "But keep it vague. Tell Michael that we have a lead. By all means, mention Crossley, but nothing further. I will visit Mr Hickman. He only lives across the river in Courtfield Gardens. It's in Chelsea. Nice and close. And if he's not convincing, then I'll drop it."

"You won't," said Violet. "I know that look of yours. You'll see this through, come hell or high water. But don't forget your priorities, Lawrence. You have a little girl at home who misses you very much."

Lawrence smiled, his face alight at the thought of Daisy. He did not take fatherhood for granted and could well imagine the pain Sophia's father had endured at the loss of his daughter. "I'm lucky enough to have my child still," he said. "Which is why I must satisfy myself that there's nothing untoward with this death. I won't let it run away with me."

Violet raised an eyebrow. "Do what you must," she said.

Chapter Nineteen

EDWIN HICKMAN

Lawrence stood outside Edwin Hickman's handsome terraced property, trying to count the floors, and wondering why one family needed quite so much space. He had walked from the hotel with the sun at its zenith, high in the sky and casting dappled rays over the honey-coloured bricks before him. Each property exactly resembled its neighbour, rising from iron-railed basements to a barely visible triple row of garret windows via an ornate iron balcony on the first floor. Lawrence estimated the buildings to be no more than thirty years old, sympathetically modelled as if they had always been there and complementing the park around which they lay. He glanced from door to door, looking for a window or cornerstone out of place. But they were faultlessly identical, and Lawrence wholeheartedly approved. Nothing bothered him more than haphazardness, and he decided he could live here if funds allowed. Not all of London was loathsome, it appeared. But though Lawrence was wealthy, he doubted his bank balance would stretch that far, and he wondered what profession Mr Hickman enjoyed affording such a fine dwelling.

Conscious that he had been standing still for so long that it was becoming suspicious, Lawrence headed for the darkly painted door set beneath four Doric pillars. He rapped loudly, exhibiting confidence he didn't feel. Ada Whittall might well desire his presence at her friend's father's house, but at no stage had she confirmed that Edwin Hickman had agreed to see him. For all Lawrence knew, the butler might meet him at the door brandishing a shotgun before ordering him from the premises. As it happened, the smartly dressed gentleman who answered the door smiled benignly.

"Mr Harpham, I presume."

Lawrence concealed a flicker of surprise. "Mr Hickman?"

"Indeed." Hickman offered his hand, and Lawrence accepted the firm shake. "Miss Whittall said you might call. Please follow me," he said, leading Lawrence down a long, black-and-white tiled passageway.

"It's too hot to talk inside," said Hickman. "And I'd prefer to keep this conversation away from my wife and children. They've suffered enough."

"Of course," murmured Lawrence as they passed through an orangery at the rear of the house. Tall, silver, elephant-shaped gilt planters contained exotic blooms that Lawrence did not recognise, while an enormous pair of feathered fans adorned one wall.

They emerged into a walled garden, and Edwin Hickman gestured to Lawrence to sit.

"A remarkable room," said Lawrence, nodding towards the orangery.

"Ah. Yes. A few memories from Spain. Another voyage looms, and I cannot put it off for much longer, but my wife is in no condition to be left alone. I am fortunate that Sir William understands."

Lawrence raised an eyebrow, desiring to know more but reluctant to pry while the man was still dealing with the aftermath of his daughter's death.

"I am a merchant," Hickman explained. "A Spanish merchant."

"Hence the travel," said Lawrence, nodding his head. "It must be an interesting life."

"But not glamourous," said Edwin Hickman with the ghost of a smile. "If I told you I mainly trade in Seville, you would doubtless think of exotic spices, Spanish antiquities and the like. But I deal in guano, sourced from the Peruvian isles. And it is a declining trade, Mr Harpham. It is as well that I am on the cusp of retirement."

"For fertiliser, I suppose?"

"Naturally. But fashions move on, and science too. It is only a matter of time before man improves upon nature and the guano trade declines."

"I am sorry to hear that."

"Well, I am not. I cannot feel any joy from travel and business while my daughter lays in the ground, and I don't know why."

"May I speak bluntly?"

"By all means. Nothing you can say could be worse than the ill-conceived verdict from my daughter's inquest."

"That's what I was about to mention. I spoke to Miss Whittall last night, and she said that the coroner was in no doubt about the verdict. Why would you think otherwise?"

"Because I know my daughter. She did not harbour inclinations of self-destruction."

"How do you know?"

"Sophia had no secrets. She would have told me."

"Is there any history of insanity in your family?"

Edwin Hickman's face flushed, and a vein throbbed in his forehead. "No, there is not."

"Any hysteria or nervous complaint?"

"Lower your voice, man." Hickman raised his finger to his lips.

"Well?"

"My youngest daughter, Mary, fell ill under the strain of her studies. But, and I cannot stress this enough, she recovered, completed her work and has shown no further signs of nerves."

"What was the nature of her breakdown?"

"She took to her bed for a fortnight – wouldn't eat and slept most of the time. Naturally, I called the doctor, and he said that Mary had taken on too much and must rest if she was to recover. She did and swiftly improved."

"Did Mary show any suicidal tendencies?"

"Mr Harpham. You are singularly unkind in your manner. I expected a more sympathetic approach from a man hand-picked by Sophia's best friend. If you understood what it was like to suffer the loss of a daughter, you might not be so direct in your questioning."

Lawrence felt a familiar combination of nausea and ire as he fought to answer in a dignified manner. "My closest friend killed my eldest daughter," he said. "Her name was Lily." He paused for a moment, trying to stop the words from spilling out. Words that signalled despair at Lily's loss and that she may not have been his child at all. Lawrence licked his lips. "Yes, I know loss. Believe me. And my questions are hard-hitting because I am away from my only living child and must return soon. I have little time left in London with other cases to unravel. If I am to investigate your daughter's death, there must be a good reason to do so.

I could pussyfoot around and consider your finer feelings, but it would only cause a delay. And so far, you have said nothing to convince me that Sophia did not take her own life. I am sorry if that is an uncomfortable fact."

Edwin Hickman's face flushed as he blinked and looked away. "I understand your position," he said, his grey eyes staring distantly from a tanned, weather-beaten face. "But I must ask if you would know if your daughter was unhappy?"

"Undoubtedly. Daisy is only eight years old. She has not yet mastered the art of keeping her feelings to herself."

"Is your wife alive?"

Lawrence nodded.

"Would you know if she was depressed and likely to harm herself?"

Lawrence considered the question. "I believe so," he said.

"I know so."

"It is not enough."

"Then how can I convince you?"

"Tell me what happened, as far as you are concerned. Not just the facts but how your daughter felt, her demeanour, her hopes and wishes. I want to hear all of it."

"Very well. It may take a while. Shall I ring for tea?"

"I can only spare an hour. But a glass of water would be welcome."

Edwin Hickman reached for a bell on a table directly outside the door. Shortly after, a uniformed maid came scurrying through. "A jug of water and another with lemonade, please," he said.

Lawrence glanced at his watch.

"I know time is pressing, but finding the right words isn't easy."

"Nothing important ever is."

"Very well. My daughter, Sophia, left my house for the last time on the fifteenth of August last year."

"Under what circumstances?"

"To attend the Royal Free Hospital where she was on duty and covering for another doctor who was on holiday."

"Which doctor?"

"I can't remember."

"No matter. I have contacts at the hospital. I can find out. How was Sophia in herself?"

"Very bright. She had replaced some equipment at the Medical Supply Association the previous day and was keen to start the morning's operations."

"Would you say she was happy?"

"I'd describe her as content. Sophia did not show extremes of emotion."

"Then what occurred?"

"Sophia did not return home. We were worried, of course. When she didn't arrive for afternoon duty, a nurse in Sophia's ward called to see if she was home but soothed our concerns by supposing that there might have been unexpected activity elsewhere at the hospital. But after two days, I visited the Royal Free to ask after her. Nobody had seen my daughter since the fifteenth, so I contacted the police."

"And did they take Sophia's disappearance seriously?"

"They did. But their enquiries were fruitless. They searched, and we searched. We contacted friends, family and eventually the press to find Sophia, to no avail. Her case captured public interest. All manner of theories abounded, some sensible, some ridiculous. I regretted the press involvement in the end. Sophia's disappearance became less tragic, spiralling into the realm of absurdity. I found myself advancing ideas that, in hindsight, were irrational. People forgot their compassion and sent detailed accounts of their various theories, which soon emblazoned the newspaper headlines. Sophia's mother nearly lost—" Edwin Hickman stopped abruptly.

"Nearly lost her mind?" offered Lawrence.

"It was just a turn of phrase," said Edwin. "She was distraught as any mother would be."

"I understand," said Lawrence. "Do continue."

"We endured this for two months," said Edwin. "And then, one day towards the end of October, a policeman arrived at our door with the worst possible news. Four young boys had been playing near Sidmouth plantation in Richmond Park and had found human remains. They had good reason to fear that they were Fanny's?"

"Fanny?" asked Lawrence.

"Sorry. We christened our daughter Sophia Frances and called her Fanny in private. But I won't complicate matters further by using her pet name."

"How did they identify Sophia?"

"By her personal items: a fountain pen engraved with a swan and a watch. They also showed me a pair of Sophia's spectacles which I recognised at once. And her handbag contained a swimming medal and a St John Ambulance fob, both engraved."

"Odd that she carried them with her. Wouldn't that suggest a deliberate intent to kill herself?"

"No. Sophia carried many objects in her handbag. She was a practical girl, not in the least fashion-conscious. She did not adopt the modern trend where young ladies change bags to match their outfits. Sophia carried the same handbag for more years than I care to mention. It was shabby and needed replacing. I expect those items had been in it for a long time."

"Her death must have come as a terrible shock."

"Indescribable," said Edwin. "I held out hope until the very end that they would find her alive. But Sophia's mother feared the worst. The guilt of her relief that Sophia would not remain missing indefinitely will never fade. She wanted them to locate her, even if it meant finding a body."

"An entirely understandable reaction," said Lawrence. "The weight of never knowing would be unbearable."

"Exactly. It was a truly terrible moment."

"Did the police find anything else?"

Edwin nodded. "They discovered a medicine bottle a few feet from her body. And some further medical supplies, including a syringe."

"What was inside the syringe?"

"Morphine."

"And the medicine bottle?"

"The same."

"And morphine was found in her body?"

"It was."

It seems conclusive to me.

"When the police first arrived at my door, they told me someone had cut Sophia's throat."

Lawrence raised an eyebrow.

"The pathologist disagreed. He concluded rats disturbed her remains."

"I see," said Lawrence, trying to decipher Hickman's logic.

"A musician picked up a knife near the plantation and submitted it as evidence."

"So?"

"My daughter's body was so mangled that the authorities couldn't deduce whether someone had cut her throat or scavengers had eaten her. Meanwhile, the police conveniently ignored a knife found in the vicinity."

"But that could equally prove your daughter cut her own throat to be on the safe side. And why would she do that with two sources of morphia in her possession?"

"What if somebody made her take it? Threatened her with physical harm?"

"Why would they? Your daughter brought the morphia with her."

Hickman placed his hand over his eyes and sighed.

"Why Richmond?" asked Lawrence.

"We lived there for a while," said Hickman, wiping his face.

"So, she was familiar with the area?"

"Yes. But it is a fair trek from the hospital. She could have found any number of parks much closer to home. And oddly, Sophia wasn't wearing her overcoat."

"Would she have required it in August?"

"On that particular day, yes."

Lawrence poured himself another glass of water from the tray the housemaid had obligingly brought. "Have you anything else to add?" he asked.

"I wondered if Sophia had died elsewhere," said Hickman. "Perhaps someone killed her and took her to the park. Her bag was there, but her purse was missing, you see. She had no money, which I found very odd. I wrote to one of the newspapers about it. The editor telephoned me, and I wish I had refused his call. I should have known better."

"Editor?"

"Mr Stead."

"Good Lord. Stead of *The Pall Mall Gazette*?"

"Not for some time. He was editing a different newspaper when he called me."

"Stead is a spiritualist. Not very sound at all. You're jolly lucky he didn't start table rapping."

Hickman's cheeks glowed pinkly, and he looked away.

"Oh, no."

"It was stupid. I regretted it immediately. They were a pair of charlatans who raised our hopes when we ought to have known better."

"What did they tell you?"

"That Sophia was being held captive in an attic room. They even supplied an address, and to my shame, I insisted the police act. They did and entered the premises, finding nothing but an elderly woman unaware of Sophia's disappearance."

"Who was she?" barked Lawrence, a sudden thought arising.

"I don't know. She was on her last legs. Probably dead by now."

"Not the old woman. The clairvoyant."

"Savage. Jane Savage."

"I don't believe it."

"I'm sure that's the right name."

"I mean, I am familiar with her. I've met her. And you are right. She is a charlatan, through and through."

"How odd that you know her."

"Hmmm. I intensely dislike coincidences. Even so. I still can't see a way past the evidence surrounding your daughter's death."

"More lemonade, sir?" The housemaid appeared at Hickman's elbow, flashing a respectful smile.

"No, thank you. Would you ask Barker to look out my brogues and give them a good polish? I'll need them later."

"Yes, sir."

The reference triggered a memory, not of Barker, who

Lawrence assumed to be a butler or valet, but of Baxter, domestic to the loathsome Savages. At the time, he'd paid scant attention, but Violet had discussed another Richmond suicide mentioned by Baxter. Who was it? He couldn't remember, but she had said something about a doctor.

"Did you know Dr and Mrs Johnstone when you lived in Richmond?" asked Lawrence.

"A little. Only by acquaintance. He lived next to the park."

"One of his house guests killed themselves last year."

"How sad. Poor chap."

"And more recently, an acquaintance of my kinswoman Ann died in Richmond Park," mused Lawrence.

"Not forgetting that poor soldier," said Edwin Hickman. "He died a few months before Sophia disappeared."

"Who did?"

"A young trooper with everything to live for. He walked in front of a train on the eve of his wedding. Imagine the despair. Hard to believe there wasn't another way. If a young man with his whole life in front of him can do it, then anyone can. Perhaps I have been wrong about Sophia, and it's wishful thinking."

"No. Richmond Park isn't Beachy Head." Lawrence snapped his head up. "It is not a natural place to end one's life. We should ask why four people have done away with themselves in under a year?"

Edwin Hickman nodded. "Something has always felt wrong about Sophia's death. Perhaps that is it."

Lawrence removed his notebook and pencil. "I need names and addresses. Anything that comes to you that might help with your daughter's case. I have little free time, but I'll do what I can with what is available."

Edwin Hickman's despair-filled eyes cleared momentarily. "I'll take anything you can offer," he said.

Chapter Twenty

TALKING TACTICS

"I can put it off no longer," said Lawrence, folding his newspaper and getting to his feet. He had spent a pleasant hour catching up with Violet in the hotel lounge over afternoon tea, knowing he must forgo his evening meal to attend the seance.

"What a shame. I'm very comfortable and could sit here all night."

"No reason you shouldn't," said Lawrence.

"There is. I'm coming with you."

"I thought you didn't want to see the Savages again."

"I hope never to clap eyes on them, but I forgot to mention that I've made other plans."

"Oh, yes?" Lawrence raised a quizzical eyebrow.

"Sorry, I should have said sooner, but I got carried away with your description of the Hickman house. Anyway, I telephoned the Johnstones earlier."

"Johnstones?"

"Yes. Dr and Mrs Johnstone. They have agreed to meet

me at six thirty prompt. I'll travel to the Savages' house with you and then to their property farther along Sheen Road."

"May I ask why you're seeing them?"

"I thought I told you. Baxter mentioned the untimely death of their house guest, and I want to find out more."

"Indeed. And I spoke of it to Edwin Hickman only hours ago. But I don't recall us making this decision."

"Don't be so stuffy, Lawrence. I don't need your permission. Do you mind?"

"No. Except that I would rather go with you. What with the hedgehog nuisance and your peculiar phone calls."

"I will be fine. I'll ask the coachman to wait for me and return via the Savages. We can go home together."

"Good. In that case, feel free. But why now?"

"Because I picked up an old copy of *The Standard* earlier, and I came across yet another death in Richmond."

"Really? Who and where?"

"A gentleman named Hedley who lived a few roads north of the park. He passed away in May."

"This year?"

Violet nodded.

"How did he die?"

"By bullet."

"Not the same thing at all, I'm relieved to say," replied Lawrence. "I'm surprised I haven't heard of such a recent murder. Or was it manslaughter?"

"Murder and suicide," said Violet. "A dreadfully sad affair. According to the article, Mr Hedley had a two-year-old boy upon whom he doted. But he woke up one morning and inexplicably cut the boy's throat while his wife was away from home before attempting to do the same to himself. And when that didn't work, he found a pistol and shot himself."

"Good Lord. Why?"

"A fit of mania, according to *The Standard*. Though temperate and studious, Hedley was excitable by nature."

"That doesn't explain why he ended the life of a treasured child." The colour drained from Lawrence's face as he imagined standing over Daisy's bloodless body, knife in hand. He shook his head, and the vision vanished.

"He must be mad," said Violet. "But it got me thinking. Yet another case of self-destruction in a small locality. It doesn't seem right. And there's something else."

"Yes?"

"Mr Hedley was a medical student."

Lawrence chewed his lip thoughtfully. "I shouldn't read too much into that," he said.

"I know. But it makes you think."

"Can you find out more about him?"

"I doubt it. There is no obvious route, so I decided that asking the Johnstones about their house guest would be more fruitful. She was a friend of the family rather than a relative, bringing a degree of separation which might produce some real objectivity."

Lawrence nodded. "You are right, of course. But I don't know what they could tell you that might help with Sophia Hickman."

"Nor do I. But where else can we look?"

"The hospital for one place, and Doctor Greville's for another. Seeing him clad in ceremonial garb at the order was odd, but he didn't take himself too seriously, and we got on jolly well. He should be willing to talk about Miss Hickman if he can remember her."

"Why would he?"

"She was a regular customer. The doctors at the Royal

Free Hospital purchase and repair their own equipment. You'd think the hospital would provide it, but they don't."

"I didn't realise," said Violet. "And I'm not impressed. If the medics work for the poor, the hospital should stock their medical supplies. It's not good enough."

"I agree, but there's nothing we can do about it. So, the Royal Free is our next port of call tomorrow."

"And tonight?"

"Go to the Johnstones' by all means. I will be glad of your company."

Violet smiled and linked her arm with her husband's as they left the room to prepare for the evening ahead.

Lawrence eyed Major Savage with the wary look of someone half expecting to see his host slipping his hand inside his breast pocket and relieving him of his wallet. The more he saw, the less he trusted him, and the major looked especially shifty tonight, dressed from head to foot in black and with an excess of hair oil that had seeped onto his forehead.

"Ah, Harpham. Good to see you, old man," he said with forced bonhomie.

Lawrence responded in kind. "Likewise," he replied. "I am keen to get started. Finding my uncle's will means a lot, you know. I don't just mean the money. Uncle Max was a dear man."

"A kindred spirit indeed," said Cameron Curzon, standing shoulder to shoulder with the major, hanging on his every word. "I hope you are as lucky as me and that your uncle takes a shine to Mrs Savage too. It is reassuring to have such easy access to Mother. I would be lost without her wise counsel, especially in financial matters. I can't be doing with all that nonsense about money."

"Don't you take any interest in your financial affairs?" asked Lawrence.

"As little as possible," replied Cameron. "I'm planning my next trip up the Niger River from Senegal and have no time for such trivialities."

"And no need to worry either," said the major cordially. "Your dear mother has placed you in safe hands."

Curzon beamed, and Lawrence concentrated hard to avoid raising his eyes heavenward. Cameron Curzon's mother had shown terrible judgement in leaving so much wealth in the hands of one so naïve and incapable. If the Savages weren't fleecing him, someone else would be.

"Just the two of us?" asked Lawrence, nodding to Curzon.

"Yes," said the major. "My wife thinks she will get a better response from Hepzibah with fewer distractions."

"Capital," said Lawrence. "I'm expecting great things of her."

"Yes, well. I'm sure she will do her best. These events can take time," muttered the major trying to manage expectations. But Lawrence was having none of it. Tonight would be his last appearance at East Sheen Road, however much they wanted to lure him into spending ever-increasing sums of money to locate the missing will. He would push them to the brink of discomfort, even if it meant asking awkward questions about the children.

"No. Two visits are quite enough. I expect Hepzibah to come through," said Lawrence firmly. "Otherwise, I might wonder if she is the real thing."

The major scowled. "No need for that tone."

"What's that?" Lawrence cocked his head to one side and peered at the ceiling.

"I heard nothing. Did you, Curzon?"

"Not a word."

"Surely you heard chattering and giggling?" asked Lawrence disingenuously. "Do you have children, Major?"

A pink glow settled over the major's cheeks. "I do not. You must have heard my wife or Baxter talking."

But as he spoke, the door swung open to reveal both women as they entered the room.

"Good evening, Mrs Savage," said Lawrence, thrusting his hand towards her. "I was asking the major about your children. I thought I heard them."

Jane Savage opened and closed her mouth, thought for a second, and answered. "William and Millicent belong to my sister. They are only here for a few weeks."

"How kind of you to put them up," said Lawrence, noting a warning glare shoot between the major and his wife. Lawrence hadn't been sure how best to perform before arriving that night. His plans had vacillated between asking the Savages polite, easily answered questions to downright brazen demands for information, only settling on the latter at the last minute because of his instinctive dislike of the major. But the tactic was working. A flushed and anxious Major Savage glanced furtively around the room while Mrs Savage looked bemused. Only Cameron Curzon seemed settled, happily awaiting another third-party conversation with his dear departed mother.

"Has my husband offered you a drink?" asked Jane Savage.

"Didn't get to it," said the major. "Don't suppose we have time now."

"I'd love one," said Lawrence, knowing he couldn't face

half an hour pretending to commune with the dead if he didn't have something alcoholic to take his mind off it.

"Baxter." The major clicked his fingers, and Baxter lumbered to Lawrence's side.

"A whisky, please," he said. Moments later, she reappeared and handed him a fingerprint-covered glass with a disappointingly small serving of a watery-looking cheap blend.

"Shall we begin?" asked Jane Savage, and they trooped through to the dining room again.

Jane Savage tried to start the seance as previously, but Lawrence pursed his lips when she suggested another hymn. "I think not," he said coldly.

"Don't interrupt," hissed the major, eyes glinting in the candlelight.

"Very well. I will try to invoke Hepzibah without our usual uplifting praise, but I insist on your complete silence. Any more outbursts, and we must call it a night."

Lawrence understood her threat all too well. The major had already trousered his fee, and Lawrence was in enemy territory. If he didn't toe the line, the Savages could close the seance and throw him out on his ear. He must be patient for a little longer until the opportunity arose to move around the house and assess the situation with the children.

"Let us pray."

Jane Savage lowered her head and thanked God for life after death. Lawrence clenched his teeth. Religion sat uneasily with him at the best of times, but for Michael's sake, he resented her taking the Lord's name in vain for the sake of trickery. He grudgingly muttered an Amen at the end of the simple prayer and waited for Hepzibah to appear.

Major Savage spat on his fingers, leaned over, and extinguished a candle, leaving Jane Savage in semi-darkness. And suddenly, from nowhere, a sound like the banging of a gong crashed through the room, making Lawrence jump. The thunderous sound rang once, twice, and once again, resonating around the room with a sinister echoing noise. Chills snaked up Lawrence's arms as the ringing sound died away, and he tried to fathom its origin. The room fell silent, and Hepzibah announced herself in a deep, broken voice from Jane Savage. She didn't beat about the bush.

"I must give way to Elizabeth Curzon. She demands access."

"Mother?"

"I am here, Cameron."

"Dear Mother."

Lawrence squinted through the darkness to see Curzon's face tip upwards, casting puppy-like eyes towards Jane.

"Do you trust me, son?"

"Of course."

"Will you obey me?"

"Always."

"Is your chequebook about your person?"

Curzon patted his jacket pockets. "It is, Mother."

"When we have finished tonight, you must write a cheque for five thousand guineas."

"To whom?"

"Major Savage. I have instructed him to invest it for you."

"Mr Baker will not like it."

"You do not need an accountant now. I will look after your affairs."

"Very well, Mother."

"And another thing, my dear son."

"What?"

"You must dispense with your valet."

"But Fenning has been with me for years. I cannot manage without him."

"You must. The spirits insist."

"Why?"

"Are you questioning my judgement?"

"No. Of course not."

"Did not my advice about the East India bonds prove fruitful?"

"It did. Very much. I made a handsome profit."

"And did I not pass sound judgement upon that girl?"

Curzon sighed and lowered his head. "Yes. She was greedy for my money."

"Then trust me now, through my mouthpiece on earth, dear Mrs Savage. And tell your friend to do likewise."

"My friend?"

"The man seated around the table with you."

"I barely know him."

"Nevertheless. Do as I say. Another spirit draws me away. It is coming for him."

"No. Stay longer, Mother."

"I cannot. Do everything I have asked, and I will come again soon."

"When?"

"Goodbye."

Lawrence waited tensely as the room fell quiet again. But within moments, a ripple of movement crossed the table, followed by a rapid tapping. His eyes darted from one side of the room to the other, forward, and back, but the sound echoed, and he couldn't locate its source. Once again, a large room divider loomed behind Jane Savage, and Lawrence determined to discover what lay beyond it.

The tapping stilled, the silences getting longer until it died away altogether.

"Is my nephew there?" The gruff tones emanating from Jane Savage's mouth bore no resemblance to Uncle Max, nor any red-blooded male, sounding for all the world like a bad imitation from a poor actress.

"Uncle Max," enthused Lawrence. "Thank goodness."

"Have you missed me, dear boy?"

"Of course. You left so abruptly earlier this week."

"Tis the way of the spirit world. We cannot linger past our time. Were it not for conduits such as dear Hepzibah through Mrs Savage, I could not speak at all."

"Then, if time is pressing, tell me more about your will, dear Uncle."

"I will."

"Then where is it?"

Jane Savage took a sharp breath as a choking noise emanated from her throat.

"Oh, no, you don't," said Lawrence. "Uncle, you must stay. Mrs Savage's maid will bring her a glass of water."

He glowered at Baxter across the room, throwing himself into the part of a greedy nephew.

Acknowledging his anger and suspicion of trickery, Jane Savage capitulated. As Baxter surreptitiously slid a glass of water onto the table, she drank deeply, then resumed in a poor imitation of Max Harpham's voice.

"I am back, dear boy," he said. "My speaker has rallied. A brave woman, indeed."

"Never mind that. Where is the will?"

"In the house of my kinsman."

"Who?"

"One who seeks to cheat you of your inheritance?"

Lawrence paused for a moment. It would be easy to suggest names, but the Savages' control over the idiot Curzon had deeply annoyed him, and he was determined to make them work for their ill-gotten gains.

"I have no such kinsman."

"A friend, then."

"Nor friends who would seek to deprive me."

"You cannot trust the women in your life."

"I hope you are not referring to Violet."

"There are others."

"Who?"

"Your cousins."

Uncle Max appeared to be growing increasingly desperate with his guesses, while Jane Savage's voice became shriller and less masculine at every new suggestion.

"You mean Harriet?"

"Yes," she said, grasping his offered straw with relief.

"My cousin, Harriet?"

"The very one." Max's voice deepened and became more measured.

"Where is the will?"

"In her dwelling."

"Are you sure?"

"Certain."

"Why did you leave it there?"

"I did not. She removed it from my property."

"Why?"

"She does not wish you to have it."

"Harriet cannot prosper from your will if I am the named beneficiary."

"She seeks only to deprive you."

"What have I ever done to Harriet?"

"I do not know. But I must go now. You have what you require. Leave at once and claim your inheritance."

Jane Savage threw back her head, gyrated it a few times and prepared to complete her finale with her head in her hands when a low sneeze broke the silence. A gentle gasp followed, and the major jumped to his feet.

"Are you alright, my dear?" he boomed, placing an arm around his wife.

"What was that?" asked Lawrence.

"Probably the cat. The damned thing coughed up a furball earlier today. Revolting creature. Anyway, that's enough of that. Time to go," the major replied.

He ushered Lawrence from the room and back down the corridor. "You'll want to be straight off now, I suppose."

"Why would you think that?"

"Your uncle. The will. No time to lose, I fancy."

"My cousin Harriet lives in Penzance," lied Lawrence. "It will take some time to get there, and I need to prompt an invitation first. No, I have time for a refill before I depart."

A frown slid over the major's features. "Well, I suppose a quick one won't do any harm."

"Thank you. And I'll use your facilities while I'm waiting."

The major cast a panicky eye for Baxter, but she was still with her mistress. Lawrence did not wait for further comment but strode back down the corridor towards the washroom, passing the dining room en route. Inside the now-lit room, Cameron Curzon was studiously writing a cheque while Jane Savage stood at his side like a prison warden. "Damned fool," muttered Lawrence under his breath.

He entered the washroom and wasted five minutes until he heard sounds from farther up the corridor. Then he quietly shut the door and emerged, tiptoeing into the now vacant dining room. He stood near the door for a few seconds before hearing a rustling from the other side of the divider and quietly stepped closer to the middle of the room. An idea occurred to him before he reached the midway point, and he shimmied to the side and released the window latch. He advanced farther and was about to touch the ebony divider when a voice roared from the passageway.

"What are you doing, Harpham?"

Lawrence spun around. "Nothing, Major. I thought I heard a scrabbling sound. You may have an infestation of mice."

"Don't be ridiculous. My wife's flea-bitten moggy sees off any unwanted vermin."

"I can't help what I heard. I thought I was assisting."

"That may be so, but the drink is off. My wife is unwell, and Curzon has left. It's time for you to depart."

"But my carriage hasn't arrived."

"Walk to the end of the road. It is easy to hail one from there."

"At this time of night?"

"It is the principal thoroughfare. There will be plenty of cabs." The major snapped out the words impatiently, and Lawrence pushed it no further.

"Very well. Wish your wife a good evening and thank her."

"I will. Good day to you."

And with that, Lawrence left and walked into the night.

Chapter Twenty-One

ENTERING THE LION'S DEN

Lawrence thanked his lucky stars that the weather was clement as he waited on the corner of East Sheen Road, out of sight of the house. He had arranged to meet Violet and return to the hotel together, but having loosened the dining-room window latch, he now had an alternative plan. It could only work under cover of darkness, and the Savages must think he had left. Above all, he must intercept Violet before she reached the Savages' home. Lawrence checked his watch for the umpteenth time before hearing the clip-clop of hooves farther up the road. A carriage was heading straight towards him, but he couldn't see inside. Sighing, he ventured into the street and faced the oncoming horse.

"Oi, you. Move over."

Lawrence winced as the cab driver's voice bellowed in the still night but stood his ground.

"Are you simple? I said sling your hook."

Lawrence held up his hand. "Are you carrying a lady?"

"None of your business," said the cabby before cocking

his head anxiously as he tightened the reins. "You're not about to rob us, are you?"

"Don't be ridiculous. I'm waiting for my wife."

"In the middle of the road? I don't believe it."

"That's your choice. Now, is Violet with you or not?"

"What's your name?"

"Lawrence Harpham."

"Ah, yes. I have your wife. She's inside. Are you coming aboard?"

"Not now. But I need a few moments to speak with Violet. Kindly move your carriage to the side of the road. I'll only be a moment."

"It will cost you," growled the cabbie under his breath.

Lawrence strode to the door and rapped with his knuckles.

"Ah, there you are," said Violet. "Why have we stopped here?"

"I've created an opportunity to do some snooping, but it will take a few hours."

"Oh, bother. I've been yawning all night. Can't it wait?"

"No. And I must go alone. You should return to the hotel."

"Why?"

"I won't spell it out with another pair of ears listening," said Lawrence.

"Fair enough. But how will you get home?"

"The cabs run all night. Did you learn anything useful tonight?"

"I'm not sure. But the Johnstones were very generous with their time and offered me supper."

"Lucky you. I'm ravenous. Off you go, then. We'll catch up tomorrow."

Lawrence leaned over and kissed Violet on the cheek,

then patted the horse on the behind. "Take the lady home safely," he instructed, nodding to the cab driver in a more conciliatory manner. The driver gave a mock salute and trotted the horses away.

Lawrence approached a street parallel with the major's house and stopped at a large home on Park Drive with a substantial plot of land to the side. He watched until darkness fell, entered the grounds, and made his way to the rear, where the garden abutted those along East Sheen Avenue. Climbing the fence, Lawrence hauled himself up, gritting his teeth as his body weight strained his weakened left hand and dropped quietly to the other side. But something was awry with the rear windows. They were facing the wrong way. Lawrence groaned as he realised, he had landed on the wrong property, but a side door opened before he could turn tail and leave. Paws scratched along an uneven pathway, heralding the arrival of a friendly retriever. Tail wagging, it darted towards Lawrence, snuffling at his coat, and reminding him of a long-forgotten cinder toffee in his pocket. He handed the sweet over, and the dog busied itself with its newfound treat, leaving Lawrence time to disentangle himself and move to the corner out of sight. Eventually, the dog's owner whistled, and the animal trotted inside, but Lawrence waited until the lights dimmed before daring to launch himself over the fence again. This time, the climb was uneventful, and before long, Lawrence found himself directly outside the Savages' dining room, gently illuminated by the hall light shining through the open door.

He manoeuvred himself until he could see beyond the room divider, where his suspicions were confirmed. A gong and a pair of coconuts lay against a wooden crate. Above, a rope stretched beyond the partition, carefully tied beneath the table. A flimsy white veil hung from a hook on the side by a length of wire. All the tricks of the trade, just as he had expected. But the collection of wooden objects on the floor was more interesting than the seance props. Lawrence counted three wooden cars and a peg doll, all indicating that children had been in this room to operate the gadgets rigged by their unscrupulous guardians. They were nothing more than stooges in the Savages' deception. But where had they come from? Did they really belong to Jane Savage's sister? Lawrence gripped the bottom of the window with his fingers, testing to see if it came away. So far, so good. Major Savage had not yet spotted the unlocked window. But the night was young, and Lawrence would need to be patient for a few more hours until the house fell quiet. He found a patch of dry, even ground near an unlit corner of the house and settled down for a long wait.

It was well after midnight before darkness finally fell in the household, but the temperature had held, and Lawrence dropped off for the best part of an hour, bringing welcome relief from the boredom. He allowed a further half hour before risking entry, but as he stood, his legs almost buckled from lack of activity, and he wasted more time pacing silently along the rear of the house until he felt ready to climb through. Lawrence pulled open the window to its fullest extent and slipped inside, landing neatly with hardly any noise. Then he passed through the dining room, seeing no more of note.

Initially, Lawrence had no further plan beyond releasing the window latch, but having had hours to think, he decided to take another look inside the major's office. He trusted

Violet had made a comprehensive search, but something might have changed since she checked.

Lawrence tiptoed along the floor, reacquainting himself with the layout of the hall, and tried the only closed door. As he hoped, it led to the study, and he closed it behind him before rifling through the unlocked drawers. Lawrence hit his objective with little effort, smiling with quiet satisfaction at the sight of Cameron Curzon's cheque poking out from the top of an accounting journal. He ripped it into four pieces and stowed them in his pocket in a potentially futile gesture. The young fool would write another one in due course. He was stupid enough to give the Savages the shirt off his back if they asked, but the act could buy Lawrence a few days. And he intended to use the time wisely by unmasking the major and his wife for the charlatans they were. But, for now, the house was quiet, and opportunity knocked. Even the cat lay quietly purring, unperturbed by his presence. So, Lawrence searched every drawer of the major's desk, removing several letters that proved fraudulent activity, including one showing proof that he had used one of Curzon's investment cheques to pay part of his bill at the local vintners. Lawrence lifted the cash book again, knowing Violet had checked it, so he didn't need to. But Lawrence's meticulous nature would not allow carelessness. And, starting from the first page, he scanned through the mundanity of the Savages' financial affairs until a column on page five revealed an interesting creditor. "Well, well," said Lawrence under his breath as he ran his finger along the page. "You're in debt to Felix Crossley, you damned fool." Flicking through the rest of the book, he found a further three entries, one repaying some of Crossley's initial loan and the other two increasing it.

Buoyed with success, Lawrence persevered and was

about to call it a night when he picked up a journal and a folded piece of paper dropped to the floor. He picked it up and held it under a candle, his forehead furrowing as he read a letter from an orphanage in Surrey refusing an offer of adoption from Colonel and Mrs Wilmott. A second, older document in the same journal agreed that William and Millicent were a good fit for the Wilmott family. Lawrence smelled a resolution to the mystery. The Savages had taken the children using false names, but the letter bore an address, and he now knew where they came from. The investigation was over, and he could now report back to Cora and commit himself wholeheartedly to the more complex problems surrounding Aurora and Sophia Hickman. Lawrence stifled a sneeze with his handkerchief, congratulating himself on a good evening's work. He was so pleased that he left the room without noticing his business card had fallen from his pocket and was lying face-up on the rug.

Lawrence was still in good spirits as he tiptoed down the corridor towards the dining room. Though tired and ready for home, he couldn't help pausing as he passed the kitchen door, inhaling the lingering smells of a late-night supper. His stomach growled. He was starving and doubtless only inches from food. His eyes darted between the dining room and the kitchen door, torn between leaving and eating. But it was no contest. Lawrence was famished and couldn't face the prospect of searching for a late-night cab on an empty stomach. He grasped the handle and slowly pushed the kitchen door open to a rusty creak that screeched through the night. Lawrence froze, holding his breath, as fear coursed through his body. But, after a few seconds of thought, he rationalised that although it sounded loud to him, they might not hear it upstairs. Still, the incident had put him on edge, and he was sweating beneath his coat. He almost called it a night, but his stomach growled again, and Lawrence tiptoed farther into the kitchen towards a metal dome glinting on the table in the moonlight. He carefully lifted the shiny handle and rested it beside the table, then lit his trusty candle and examined the contents. Lawrence's mouth watered at the sight of a raised game pie. Better still, the major had already started it, and he ought to be able to extract a slice without detection.

Lawrence headed for the nearest kitchen drawer, finding only napkins. But a further search revealed a cutlery drawer, and he took the largest, sharpest knife and cut himself a modestly sized piece. For one moment, Lawrence considered eating it there but, on second thoughts, wrapped it inside a napkin to eat at his leisure in the cab while journeying back. Lawrence reached to stow the pie in his pocket, but as he moved, his elbow brushed against the knife, pushing the blade beneath the domed lid, and levering it from the table. It landed on the kitchen tiles with a sound like clashing cymbals. Lawrence froze.

He waited for a moment, barely breathing, hoping against hope that no one had heard. But a bellowing from upstairs told him otherwise. The major was yelling while stomping around his bedroom, looking for clothes. Lawrence dropped the piece of pie and ran for it, racing into the dining room as the major clumped downstairs. Hurling the window open, Lawrence dived outside, landing badly on his ankle and wincing. He jumped to his feet but could barely move for the pain and didn't have time to recover. He'd left the dining room window open, and the major could only be a few short yards away. Lawrence ducked towards the darkest side of the garden where the irritatingly full moon hadn't quite made its mark and limped along the fence towards the rear.

"You damned bloody villain," yelled the major, poking his head outside the window. Lawrence stopped and crouched stock-still under a bush, not daring to move in case the rustling foliage gave his location away.

A mighty bang followed, and a projectile whistled past his ear. "I'll give you what for, you common little thief!" screamed the major. "Nobody breaks into my house. I'll have the law on you."

Lawrence chanced a backward look to see Major Savage crouching over the dining room window sill, brandishing a crow rifle. "Stay where you are," he snarled, loosing off another shot. But Lawrence had no intention of risking further injury. Steeling himself for the inevitable ankle pain, he darted towards a large shrub in the bottommost corner of the garden, leapt up the fence and shimmied over the other side before the major could cock the rifle again. Ignoring the stream of invectives hailing from East Sheen Road, he ran pell-mell towards the cab rank as fast as his legs could carry him.

Chapter Twenty-Two

A TRICK TOO FAR

Friday, June 17, 1904

"It wasn't my doing," said Violet tersely, dipping a chunk of brown toast into a perfectly cooked egg.

"I'm not saying you did it intentionally, but you left the hotel staff under the impression that I wasn't to enter my bedroom. Not amusing after the shocking night I've had. I mean, really – how could it possibly happen?"

"Because I had no choice in the matter."

"Sorry. I don't understand," sighed Lawrence, trying to be patient.

"Didn't the receptionist explain?"

"Funnily enough, she wasn't that interested in the whys and wherefores during the early hours of the morning. And being dog-tired and starving, I was hardly in the mood for a protracted discussion. The girl explained you were in my room and had left instructions not to disturb you under any circumstances. I tried to knock on the door, but you didn't respond."

"I had earplugs in, as usual."

"Of course, you did."

"Where did you spend the night, Lawrence?"

"In the caretaker's room."

"Then what are you complaining about?"

"The caretaker was there too. My bed was about two feet away from his, and when the delightful man wasn't mumbling in his sleep, he was snoring his head off."

"Oh."

"Oh, is right. The so-called supervisor, Mr Cannon, offered me the choice of bunking down with his staff or finding another hotel. Oh, and a third option was to evict you from my room, none of which appealed at quarter to three this morning. So, once again, please enlighten me on how this happened?"

A waiter strode across the dining room towards Violet. "More toast and tea, madam?"

"Not for me," said Violet calmly. "But please bring a cup of coffee and a large plate of eggs and bacon for my husband. He has had rather a night of it and needs cheering up."

"Very good."

The waiter shimmied off, and Lawrence pursed his lips. "Well? I'm waiting?"

Violet sighed. "If the hotel staff locked you out, they misunderstood my instructions. I simply said I was taking your room and asked them not to disturb me."

"What the hell was wrong with your room? And why wouldn't they let me swap?"

"There was only one room left. That was the problem."

"What do you mean? We each had a room when we left for Richmond yesterday. Did the cleaners lose it, or has it vanished into the ether?" asked Lawrence, bristling with indignation. Violet's face darkened.

"Calm down and listen. The girl wouldn't give me the key to my room when I returned to the hotel last night," she said, slowly enunciating as if Lawrence was a small child finding it difficult to comprehend. "The maid had packed up the contents of my wardrobe and sent it over to left luggage at Liverpool Street Station."

"Why would she do that? It sounds like nonsense."

"I'm telling you, she did."

"Any particular reason why, or just a passing whim?"

"Try not to be facetious, Lawrence. It's not in the least bit funny. I've had no nightwear or clean undergarments and no choice but to use your toothbrush last night."

"That's the least of our troubles. Who told the domestic staff to pack your things away?"

"I did, apparently, according to Mr Cannon. He said that the receptionist had taken a phone call from me yesterday evening. I allegedly told Miss Clark that I was getting the late train back to Suffolk and asked her to send my luggage to the station."

"But you didn't?"

"Of course not. I was with you until we parted outside the Savages'."

"Do you think…?"

"Naturally. The call was quite deliberate. Somebody is trying to upset me, and I've had enough. Hedgehogs are one thing, but this is spiteful by any measure. My bags are at the station, and it's too much trouble to fetch them back, so I'm taking it as my cue to go home. Daisy must be missing us dreadfully by now. You can stay here a little longer if you like, but I'm leaving on the ten-thirty train."

"But I've so much to tell you. I've learned more about

the children, and the major is in debt to Crossley. I must stay here and sort things out."

"I never doubted you would, but I'm going home."

"Are you sure?"

"Sure I want to go, or sure I don't mind you staying?"

"Both. Either."

"Yes, I want to go, and I would prefer it if you came with me, but I understand your commitment to Michael. Try not to get too distracted by the other matters."

"Will you tell me what the Johnstones said before you leave?"

"Of course. Here, have the rest of my toast while you wait for breakfast. It might improve your mood."

Violet was right. Two cups of coffee and a large breakfast later, Lawrence was a different man. "I wish you would stay," he said, stroking the back of her hand. "I will miss you dreadfully."

"I must leave," said Violet. "But I will telephone regularly, and you must keep in touch too. I would still like to play an active part in this investigation."

"And you shall," said Lawrence. "I'll only be in London for a few more days, at most."

"Not if you mean to get to the bottom of Sophia's death."

"If it's even possible."

"Are you having doubts?"

"Always. But I'll try my best."

"I know. And for what it's worth, I think there's something sinister behind Emily Locker's death."

"Did the Johnstones say so?"

"Not in so many words. They have taken the suicide verdict at face value. The coroner said it was deliberate, and naturally, they believe him."

"Have you got time to tell me now, or shall I call a cab?"

"I've already spoken to Miss Clark. An automobile will collect me at ten o'clock. We can talk until then."

"Then, tell me… what did the Johnstones say?"

"Well, the Johnstones' friends Emily Locker and her husband Benjamin usually lived in Surbiton. Emily was of a nervous disposition, had been unwell before the visit, and was pessimistic about her prospects of getting better. On the day she died, Emily was unusually cheerful. She had been to the park and told Mrs Johnstone that she'd spoken to someone who had given her helpful advice on dealing with her low spirits. Mrs Johnstone, relieved to see an improvement in her guest's mood, was even happier to see her head upstairs early to read a book before bed."

Violet paused as Lawrence lowered his head and scribbled furiously in his notebook. I wish you wouldn't do that," she said.

Lawrence looked up. "I'm sorry. I don't mean to be rude, but I'll forget what you said if I don't write it down."

"I know. Forget I mentioned it. Anyway, Mrs Johnstone set an early alarm for four o'clock."

"Seems unnecessary. Whatever for?"

"She didn't say, and it's by the by. So, she tiptoed past Mrs Locker's bedroom and saw her sleeping. Mrs Johnstone did whatever chore was necessary, returned to her bedroom, and heard Mrs Locker's door creaking open about five o'clock. She continued listening as Emily Locker went downstairs, and after a short time, she heard a thudding sound."

"A thud?"

"Exactly that. Mrs Johnstone was quite taken aback and went downstairs to find her guest slumped against the hallway wall, holding a box of matches in her hand, her face wild with fright. Mrs Johnstone helped Mrs Locker to the bathroom but could move her no further. Her struggles roused the locum, Dr Hey, who assisted Mrs Locker back to her bed. But as they settled her, Mrs Johnstone noticed that Emily's breath smelled of lavender, and being a doctor's wife, understood the implications."

"Which were?"

"That certain drugs contain lavender. So, Mrs Johnstone hastened to the room where her husband took his surgeries to see if anything was missing. There, lying on the floor with the stopper out, was a bottle labelled *liquor arsenicalis*."

"Oh dear," said Lawrence. "Presumably, death soon followed."

Violet nodded. "Emily Locker passed away at five thirty."

"And the coroner doubtless ruled a suicide?"

"Yes, suicide during temporary insanity, with no one else to blame."

"Which sounds perfectly reasonable," said Lawrence.

"Well, it does until you consider the conversation in the park."

"What about it?"

"As I told you, Emily Locker spoke to someone who made her feel so much better that she was almost euphoric by the time she returned."

"It doesn't help unless you know who she spoke to?"

"I don't, and neither did the Johnstones, but they had high hopes for their guest's swift recovery. Not only was she in much better spirits, but she appeared so much healthier."

"Low spirits often cause physical ailments," said Lawrence.

"Quite. But the question is, why would someone who seemed so improved deliberately destroy themselves?"

"What are you getting at, Violet?"

"Can someone persuade a low-spirited person to take their own life?"

"I suppose so, though hardly during a single conversation. It would involve much persuasion and could only happen over time. Certainly not in the course of an afternoon's casual chat."

"But who's to say there weren't other conversations?"

"Are you suggesting Mrs Locker was happy because she'd finally found a way out of her misery?"

Violet nodded.

"But why assume another person is involved?"

"I'm only guessing. But compare this to Maria's death. Remember, someone gave her money to take the pain away. Doesn't it make you think?"

Lawrence covered his eyes with his palms and considered her words for a moment. "You might be on to something," he said. "But for the life of me, I don't know what we can do about it."

Chapter Twenty-Three

BILLY & MILLY

Lawrence turned an uncomfortable shade of pink as he walked towards the offices of Ponsonby & Cream. He had left Violet at Liverpool Street station, waving her off while battling a pall of gloom threatening to wake the black dog. But less than an hour later, he was striding towards a woman who, at every recent encounter, had set his bodily urges off in directions his heart and mind had no intention of following. He opened their office door with resigned trepidation, immediately relieved to see Vera Ponsonby alone at her desk with no sign of Cora.

"Mr Harpham," she said, jumping to her feet and offering her hand. "I wasn't expecting you."

"I know. But I thought it better to come while things are fresh in my head."

"Did you go to a second seance?"

"I did. And it was fruitful if a little unedifying."

"Let me make you a coffee, and you can tell me all about it."

Lawrence sat in front of her desk as she bustled into the

kitchen, arriving a few minutes later with two steaming cups. "Lucky for you, I've only just boiled the kettle," said Vera. "Cora will be along at any moment. You will stay for a while, won't you?"

"Not for long," said Lawrence. "I'm running out of time to resolve this latest mystery."

"Not the Hickman thing? I rather think you are wasting your time."

"We've uncovered several more Richmond suicides," said Lawrence. "One very recent. Violet thinks someone is taking advantage of distressed, unhappy people for their own amusement."

"Well, it's possible," said Vera, cupping her hands around her drink. "And a lot more credible than your previous suggestion. But how would you prove it one way or the other?"

Lawrence shrugged. "Therein lies the problem. I've listed a few people at the hospital worth speaking to, and I'll have another chat with Doctor Greville."

"You'll be lucky if they give you the time of day. It's jolly difficult getting medical men to talk."

"Two of them are women," said Lawrence. "Not that it matters. It's my job to tease the information from them. I'm confident about Greville. He's a decent chap, considering the company he keeps. Did I tell you he's a friend of Crossley's?"

"No. Your friend has poor taste, but that's a matter for him. As long as you don't cross paths with Felix Crossley."

"I haven't met him yet, although it may become unavoidable."

An opening door cut their conversation short as Coralie Cream waltzed into the office, shedding a light coat as she entered.

"Well, hello," she said, gazing at Lawrence as she hung her coat on the stand.

"Good day, Miss Cream," he said awkwardly.

"Cora. Call me Cora."

"How did you get on?" Vera Ponsonby replaced her cup on the saucer and leaned back in her chair.

"Jolly good, actually. Andrew is quite pleasant for a politician."

"But did he tell you anything?"

"Not enough to make a difference to our plans, but I'll keep working on him. He's invited me to dinner, you know."

"Good work." Vera Ponsonby nodded approvingly. "A new case," she said to Lawrence. "Quite an interesting one, actually. I shouldn't tell you this, but you are the soul of discretion, and I trust you. There's a mole in the foreign office."

"A spy?"

"Gosh, no. We wouldn't be involved in something like that. This is low-level stuff involving the press. Our client, Mr Pennington, is eager to stop information leaking into the newspapers. He thinks it's coming from the typing pool. There are dozens of suspects, as I'm sure you can imagine. We want to work from the inside and gain temporary employment as typists, but Pennington is dead against it. He likes Cora and feels protective of her."

Cora Cream winked. "As I intended," she said.

Lawrence averted his eyes from her face. Her plump lips and sparkling blue eyes made him hot under the collar in a way he couldn't control. Women like Coralie were dangerous – all too aware of their power over men and willing and able to use it.

"Have you brought news?" she asked.

Lawrence nodded and recounted his experience the

previous night. Cora raised a wry smile at his story, but her face fell when he mentioned the orphanage. "The location rings a bell," she said, glancing at Vera.

"Does it?"

"I've heard about a couple of children missing from an orphanage."

"Have you? You didn't mention it. Should I check with Isabel?"

"Good idea."

Vera stood and walked towards the door.

"Where are you going?" asked Lawrence.

"Next door. Our neighbour, Mr Rodman, has a telephone. He won't mind me using it."

"Don't worry. You're safe with me. I won't eat you," smiled Cora.

Lawrence licked his lips, searching for another topic of conversation. "Oh. Something else you should know. Major Savage is spending Curzon's investment money on his debts."

"Good work. But can you prove it?"

"Only if someone in authority goes to the house. Savage keeps a journal in his desk. The evidence is in the bottom drawer on the left."

"That's good to know. We are nearly ready to intervene if Isabel agrees."

"She must. The Savages are using the children to make their awful seances credible. They sit behind screens making spectral sounds at the appropriate times."

Cora shook her head. "Poor little mites. But it's not against the law. Let's hope Isabel comes up with something."

"In any case, Savage won't be happy when he tries to bank Curzon's cheque."

"Why not?"

"He won't find it." Lawrence reached into his pocket and withdrew the torn pieces of paper.

"Oh, well done, you clever thing," beamed Cora.

"I found it rather satisfying. And despite Savage's best efforts in the garden, he didn't see me. A good thing too. He's another one with links to Crossley."

"Really? That's another black mark against him. Oh, look. There she is."

Vera Ponsonby strode through the door and stood in front of them with her hands on her hips. "We've got them now," she said. "The Savages, I mean. Isabel had already heard about the missing orphanage children but didn't put the two things together."

"How could she have known?" asked Coralie.

Lawrence crossed his legs. "It was possible at a stretch. The Savages didn't alter the children's names but lengthened them. Milly and Billy became Millicent and William."

"But how silly to steal the children after corresponding with the orphanage. Surely, the Savages made themselves prime suspects? Why weren't they approached when the children disappeared?"

"Because the Savages used false names," said Lawrence. "I found a letter addressed to Colonel and Mrs Willmott. But I don't understand why they went to the trouble of starting the adoption process if they intended to steal them all along?"

"To get to know the children well enough to lure them away without a fuss," said Vera. "William and Millicent are old enough to protest if they encounter a stranger."

"There must be more to it," said Lawrence. "The Savages have taken a lot of effort to secure these particular children. They could have lifted any waif from the street without notice but specifically wanted these two. Why?"

Vera and Coralie exchanged glances. "A good point," said Cora. "I wonder where they came from before they were orphaned?"

"Coggeshall," said Vera. "A little town in Essex."

"I know it." Lawrence crossed his legs. "What happened to their parents?"

"I don't know, but Isabel said their father was the parish vicar."

"What a shame they had no relatives to take them in."

"Isn't it?"

"What will happen to William and Millicent now?" asked Lawrence.

"They'll go back to the orphanage."

"How sad. They'll be no better off."

"I'll speak to Isabel," said Cora. "They need a loving family, and Isabel will ensure they get one. She'll leave no stone unturned trying to make this right."

"And this information is enough to take action against the Savages?"

"Oh yes. Isabel says she will involve the authorities as soon as we finish the call. Major and Mrs Savage should be in chokey by the end of the day."

Chapter Twenty-Four

BREAKING RETREAT

Lawrence's instinct was troubling him. He should be *en route* to the hospital to speak to the various medical staff, but something was niggling in the back of his mind, and he found himself walking in the opposite direction. He perambulated distractedly, thoughts of the children churning through his mind. Violet should be in Suffolk by now. Probably not yet home, but ever closer to Daisy. He envied the moment she would put her arms around their daughter, holding her close, and quietly promising never to leave her again. And while Lawrence knew he must stay in London for another few days, it was primarily a matter of pride. He wished it were otherwise, but practically, there was little left to do. Lawrence couldn't simply walk away. He always followed his instinct, remaining dedicated to the job at hand at a significant cost to his family and peace of mind. But things weren't going his way, and with little left to achieve, he would soon join Violet in a day, two at the most. Aurora was still missing; probably in Scotland and too far away to pursue. Lawrence was increasingly sympathetic to Violet's theory about the Richmond Park suicides but could do little about it. His time in London was now a matter of tying up loose ends. Once he had spoken to Doctor Janet Campbell, her colleagues, and Doctor Greville, his job was finished. And it was a liberating realisation. He could go home knowing he'd done everything possible to help the grieving family and Sophia's friend, Ada. And when it came down to it, he hadn't even met Miss Whittall. He shouldn't feel obligated to any case, and if it weren't for his overdeveloped instinct, he would pack and go today. But something was bothering him, and he found himself drawn back to the hotel, passing through the door with a feeling of resignation.

"Good afternoon," said Miss Clark as he entered. Lawrence glanced at his watch, too tired to comprehend how much time had passed. It seemed like he'd only been away from the hotel for a while, but it was closer to four hours. He would go to his room and lie down, assuming they hadn't allocated it to someone else while he was out, but when Lawrence asked for his key, the receptionist offered it with a knowing smile. He grasped it, and as he walked away, she called him back.

"I took a phone call for Mrs Harpham this morning," said Miss Clark. "Will she be back soon?"

"Mrs Harpham has gone. Didn't see the point of staying when her luggage was resident at the station," Lawrence replied testily, still angry at the hotel's refusal to accept the blame.

"Oh."

"And she could hardly stay with no room to go to."

"That's a pity. We intended to offer you a junior suite. Mr and Mrs Phillips have vacated theirs today."

"Well, it's too late," said Lawrence.

"Would you like to see the message?"

Lawrence sighed, expecting the worst. With Violet recently plagued by a series of foolish pranks, he feared this was another silly trick in the same vein.

"Not really."

"As you wish. But he sounded like a nice man."

"Who did?"

"Mr Farrow. Mr Michael Farrow."

"Good grief. Why didn't you say? Hand me the note at once."

The girl hesitated, then reached for a cream-coloured message neatly folded in two. "Here it is," she said.

Lawrence snatched it and walked away, then turned back. "Sorry for my curtness," he muttered. "This is important. Thank you for bringing it to my attention."

She smiled half-heartedly, but Lawrence was halfway to the snug in case he needed the telephone. Checking inside and relieved at the absence of guests, he shut the door and locked it with a key someone had conveniently left outside.

Then he reclined on the sofa and opened the note.

Dear Violet

How did you track me down? I received your message and broke my retreat immediately. I am on the mainland, with access to a telephone for the next two hours, and I will call again before catching the train. If all else fails, I will meet you in London, God willing.
Yours Michael Farrow. 11.15 am.

"Damn it, Michael," hissed Lawrence impatiently. "Why didn't you give the girl your telephone number?" He glanced at his watch, glad to see that there was still another half hour before the two-hour window ended "Ring, will you?" he exclaimed, eyeing the silent telephone with contempt. Lawrence stood and paced the room, hoping that Michael wouldn't be angry at the paucity of information for which he had broken his retreat. He tried to put himself in Michael's position. Lawrence lacked detail about Aurora's location and whether she was safe. Michael would want to know, and without the information, was likely to think Lawrence was wasting his time.

Lawrence stood by the window, glancing over the road towards Battersea Park and watching a grey horse twitching its tail from side to side to dislodge an unwelcome fly buzzing around its rear. The cab driver approached his mount and offered it a nosebag of food, distracting it from the irritating insect. The horse settled, the driver disappeared, and Lawrence stared vacantly at the grass, trying to resist the temptation to look at the telephone.

Suddenly, a ringing pealed out behind him, and he snatched the receiver before it could attract the attention of anyone else in the hotel. "Call from Strathclyde 201," announced the operator.

"I'll take it."

Lawrence waited a moment before a familiar voice came over the crackling line.

"Violet. Are you there?"

"It's me. Lawrence."

"Oh. How are you? And where is Violet?"

"Back in Bury. It's a long story. I'll fill you in another time."

"What's this about Aurora? And who is Crossley?"

Lawrence paused. He had hoped that Michael might have heard of Felix Crossley so that Aurora's entanglement with him did not come as too much of a shock. But Michael was oblivious to the existence of the wickedest man in Britain. "How much time have you got?" asked Lawrence.

"As long as this line holds. It's blowing a gale outside, and I don't know what effect it might have. I can barely hear you as it is."

"Right. I'll try to be quick, but, Michael. It's not good news."

"You haven't found her, then?" Michael's voice was heavy with disappointment.

"No. We don't know where she is."

"Then why bother me? I would have left Iona in ten days."

"We may not have that much time."

"I don't understand."

"Look, Aurora is mixed up in something sinister. A cult."

"I'm not surprised after her reaction to my brother's secret room. What do you mean by a cult?"

"The kind that practices blood magic."

The line fell quiet.

"Are you still there, Michael?"

"Yes. I'm trying to take it in. As a parish priest, I can barely accept the idea of men prostrating themselves before the devil. That's what you are talking about, isn't it? Satanism?"

"Not exactly. But we have good reason to believe that Aurora has been under the influence of Felix Crossley. He started in a fairly harmless esoteric movement called The Order of The Crescent Moon."

"The same organisation Francis supported?"

"Exactly. But Crossley outgrew the order and was rejected by his peers. His naked ambition has pushed his interest into other, more dangerous pursuits. Crossley has chosen to travel the path of black magic. It's filthy stuff, Michael. Sex magic, rituals and devil worship."

"Is Aurora in danger?"

"Not directly, not now. And we can't be certain she's with Crossley at all. Even if she is, you must understand these rituals are side shows to create a certain atmosphere. They are gimmicks, ways of enticing fresh blood into the order. These men don't really believe Lucifer will jump from a hole in the ground if they walk around a churchyard in a certain direction."

"Why do you say that?"

"Do you remember Frank Podmore?"

"The chap from the SPR?"

"Yes. Him. Podmore says that Felix Crossley intends to conduct his next ritual in Suffolk."

"Why?"

"Because of the history surrounding a particular church – a legend of old, claiming that the devil lies beneath. All nonsense, of course."

"And where is this man, Crossley?"

He lives in a little village called Duncryne. Did the operator say you were calling from Strathclyde?"

"She did."

"Well, it can't be far from you. Duncryne House is on the shores of Loch Lomond."

"You said that Aurora had connections to Crossley. How do you know?"

Lawrence hesitated.

"Tell me now," said Michael with unfamiliar firmness.

"I hoped to spare you the details."

"Don't. I want to hear every word of everything you know."

"We chanced upon an item of jewellery belonging to Aurora."

"How?"

"Through her previous employer. The object was a ruby brooch fashioned like a crescent moon."

Michael hesitated. "A brooch, you say? I've never seen her wear one."

"You wouldn't have. Aurora left it in London. We removed the brooch from its box and found an inscription beneath."

"What did it say?"

"It doesn't matter. Now is not the time."

"What did it say?"

Lawrence sighed. "To Aurora. Loveliest of the scarlet women. Your Felix."

"No."

"I'm sorry, Michael."

"What does it mean?"

"It's a term for Crossley's female disciples."

"I won't ask what you mean by that." Michael's voice cracked uncertainly on the other end.

"I wish I had better news."

"Are you still looking for Aurora?"

"To a certain extent. I can't do much about it if she is with Crossley. Especially if she is there by choice."

"She's not. Aurora was running away from something. The poor girl was terrified, Lawrence. I knew her at her most vulnerable, just as she'd learned to trust again. And don't forget, Aurora took on domestic work at a lower wage to be in the house of a man of God. She is a reformed character. Aurora would never follow Crossley by choice."

"If you say so."

"I know so." Michael Farrow's voice was firm again.

"But what if you are wrong?"

"We don't choose who we fall in love with," said Michael. "I only knew Aurora for a few short weeks, and it feels like she has been gone for a lifetime. But I will never find another woman like her. I forgive her for any unfortunate decisions made in the past. And I will spend the rest of my life trying to find her, no matter what the future brings. She is the one, Harpham. The only one, and if that makes me a fool, then so be it."

"I don't think you're foolish."

"Then help me."

"I will. But we have limited options Why not join me here? I need a little longer in London, and then we will go to Akenham in time for the pagan festival of Litha. Crossley may be there. We can intercept him and hope he will lead us to Aurora. But, Michael. It's a long shot. There are no guarantees. How soon can you get here?"

"I'll travel overnight. Should be with you tomorrow."

"Why not sooner?"

"I must do something else first."

"What?"

"I'll tell you when I see you."

"Michael?"

"Goodbye, Lawrence."

The line went dead, and Lawrence hammered the cradle until the operator answered. "Can you reconnect me?"

"What number?" said the girl in a monotone voice.

"Blast it. I don't know."

"Then I can't help you, sir."

Lawrence slammed the handset onto the cradle, cursing under his breath. Michael was clearly planning a detour before boarding the train. And Lawrence would bet his last silver sixpence that he knew where.

Chapter Twenty-Five

DUNCRYNE HOUSE

Michael Farrow picked his way through the ancient cemetery at the foot of Duncryne House, wishing he had company. A pale sun lurked beneath a burgeoning rain cloud while a chill wind more reminiscent of an autumn day cut through his light clothing. But it wasn't the weather that caused his heart to thump in his chest, more the prospect of encountering something unholy in the ancient house squatting beneath towering chimneys ahead.

Duncryne House was an ugly brute of a building made from solid stone blocks with projecting quoins set beneath an unruly tiled roof. Two low wings flanked the central part of the house with gothic-style arched windows that peered imperviously across the barren landscape, spying on the banks of the loch, and casting a wary, hostile gaze for strangers. Michael stopped short and considered his options.

Coming alone had been rash, but he'd had no choice. Lawrence was in London. Michael had unintentionally angered the bishop by breaking his retreat and could expect no help from his peers at St Columba's House. Not that he felt worthy of asking anything of the dedicated, kindly men of God who would never turn tail and run at the sight of a letter from home. Shards of guilt pierced Michael's heart, almost bending him double with the weight of his self-loathing. He'd only ten days to go; ten days of self-imposed imprisonment designed to heal and bring him closer to God. But he couldn't even manage that without bolting at the first sign of trouble. Closing his eyes, Michael willed a vision of Aurora, straining until she appeared in his memory. There she was, her heart-shaped face staring into his as if he were the only man in the world, brown eyes hazy with admiration and, dare he say it, affection. Because of him, she'd changed from a frightened child to a trusting woman in a few short days. Because of his kindness and her faith. A heady combination that could last a lifetime if he could only find her. No. Michael would banish all feelings of remorse. Leaving the retreat was the right thing to do and his only course of action. And if the Anglican order had not wanted him to react, they shouldn't have shown him the letter; unless they had done it as a test of faith. If so, he had failed them, but he would not abandon Aurora, even though the drab, grey, soulless manse before him put the fear of God into his heart.

He pushed on, striding through the long grass towards the wall surrounding the house. From a distance, the structures looked close, but as he drew nearer, the vast grounds stretched farther away, with the unscalable wall seeming acres from the front of the building. Michael had no plan of action. A calm man and peaceful by nature, words were his preferred weapon, and in an ideal world, he would stroll up the driveway, feigning an innocent reason to be there before requesting an audience with Felix Crossley. Then, he might gain entry to the house at little bodily risk. But he hadn't considered the effect of the ivy-clad stone walls looming above him, and the ominous presence of gargoyles carved to such frightening accuracy that they might be sentient. Terror streaked up his back like lightning, and a vein on his forehead throbbed to the rhythm of his fear.

A low, guttural rumble disturbed his musings, and he wondered if it was his imagination. He heard it again, followed by a deep, throaty bark from a large dog, then another. Michael swallowed. Crossley had guard dogs on his property. Security mattered to him, which didn't bode well. Michael's spirits faltered as he realised that a legitimate entry to the house would not be possible. He would need to break inside, and he'd never done such a thing alone. Steeling himself, Michael took advantage of the high walls shielding him from view, slowly following the stones to the side of the property, where he found a small arched gate set into the wall. He tried the ancient doorknob. To his shameful relief, it didn't move, and he walked on.

Step by step, Michael closed the distance, soon finding himself at the rear of the manse. Storm clouds hovered above, and raindrops streaked down the back of his neck. He brushed them aside and mentally bargained that if he couldn't find a way through the wall, he would give up and return to the railway station. But even as the thought emerged, his heart flipped with disgust at his cowardly abrogation of duty. He would get inside the house or die trying.

The skies darkened, and rain pelted down, splashing against the rough, badly hewn stones, now increasingly uneven, indicating a change to the structure. Michael donned his gloves, running a hand along the irregular mass until it fell away, revealing another arch carved into the stone and another wooden door. A door without a keyhole but with the benefit of an ancient iron latch which Michael lifted before gently pushing forward. The door gave slightly, but something stopped it. Michael jerked the latch, first cautiously and then with abandon. Something snapped on the other side, and he pushed the door ajar and peered beyond. The entrance must have been largely unused, and long, unkempt clumps of grass grew immediately behind it, with a fortuitously placed, low-spreading bush. He moved his head to one side, using the shrub for cover, and examined the house ahead.

The rear was less grim than the front, with a triple row of floor-to-ceiling windows immediately across the lawns. Michael pursed his lips as he considered his dilemma. He could not advance towards the property without detection unless he crossed under cover of darkness. He had already promised Lawrence that he would meet him in London in the morning, which meant catching the overnight train. But that would mean leaving Duncryne in the next hour. What if Aurora was inside the house and needed his help? He would never forgive himself if he left without checking. Michael retreated behind the bush and inspected the left-hand side of the garden. He couldn't see from his previous vantage point but now noticed a narrow run of stone outhouses lying down the side parallel to the wall. If they abutted, he couldn't sneak behind them, but at worst, he could get inside and seek shelter until darkness fell. And with dense shrubbery to the rear, he should be able to make his way towards them with little risk of being seen. Michael fingered his neck and touched the dog collar he still wore from his time in retreat. He was already on the wrong side of the law and disinclined to proceed any further while dressed in the garb of his profession. Snatching it from his neck, he stowed it in his inner jacket pocket and pulled his coat collar higher. Then he tiptoed towards the first of the outbuildings.

As Michael feared, the coal shed was flush with the wall. He slinked past the shrub and stepped inside the cold stone wall, but the structure was only a few feet square and almost full, with standing room only. Michael knew he must move on, but that meant stepping away from cover where an eagle-eyed household member could easily see him. He swallowed, wondering what to do next when he saw a dog from the corner of his eye and froze. Michael liked dogs as much as the next man, but he was not especially keen on large ones. And this dark-coated devil dog with a flat face and slavering jowls looked a little too hungry for his liking. He waited, heart thumping, for the dog to move, but another identical version appeared. With sweat prickling his armpits, Michael unbuttoned his jacket. One wrong move, one sound, and the dogs would hear, racing towards their prey in a heartbeat. He watched as one dog pawed the ground while the other looked on. But to his relief, a noise from the house startled them, and they thundered away like a pair of racehorses. Michael needed to move, and common sense told him to retreat. But his heart said otherwise, and he crept from the outbuilding towards its neighbour, relieved that the second building was closer to the lawn with a narrow gap behind, through which a man could squeeze. He slid into the space, using his hands to move ivy, vegetation, and spiders' webs as he travelled several yards past smaller stone buildings. By the time he emerged blinking into the daylight, he realised he was only yards away from the closest wing, which protruded into the grounds with the lowest windows inches away from the narrow basement wall surrounding it. Michael shuffled closer, but there was no room to drop below. Squatting, he peered inside, seeing nothing but dirty windows.

Options limited, Michael circumnavigated the wing, veering towards the left-hand side to avoid any prospect of encountering the dogs. The side of the house provided more opportunity with a large rhododendron giving ample cover while he peered into one of the ground-floor rooms. Inside, a man reclined in a chair with his legs crossed while reading a newspaper. The ordinariness of the act confounded Michael, who doubted his suspicions. Could he misguidedly have broken into the grounds of a perfectly normal property because of fanciful notions encouraged by Lawrence? Shaking his head, he decided to leave. But the window was ajar, and as Michael turned to go, a voice boomed from inside.

"Ah. I thought I might find you here. All set?"

"Of course. We'll start at five o'clock, as agreed. No point in making a late night of it with everyone already here, and an imminent journey to consider."

"Will you require the girl?"

"No. She can stay where she is. Ramona is increasingly intolerant in her advanced condition, and the child could arrive any time. No, we must press on with the practice run, and that will do."

"I'll get changed then."

"I would. The others will be along shortly."

Michael watched as one man retreated while the other stretched his legs and picked up the newspaper again. But within a few moments, he was also on the move, making his way towards a buffet, where he poured himself a large drink. He knocked it back in one gulp and wiped his mouth with the back of his hand. Then he turned sharply as the door opened.

"What are you doing here?" he asked rudely.

"Looking for you."

"I asked you to stay out of sight." The man's voice was abrupt and discourteous.

"It's my house too," said the woman, walking towards the drink cabinet. She reached out a hand, and her flowing robes fell open, revealing a distended stomach.

"What do you think you're doing?"

"Oh, come on, Felix. Baby is nearly here. What difference can it make?"

"None. Except I don't want you mixing with the others. If you must drink, do it in your room."

"I'm lonely."

"And I am about to conduct an important rehearsal. You know what this means."

"You care more about loyalty to the order than you ever will to me."

"Correct. And your point?"

Michael shifted slightly as the woman crossed the room again. His heartbeat quickened at the sight of the man he now knew must be Felix Crossley. And from the disdainful expression on Crossley's face, he had little regard for the heavily pregnant woman in front of him, who appeared to be his wife.

"You're about to be a father. Don't we matter?"

Crossley strode towards the woman and took her chin in his hand. He moved her face towards him and lowered his until his lips were almost upon hers. "Some days you do, and some days you don't. It depends on what else demands my attention. Tonight, you are an irrelevance. Go to your room, Ramona." He relaxed his hold, and she turned towards the window, tears sparkling in her eyes. Michael ducked backwards, fearful that she had seen him, but she stared into the distance, oblivious to his presence.

"This child will be the death of us."

"Don't be ridiculous."

"You don't care anymore. You don't want me."

"Not true."

"Then make love to me, Felix. Do it here. Do it now."

"I will not. You are days away from giving birth, and I have duties to perform later."

"With her."

"Not with her. She must be left alone until the ceremony."

"Ha. You won't last until next week."

"I must. Now push off, will you?"

"But…"

"I said go." Crossley's mouth contorted into a sneer as he hissed the words. Ramona fastened her robes, lowered her head, and barged from the room, sobbing.

"Stupid bitch," he muttered loudly, and Michael fingered the cross around his neck, wishing he were far away from the unedifying spectacle before him.

Crossley poured another drink, swigged it down and strode from the room. Michael inched towards the window, stuck his hand inside, and loosened the latch. Then, placing his hands together in silent prayer, he hopped inside the low window and ducked behind the sofa. He remained there for a moment, hardly believing he had dared to go inside, and then, buoyed by the silence and lack of movement, he crept towards the door. Before him, a long passage ran towards the rear of the house, but to his right, a steep flight of stairs descended to a basement level. Hearing voices ahead, he chanced the stairs and jogged down two at a time until he reached a wooden latched door. Silently, he opened it and made his way into a series of basement storage rooms, all with shut doors except one at the far end, which doubled as a rudimentary kitchen with an external door to the rear.

Michael took stock of his surroundings. To one side stood a range, heavy with dust and cobwebs, with tins and boxes stacked on a large table nearby. Michael peered inside to see that most of the food was of the canine variety and intended for the dogs. And two large stone bowls on the floor confirmed his suspicions that they fed the hounds here. But the kitchen was dog free now, and the side door afforded him the luxury of knowing he could quickly leave if he needed to. Now that he was inside, Michael wanted to explore and returned down the corridor, trying the doors one by one. Halfway down, his patience was rewarded when the narrow door swung open, revealing another passageway into an older part of the house. The temperature immediately dropped as the floor sloped towards the rear of the house. This passageway was colder, and the smell of dampness hit him, causing him to take his handkerchief and place it over his nose and mouth. Shivering, Michael proceeded farther down until he reached a room at the end with a sliding grate across the door. Taking a deep breath, he gently pulled it, waiting until his eyes grew accustomed to the darkness beyond. When they did, he saw a sleeping shape, moving ever so slightly with shallow, rhythmic breathing beneath a blanket. The dim room appeared to be a bedroom, with a single bed, a wardrobe, and a chest of drawers. Were it not for the basement location and the grated, locked door, he would not think twice about the safety of the occupant inside. But what host in their right mind locked their guests away? He opened his mouth to call out, hoping to make a sound loud enough that the occupant would hear and reveal themselves. The shape was ill-defined and could have been a man, woman, boy or girl, old or young, he couldn't tell. But before he had time to react, the scratching of nails along the stone floor caught his attention. He looked up to see a dog bounding towards him. Gasping, Michael turned to face it and, with a calmness he did not feel, stood stock-still. The dog slowed down, trotting towards him until it was only inches away. It stared at him passively, and the corner of its mouth twitched as it drew back its lips and bared its yellowing teeth.

"Good boy," breathed Michael. "I won't hurt you."

The dog remained motionless but snarled a warning.

"There's a good boy." The dog narrowed its eyes but lowered its head and relaxed before advancing towards Michael, sniffing his trouser leg.

You're a clever chap." Michael was winning. The dog calmed and became less menacing. Michael risked a step forward. The dog moved silently beside him like an unwanted shadow – one more step, then another. Michael was hopeful. All was not lost. But a sudden noise shattered the uneasy truce as a second dog galloped up the corridor, running towards Michael with saliva trailing from its teeth. It barked ferociously, and the other dog followed suit, baying in tandem. Michael inched back up the corridor, hoping his smooth, considered action would cause the dogs to falter. But as they sped towards him, he stared in fright, looking for inspiration or a way out. And as he glanced towards the grate, a pair of frightened eyes opened inside, and the shape sat bolt upright in the bed. But Michael had run out of time. The dogs were on him, their rank breath misty in the chilly corridor. The more aggressive dog launched at his leg, clamping its teeth through his trousers and into his fleshy thigh. Michael swallowed a scream and elbowed the dog in the face. It fell away, tumbling into the calmer animal. And Michael made a break for it, sprinting down the corridor, trying to ignore the stabbing pain in his leg. And as he hurtled into the west wing, blood pooling into his trousers, he thought he heard something that chilled him to the marrow – a desperate, frail voice calling his name.

Chapter Twenty-Six

GRILLING THE MEDICS

Saturday, June 18, 1904

Lawrence burst through the doors of the Royal Free Hospital, relieved that it would be his last visit for a while. His passion for resolving Sophia Hickman's disappearance ebbed and flowed like the tide, depending upon his mood that day. His current state of mind was buoyed early on by Violet's agreeable morning telephone call. After hearing the good news about Michael, she had passed the telephone receiver to Daisy. A natural chatterbox, Daisy had regaled Lawrence with details of her time with Nora and insisted on singing him two new songs she had learned at school.

"Has Nora gone back to Swaffham yet?" asked Lawrence, eager for all house guests to be long gone before he reclaimed his home.

"No, Daddy. She's staying for another few days while Mama joins you."

"Joins me? Joins me where? Give the telephone to

Mama, would you, dear? And be a good girl until I get home."

"I will, Daddy."

"What's this about joining me?" asked Lawrence as Violet came back on the line.

"You're still going to Akenham, aren't you?"

"Yes. But I'll take Michael along. You don't need to be there. After all, we've only got Podmore's word that Crossley will turn up at all."

"I'm coming, and that's the end of it," said Violet firmly.

"Right. Keep in touch, and I'll let you know where to meet us."

"I will. What are you doing today?"

"Clearing matters up with the doctors."

Lawrence had played the conversation over in his head as he'd travelled to the hospital, smiling at the thought of his little girl growing up and speaking on the telephone like an adult. He missed her and was eager to return home, which gave him the impetus to finish matters in London as soon as possible. He had left for the hospital, not knowing when to expect Michael, but had left a note advising his itinerary for the day. All things being equal, he would be back at the hotel before Michael had even stepped off the train. And with this in mind, Lawrence strode through the hospital foyer, making for the ward where Ann would be for the next few hours.

She was waiting for him at the reception desk, as they had agreed by telephone the previous day.

"I've done what you asked," she said, an anxious look on her face.

"Thank you. I'm grateful."

"It wasn't easy. It's hectic here, and the doctors are not keen on revisiting this case. They've heard it all before and

The Disappearing Doctor

want to go about their business without you dragging up unpleasant memories."

"What can I do but say thank you? I fully understand your position, Ann."

"Well, you've tried to help me, and it's the least I can do. But getting three doctors in one place in a busy hospital is like juggling cats."

"I'm sure it is. Lead the way, and I promise I won't keep them any longer than necessary."

"Follow me." Ann led Lawrence through a maze of corridors, directing him through a door, where he recognised a familiar face.

"Dickie. What are you doing here?" he asked.

"Driving duties," said the young man ruefully. "Doctor Greville has a meeting later today. Time is not his friend."

"Well, I won't keep him long," said Lawrence.

"What's it all about?"

Dickie's eyes sparkled with interest, and Lawrence found himself explaining his thought process to the charismatic young man. But Dickie stopped him in full flow. "Sorry, I shouldn't have asked. I'm holding you up."

"You're right. Another time," said Lawrence. A quiet chat with Dickie would be very worthwhile if Ernest Greville refused to help. Not that it was likely. Greville had been friendly and open during all their encounters. But it was always good to have a second source of information, just in case.

"I won't join you," said Ann, with the ghost of a smile.

"Are you sure? I don't mind."

"I'd rather not, and the doctors will speak more openly if I'm not around."

"Michael and I will see you later, anyway."

"I'll look forward to it."

Lawrence opened the door and let himself into the small room where three doctors sat silently around a table, two sipping hot drinks and the other with her hand on her chin staring fixedly ahead. Ernest Greville jumped up and greeted him.

"Good day, Mr Harpham. And how are you?"

"Well," said Lawrence. "Thank you for agreeing to see me."

"I have precisely five minutes to spare," snapped Janet Campbell. "My first operation is in half an hour."

"I won't keep you. I promise."

"Good. Because you're flogging a dead horse," said Greville. "The poor girl died by her own hand, and I don't know what you hope to achieve with another round of questioning."

"I don't know why you think I could help at all," said Janet. "Or any one of us. Sophia killed herself. It's sad but true."

"I've come to believe that she took her own life," said Lawrence. "But someone may have encouraged her to do so."

The three doctors exchanged glances, and the younger dark-haired woman spoke. "Why?"

"Explaining that theory would take more time than you have," said Lawrence. "But thank you for agreeing to help. First, tell me why Sophia Hickman was at the hospital that day?"

"She was covering for me," said Janet Campbell.

"Were you ill?"

"No. I was on holiday. Doctor Chamberlain and Miss Hickman were dealing with my patients." She gestured to the dark-haired doctor.

"Then you probably can't help. Feel free to leave."

"I knew this would be a waste of my time," she muttered, placing a half-drunk cup of tea on the table before leaving the room. Seconds later, she returned. "I will say this," she stated, pointing towards Lawrence. "Miss Hickman accompanied me on my rounds the week before I left. She was a competent doctor, showing no sign of nerves, and seemed very cheerful."

"And no problems that you knew of."

"No. Relationships between the doctors were very cordial."

"Thank you. I appreciate it."

Doctor Campbell nodded and closed the door.

Lawrence took a seat at the table. "That's the sort of thing," he said. "I know you've recounted these facts before, but I'd like to know a little more about how Sophia felt that day. What she said, how she looked, who she spoke with. Doctor Campbell was succinct in her assessment, but it's useful all the same. Now, may I start with you, Miss Chamberlain?"

"If you must." Catherine Chamberlain steepled her hands and held them under her chin, looking for one moment like a lost child.

"How well did you know Miss Hickman?"

"As well as anyone can who has only been acquainted for a few weeks."

"And did you get on?"

"Why? What have you heard?"

Lawrence paused. "Nothing."

"Sorry. Hospitals are rife with gossip. I meant nothing by it."

"Did you see Miss Hickman around the time she disappeared?"

"Yes. We lunched together the Friday before."

"How did you find her?"

"Perfectly agreeable. There was nothing unusual about her behaviour."

"She went missing on Saturday fifteenth of August. Did you see her that day?"

"Yes. Sophia joined me for breakfast."

"And?" Lawrence grimaced. Getting information from Catherine Chamberlain was like pulling teeth. He pursed his lips and allowed a long silence to settle between them.

Miss Chamberlain licked her lips and spoke. "She was in good spirits."

"How do you know?"

"Her general demeanour. She smiled."

"Did she speak?"

"Obviously."

"Are you going to help me or not?" Lawrence stood and stalked to the end of the room, trying to keep his temper in check.

"Come on, Doctor Chamberlain. You can do better than that," cajoled Ernest Greville.

"Too many bad memories," she muttered.

"Is that why you didn't get to the inquest?"

"No." Catherine Chamberlain spat the denial, and Doctor Greville raised an eyebrow.

"You didn't attend the inquest," repeated Lawrence. "Were you called as a witness?"

"I was."

"But you didn't go?"

"I couldn't."

"Doesn't that count as contempt of court?"

"Don't you start," snapped Miss Chamberlain.

Lawrence loomed over her, his hands on top of the opposite chair back.

"Would you mind explaining what took priority over a woman's death?" he asked in a firm but measured tone.

"My father was unwell. He lives in Ceylon, and I'd booked the passage before they set a date for the inquest. I couldn't be in two places at once, so I sent a note, and the coroner was satisfied with my explanation."

"I understand," said Lawrence. "What would you have told him about Doctor Hickman's state of mind that day had you attended the inquest?"

"That Sophia Hickman was happy. She asked me when she needed to be on duty, and I told her. Then she joked that there were sure to be drunks among her cases. I said the number had been lower of late, and Sophia replied she was pleased to hear it. I offered my help should she need it, which she gratefully accepted. She seemed satisfied and left to take a look at the queue in the waiting room."

"Did she return?"

"Almost immediately and with a big smile on her face. She expected a rash of cases, but there were only a few. I reiterated my offer of help, and she returned later to take me up on it."

"What did she need?"

"A second opinion."

"On what?"

"A patient."

"Well, I didn't think it would be about her choice of daywear." Anger flashed across Lawrence's face as he struggled to remain professional.

"Do you want my help, or shall I just get back to my busy ward?" Catherine moved to stand, but Lawrence waved her back down.

"Five more minutes, and you can go. You probably knew Sophia Hickman better than anyone else at the hospital. I've met her father, and he's still heartbroken. Can you imagine how your father would feel if you'd disappeared? Mr Hickman isn't satisfied with the coroner's verdict and has commissioned my services. I have a daughter myself and would dearly like to help him, but I only have a few days left in London and time is running out. If you have a shred of compassion for that poor girl, try to make the next five minutes count."

Catherine blushed scarlet as the words hit home. She tried to rein in her temper while wrestling with her conscience, and Lawrence half expected her to flee. Compassion won.

"Very well. Sophia asked me to see a medical case in the casualty ward. She wanted to admit him but wasn't sure whether she should. I agreed with her diagnosis and signed the admission papers, and I can assure you there was no unpleasantness about it."

"I neither said nor implied that there was."

"Good."

"Now, let's be clear about this. Doctor Campbell just mentioned how cordial things were between the doctors, and you just denied any unpleasantness. Those two statements together lead me to conclude that on the balance of probability, one or more disagreements arose between you. Did they?"

Catherine Chamberlain lowered her head.

"I remember something," said Ernest Greville.

"Yes?"

"Something Doctor Roberts said at the inquest?"

"Who is Doctor Roberts?" asked Lawrence.

"The resident physician," replied Greville. "I wouldn't have thought twice about this ordinarily, but Roberts made an unprompted comment at the inquest. He said there was no friction between the staff."

"Just as Doctor Campbell offered," said Lawrence, turning to face Catherine Chamberlain. "Well, Doctor. You may as well be honest. You have my word that nothing you say will leave this room."

Catherine Chamberlain put her head in her hands. "I meant nothing by it," she said.

"What happened?"

"I was tired. It was the end of a long week, and I'd had another letter about my father's failing health. Sophia should have been helping, not constantly asking silly questions. And though she seemed cheerful and confident, Sophia was indecisive. She needed her hand holding rather too much for an experienced medical woman. I didn't complain or pass comment, but I think Sophia sensed my impatience."

"Do you feel responsible for her death?"

"No. Why should I? If she were that sensitive, she'd have harmed herself, anyway."

Lawrence stared silently into her eyes and Catherine Chamberlain sighed.

"Alright. Perhaps I blame myself a little. I wish I'd been more patient with her that day."

"Let me make one thing clear," said Lawrence, standing tall. "You are not responsible for Sophia Hickman's actions. Stop feeling guilty. You are not to blame."

Catherine's eyes filled with tears at his unexpected kindness. "It's been bothering me for a long time," she admitted. "I could have been kinder."

"We are all guilty of that."

"Is there anything else I can tell you?"

"No. You have helped enormously. At least I can tell Mr

Hickman that his daughter had some self-doubt. The act of suicide is impossible to understand without reason. Her state of mind was not as healthy as everyone thought."

"You're right," said Ernest Greville. "In ways you may not yet realise."

"What do you mean?"

"Have you finished with Doctor Chamberlain?"

"Yes, if you've nothing more to add, Doctor?"

"No. I've said enough. And I'm sorry I wasn't more forthcoming."

Lawrence reached out his hand. "Good day, Doctor Chamberlain."

"Mr Harpham."

Catherine Chamberlain left the room with her head bowed, less combative than when she'd arrived.

"Nicely done," said Doctor Greville when they were alone.

"I hope so. Doctor Chamberlain is spirited, I'll give her that, but it's a matter of self-protection. She's defensive."

"Don't talk mind matters to me. You sound just like Dickie with his psychology babble."

"I'm surprised at you, Doctor. A broken spirit makes for poor health."

"If you say so. I'm afraid I've little time for it."

"You were telling me about Miss Hickman's state of mind."

"Ah. Not exactly. I was trying to explain why she hadn't committed a rash act on the spur of the moment. If Catherine Chamberlain had upset her on the day she disappeared, she wouldn't have purchased the drug that ended her life several days before that incident."

"What do you mean?"

"If you'd spoken to me before Miss Chamberlain, I

would have told you that Miss Hickman purchased fifteen grains of morphia sulphate Tabloids from me three days before she died, implying longer-standing intent. Miss Chamberlain's shortness couldn't have caused her death."

"Unless Sophia had been underconfident for some time and was merely putting a brave face on it. Could she have purchased the morphia for another reason?"

"No. They don't use it at the hospital."

"How do you know?"

"The coroner asked the same question."

"Did you serve Miss Hickman yourself?"

"Yes. I handed the tablets directly to her."

"And you recognised her?"

"Naturally. She had been a customer for the last four years."

"Did she purchase anything else?"

"No, but she collected a syringe she had left for repair a few days earlier."

"And how did she seem?"

"Cheerful. Even more so after a chat with Dickie."

Lawrence grinned. "Dickie never stops smiling," he replied. "It's infectious."

"I know. I can think of no one more suited to running our hospital stall than Dickie. He's a regular tonic. I'd be rich beyond avarice if Dickie worked there five days a week. He's a great credit to our association."

"Time for a pay rise, perhaps?" suggested Lawrence.

"I suppose I must, or someone else will snap him up. Anyway, enough about my assistant. Is there anything else?"

"What do you think happened?" asked Lawrence.

"I don't know. Sophia Hickman was a pleasant, friendly, and seemingly cheerful girl. I am surprised at what she did, but I can't think of any other explanation than suicide."

"Might someone have encouraged her?" asked Lawrence.

"Of course. Some people are suggestible, though self-preservation comes naturally to humankind. But it is unlikely that anyone could persuade another person to do something contrary to their nature."

"But not impossible?"

"Nothing is impossible."

They left the kitchenette and Lawrence walked Doctor Greville to the seated area where Dickie was waiting. "I have a note for you," said Dickie, thrusting a folded piece of paper into Greville's hand.

Greville opened it and sighed. "Damn. They want me in the fracture ward. Did Mr Spencer say when?"

"As soon as you can," replied Dickie. "It's a tricky case. I've telephoned your next appointment and asked them to put it back by an hour. I hope I did the right thing."

"You did," said Greville, relieved. "But I'm afraid it will mean a long wait for you. Go back to the shop, and I'll meet you there when I've finished. Bring the car around if I'm not with you in forty-five minutes."

"I will."

"Good luck, Mr Harpham. Might I see you at the club later this week?" Greville raised a conspiratorial eyebrow before Lawrence understood his reference to the next meeting of the Order of the Crescent Moon.

"You will," said Lawrence, hoping he was safely back in Suffolk by then. He'd had his fill of secret orders, and normality beckoned like a shining light.

"Well, that was a lucky break," said Dickie. "I'm starving. But I've gained an hour and can now purchase a slice of that delicious sausage plait in the front window of Mrs Norman's pie shop."

Lawrence's stomach rumbled loudly.

"You should try it," smiled Dickie.

"I might. Ah, excuse me," said Lawrence, placing his hand on Dickie's shoulder. "I've just seen someone. Back in a moment."

He strode towards the entrance door with his hand outstretched. "Michael. I wasn't expecting you yet. You look bloody awful."

Michael turned around and visibly sagged at the sight of Lawrence. "It's good to see you too," he said, returning the handshake.

"Sit down." Lawrence beckoned to an upholstered settee at the front of the reception hall. "Have you eaten? You look ready to pass out. And what is that on your clothes?"

Michael brushed his hand limply over the dried blood staining his grey trousers. "It's nothing," he muttered.

"Where are your bags?"

"I sent them straight to the hotel. I called first, and they read your note out, so I came straight here."

"Why? You need a good wash and a change of clothes."

"No. I need absolution."

"Don't be silly," said Lawrence jovially, looking into Michael's sunken, red-rimmed eyes as he stared unseeingly into the distance.

"What happened? Has someone hurt you?"

"Not as much as I deserve."

Lawrence changed position and sat beside Michael, placing an arm across his friend's shoulder. Michael flinched and pulled away, but Lawrence patted his arm. "Talk to me," he said.

"I went to Duncryne House."

"You silly young fool."

Michael stared at the floor. "Don't tell me you wouldn't have done the same."

"Alright. I would. But I'm not above a bit of fisticuffs if necessary. You're not made that way."

"No. I would turn the other cheek like the coward I am."

"That's not what I meant."

"Regardless, it's true."

"Michael, look at me."

The younger man ignored him and continued to gaze at the floor.

"I said, look at me." Lawrence barked the words, and Michael's head jerked upwards. "What happened to you? Did you see Crossley?"

"I did. And his pregnant wife too."

"Oh dear. Ramona Crossley is vulnerable up there alone. He's unpleasant to her, you know. Violent."

"She looked well, although she is due to deliver any moment now. Crossley was unkind to her but not cruel. And no, he didn't see me. In fact, I slipped into his house undetected."

"Well done." Lawrence glanced at his friend with undisguised admiration.

"For all the good it did. She's there, Lawrence. Aurora is there, I'm sure of it."

"Did you see her?"

"I think so. I can't be sure. But he's holding her prisoner."

"Did you call the police?"

"No. I should have. But I wasn't certain."

"Of what?"

"Whether she was there of her own free will."

"You're not making much sense. How did Aurora appear?"

"I don't know. The room was dark, and she was asleep under the covers."

"Then how do you know it was Aurora?"

Michael sighed. "I just do."

"Did you see her face?"

"No."

"Her figure?"

"No."

"What was the room like?"

"A hotel bedroom furnished in the usual way. I couldn't tell if it was clean in the poor lighting, but I noticed a sink in the corner."

"So, an unidentifiable person was sleeping in a fully equipped room."

"It was Aurora."

"Then why did you leave her?"

"Because I have no moral fibre and no courage. I am not you, Lawrence. And I encountered a problem. Look at this."

Michael rolled up his trouser leg, exposing a jagged wound above his knee. Bloody flesh glistened moistly against the inflamed, pitted skin.

"I'd get that seen to," said Lawrence.

"I don't care."

"You will if it starts rotting. I'll call the nurse."

"Don't trouble yourself. I'll do it before I leave."

"Why are you so angry with me, Michael?"

"Because the great Lawrence Harpham would have got the girl out of there. He wouldn't have let a pair of dogs chase him off the premises, nor would he have fled for the station as fast as his legs could carry him. I failed her, Lawrence... abandoned her in her hour of need. Even now, I don't know why."

"You might not know, but I do."

"Why then?"

"Because there's very little chance Aurora was there at all. And even if it was her, she might be there by choice. Did you attempt to gain access?"

"I tried the door before the dogs came."

"And was it definitely locked?"

"I pulled it. Only once, but firmly."

Lawrence glanced at his watch. "Look... change of plan since I wrote the note. Ann has invited us to lunch. I'll go there now to avoid keeping her waiting. Ask a nurse to look at your leg, return to the hotel and get your glad rags on. I'll tell Ann to expect you in an hour or two, and we can talk later."

"Must I go to Ann's?" Michael wiped his hand across his brow, wincing as he got to his feet.

"Everything alright, gentlemen?" Dickie walked towards them, concern etched over his face.

"More or less. My friend here needs some medical attention for a dog bite."

"Nurse Gloria is on duty today. She'll look after you."

"Can you show Michael where to find her? And then point him towards the nearest cabbie. He's staying at my hotel in Battersea. I'd go myself, but I must run."

"I'll do better than that. The car is outside. I'll take him to see Gloria and then run him home."

"But I thought you needed to eat?"

"There's plenty of time for that. I can get to Battersea and back in half an hour. Off you go, Mr Harpham. I'll take care of things."

Chapter Twenty-Seven

AN INDECENT PROPOSITION

Sunday, June 19, 1904

"I don't know what's got into him," grumbled Lawrence as Violet listened patiently at the other end of the telephone.

"Show a little understanding. Michael has had a terrible experience. And don't forget how odd it must have been coming out of a six-month retreat into what I can only describe as a breaking and entering situation."

"It was nothing of the kind," said Lawrence. "Michael climbed through an open window and strolled into a basement."

"Where he was set upon by savage guard dogs. Anyone would have run away."

"I daresay. But that doesn't excuse his rudeness."

"You're a grown-up. You can stand it."

"I don't mean towards me. It's poor Ann I feel sorry for. She's been desperate for news of her younger brother, and he stands her up with no explanation."

"Didn't Michael arrive for lunch?"

"No. Nor did he send word, even though Ann has a perfectly well-functioning telephone."

"Have you seen Michael today?"

"No."

"Then how do you know he's safe and well?" Lawrence detected a momentary wobble in Violet's voice. He sometimes forgot how close she had been to Michael and that, for several years, he had been her only friend and confidant; those dark, depressing years when Lawrence thought he had lost her forever. He lightened his tone.

"I asked the receptionist this morning. She said Michael hadn't left his room since Dickie drove him back yesterday. I knocked on his door last night when I returned from Ann's, and he asked me to leave him alone with his headache. So I obliged. I listened at his door before coming down this morning. He's moving around the room and quietly coming to terms with his thoughts. The expression, 'wallowing in self-pity', had been on the tip of Lawrence's tongue, but he didn't want to upset Violet again.

"How did you get on at the hospital?" she asked.

Lawrence sighed and prepared himself for a lengthy discourse. When he had finished, Violet spoke again. "Well done," she said. "It may not be the answer you hoped for, but you've provided a motive for Miss Hickman's suicide, even if you haven't proved that anyone else was involved."

"I know. And I've exhausted all witnesses. There's no one else to ask and nothing more to be said. I must speak with her father and tell her that the police were correct."

"It's a pity. I felt sure we were on to something. Perhaps we are, and Miss Hickman's death is the outlier."

"I can't spare any more time if I'm to make Akenham before Tuesday."

"If you still think it's worth it. Strathclyde is a long way from Suffolk, and from what Michael told you, Crossley was showing no signs of leaving home."

"No, but if Michael can take the overnight train, Crossley can too."

"I'll meet you there, regardless. I've been getting to know the locals."

"Good show. I wish you'd been with me yesterday, though. It took me a while to break through Miss Chamberlain's frostiness. You'd have done it in a heartbeat. Thank goodness for Greville. He guided her in the right direction."

"Don't you think he's too good to be true?"

"No. Why should I?"

"I've never met anyone quite so accommodating."

"That's just the way he is. Frankly, I'm glad of it." Lawrence hesitated as the snug door burst open and looked up.

"What's that? Hold on a minute, Violet." Lawrence placed the handset on the table as one of the hotel porters staggered inside, carrying a large wicker basket tied with a ribbon.

"Thought I saw you through the window," he boomed.

"Did you? How can I help?"

"This is for you, gov. It's just this minute arrived by carriage from Fortnum and Mason. Your birthday, is it? Many happy returns of the day."

"I am not celebrating anything," hissed Lawrence, gesturing at the man to lower his voice.

"Sorry to offend," he muttered.

"Here. Take this." Lawrence reached into his trouser pocket and thrust some coins into the porter's hand. He waited until the room was vacant again before retrieving the handset.

"Who was that?" asked Violet.

"Only the porter."

"What did he want?"

Silence.

"Are you there, Lawrence?"

"Hmm?" Lawrence had opened a white envelope tucked into the top of the hamper. He rapidly scanned it while listening to Violet. 'I thought this might bring back a few pleasant memories. Meet me at The Lavender Bush As soon as you can. I'll be waiting.'

"Lord, no," he whispered, scowling as he tossed the letter onto the table. It bounced off and settled by the door.

"Lawrence. What is it?"

"Nothing. Just a mistake. The porter's given me a parcel intended for someone else."

"How careless. What will you do about Michael?"

"I'll keep knocking on his door until he lets me in."

"Good. Do that now, and we'll speak again tomorrow."

"I'll get to it as soon as I can. There's a small matter I must attend to first."

Lawrence strode through the door of The Lavender Bush Café, glanced around the room, and made his way towards a table indiscreetly positioned in the centre of the room. The public location did not improve his mood, and he tried to temper his anger as he sat opposite Loveday Melcham, who sported an expression of quiet satisfaction.

"What's this all about?" he snapped.

"Isn't it customary to thank someone for a gift, Laurie dear?"

"Don't call me that."

"You used to like it."

"That was years ago before we married other people. Our spouses. Remember them?"

"How could I forget?" Loveday stared into Lawrence's eyes. "Perhaps I was too hasty in marrying Tom."

"Nobody forced you."

"He was very persuasive."

"I'm not here to talk about your marriage, Loveday."

"Then why did you come?"

"To see what you wanted and make it clear that Tom Melcham is my friend. We've known each other since boyhood, and my loyalties lie with him. You must understand I cannot meet you alone again and won't accept your gifts. God only knows why you thought it was appropriate, given our marital circumstances."

"Don't be so stuffy, Lawrence. We're not living in the dark ages. I have always done as I pleased. I don't care about societal conventions, and neither should you. We were happy together once and could be again. I'm not asking you to commit to a relationship. Just a little excitement every now and again."

"What?" Lawrence rubbed his ear as if he could scarcely believe her words.

"An affair. I'm offering you a discreet affair. Nothing regular. But now and again when you're in London or the Cotswolds. It would be fun."

"I thought you came to see me because you were worried that Tom was going astray?"

"It was a ruse."

"A ruse?"

"I wanted to see you, Lawrence. We have unfinished business. You know that."

"But I'm married."

"So you keep saying. I must admit, it put me off my

stride when you told me last week. I couldn't believe I hadn't heard. But then I realised you've known Violet for so long that you've grown into an old married couple early in your relationship. You bicker like a pair of old dears in their eighties. If you're not bored with her now, you soon will be. And I can offer you something exciting. What man wouldn't want a younger lover?" Loveday slowly released the top two buttons of her blouse, flashing a hint of bosom, and Lawrence felt a stirring in his loins.

"You want to, don't you?" she whispered. "You're all alone in London, and your hotel bed is empty. Just think about what we could do in it."

Lawrence leaned forwards and looked directly into her eyes. "How do you know?" he asked quietly.

"Because we're attracted to each other."

"That's not what I meant. How do you know I'm all alone?"

Loveday chewed her lip. "I supposed you must be by now. The child presumably needs its mother."

"Daisy," said Lawrence. "My daughter's name is Daisy."

"Well, I can help take your mind off her," said Loveday. "I'm sure you must be missing Daisy."

Lawrence regarded the beautiful woman before him, acknowledged the temptation of her offer, and consigned it to the back of his mind. He suspected she'd had a hand in certain events over the last few weeks, but before challenging her, he wanted to get to the truth and help Tom. "Do you have any children?" he asked.

Loveday wrinkled her pretty nose. "No. A few near misses, but it was not to be."

"You don't sound especially troubled."

"I'm not. But Thomas had certain expectations in that department, and one must be seen to be doing one's duty."

The Disappearing Doctor

"Tom is a proud man of means. He would expect to leave his assets to an heir."

"I'm not a broodmare, and children are tiring."

"Then perhaps it's as well that fate intervened."

"I don't believe in fate." Loveday raised a perfectly manicured eyebrow. "I make my own luck."

Lawrence swallowed the temptation to ask if Loveday had really conceived or, worse still, taken steps to prevent a live birth. She had implied as much, and he didn't need to hear it.

"Do you love Tom?" he asked instead.

"Will it make a difference to your decision?"

"No. But he's my friend, and I would like to know."

Loveday sighed. "Thomas gives me a good life and is tolerable company. But he's older than me and set in his ways. I am bored, Laurie, bored to tears most of the time. I want to eat out, go to plays and concerts, and be in company. It's not too much to ask."

"You should have married a man of your own age."

"I should have married you. But I'm happy to settle for less." Loveday reached for his hand, took it, and stroked the back with her thumb. Lawrence paused, then casually removed it from the table.

"The difference between us is that I am in love with my wife," he replied.

"So you say. But Violet is twenty years older than me, her skin is ageing, and her eyes are dull. As for her fashion sense, well, it's incomparable. I am sure she is a wonderful mother, but I can offer something fresh and exciting."

"You're missing the point. I love Violet."

"I don't see what that has to do with it. She need never know."

"But I would. You seem obsessed with me, Loveday, but you don't know me at all. I value fidelity."

"Tosh. You were quick enough to forget Violet in Liverpool."

"For which I have never forgiven myself. Nor will I. You are right about something. Violet and I disagree from time to time. We bicker, as you call it. And I'm glad we've had this conversation because it has reminded me not to take her for granted. And when I return to Suffolk, I will make sure she knows how much I love her daily for the rest of our lives."

Loveday's face fell. "Are you declining my offer?"

"Of course. How could you ever think I would treat Tom and Violet so badly?"

"But your precious wife doesn't think twice about staying out all night herself? She could have been anywhere."

"What do you mean?"

"I saw her returning to the hotel alone in a carriage last Thursday. And looking rather dishevelled if I may say."

"What a happy coincidence that you passed our hotel at the exact moment she returned." Lawrence's voice dripped with sarcasm.

"It just so happened that I was shopping nearby. I dare say she spun you a fine story."

"Violet was with Ann Brocklehurst."

"Whoever that is. But did you check?"

"No. I trust Violet implicitly, and Ann is a family friend. Don't try to play on my insecurities, Loveday. I have none when it comes to my marriage."

"Do you want to order anything, sir?" A waitress approached somewhat tardily, considering the time Lawrence had already been seated. He waved her away.

"No. I'm just leaving."

"Don't go." Loveday reached for his hand again, and the waitress turned away, embarrassed.

"You're making a scene," hissed Lawrence. "I'm leaving, and that's the end of it."

He strode towards the door and barged through, relieved to be away from the awkwardness of the encounter. Heart thumping with repressed anger, he walked towards the park to marshal his thoughts. But within minutes, he heard the clickety-click of heeled feet. He turned around to see Loveday storming towards him.

"How dare you humiliate me like that," she snapped.

"Try to retain some semblance of dignity," said Lawrence. "For both our sakes."

"This is your fault. You made me think we had a future."

"No, I didn't. You think you want me, Loveday, but you are mistaken. You don't care about me, Lawrence Harpham. All you see is a challenge. A man you can't have married to a woman you despise. Go home to your husband, who loves you more than you deserve."

"You're hateful, Lawrence. And I hope your horrid pig of a wife enjoyed her nasty, flea-bitten hedgehogs."

Lawrence cast a look of pity towards Loveday. "That you would spend good money on such silliness says more about you than it does about Violet. I feel truly sorry for you, Loveday. You have a good life and the love of a kind and gentle man. Yet you selfishly squander it. Nothing is ever good enough. I suppose you cancelled Violet's room too?"

"She deserved it. And so do you." Loveday was quiet now, her face a mask of rage and embarrassment.

"I'm going back to my hotel," said Lawrence. "I don't

want to hear from you or see you again. Stay away from my wife and child. Have a happy life, Loveday. I know I will."

Lawrence turned on his heel and walked purposefully towards the hotel, glad to retreat from a mistake in his past. He had more important things to deal with now. And Michael's welfare was at the top of the list.

Chapter Twenty-Eight

THE BLACK DOG PROWLS

Lawrence raced upstairs to Michael's room on the third floor. He had promised Violet to look in on their friend but had already wasted too much time dealing with Loveday and her spiteful ways. He shuddered at the notion that, under different circumstances, he might be married to her and made a mental note to write a love letter to Violet ahead of his return. Loveday had been right about one thing. He'd taken Violet for granted, and it was time to put things right.

Lawrence knocked on Michael's door.

"Go away." The muffled voice was devoid of emotion.

"It's me, Lawrence."

"I know. Leave me alone."

"Let me in. Violet wants me to speak to you."

"About what?"

"I can't exactly shout it across the corridor. Please let me in."

Lawrence heard a deep sigh and the shuffle of feet

across the room. The door clicked open and moved half an inch. Lawrence pushed it and went inside.

Michael had resumed his position, hunched over the dressing table with his head in his hands. Still dressed in his garb of the day before, his hair was grey with dust and debris, and the room smelled rank. Lawrence yanked the curtains open before unlatching the window.

"I thought you were freshening up. What happened?"

"What does Violet want?"

"For me to check on you and ensure all is well, which it clearly isn't. What happened yesterday? Your sister is worried."

"Oh, Ann. Yes, I suppose she is. Tell her I'm sorry."

"You tell her. You owe her that much, at least. She's expecting you later today."

"No."

"Why not?"

"I have other plans."

"They can wait. We're only here for another night. Two at the most. You haven't time for sightseeing."

"Have you finished?" Michael's eyes were still downcast and fixated on the wooden dressing table.

"No." Lawrence moved towards him and laid a hand on his shoulder. Michael pulled back.

"Look at me."

Michael shrugged the hand from his shoulder and remained seated.

"I said, look at me."

Finally, Michael faced him, and Lawrence stepped back. The younger man's eyes were red-rimmed, his face dusty, swollen and streaked with tears. He'd barely slept.

"Are you satisfied now?" asked Michael, turning away again.

"What is it?" Lawrence lowered himself onto the edge of the bed.

"I can't talk about it. Don't ask me to."

"Michael. You must. I cannot leave you like this. What would I say to Violet? She loves you. We love you."

Lawrence turned away, concealing his discomfort. Unused to emotional declarations, especially towards men, the awkward situation was alien. But his feelings did not matter next to Michael's obvious pain. And Lawrence understood the overwhelming despair of melancholy. God knows he had suffered enough since Catherine's loss. He had learned to recognise the craven shadow of the black dog slinking towards him. It was here, now, circling Michael in this room, its amorphous form trailing above, around, and inside his friend. He searched his memory for the most effective remedy.

"Michael. We need to get you outside. You can't stay here. It's not helping."

"What do you propose? A walk in the park? Why didn't I think of that? And when I return, perhaps the missing pieces of my life will magically reappear."

"It's not that simple. It takes time to feel better."

"Go away."

"I won't, Michael. I'll stay here all day if I must. Longer, if you need me."

"But I don't. I want to be alone."

"I thought you said you were going out?"

Michael sighed. "That's my business."

"Oh, for God's sake." Lawrence exploded in a fury of impatience, and Michael winced at the blasphemy. "You are a parish priest, Michael. Where's your compassion?"

Michael stared as if he didn't understand. "Compassion?"

"Towards me, towards Violet and Ann. We are worried about you. This is too self-indulgent. Please let me help."

His words hit their mark. "What do you want from me?" asked Michael quietly.

"Get ready and meet me at the restaurant. There's still time for a late breakfast if we hurry."

"Very well. But that's all you get. Then I must go out."

"Whatever you like. I'll see you downstairs in half an hour."

Lawrence fidgeted with his napkin as he waited at the breakfast table. He'd arrived slightly early, hoping Michael would too. But no such luck, and he sat alone, anxiously watching the entrance and rejecting two attempts at service by the friendly waitress. Michael was uncharacteristically emotional, and Lawrence, feeling unaccountably responsible for Michael's distress, couldn't bring himself to eat in his absence. Denying himself sustenance eased his guilt, but his empty stomach growled loudly, and he dropped his napkin while kneading his belly to stop the noise.

By the time he'd ducked down to retrieve it, Michael had arrived. Lawrence looked up, relieved to see a smarter, cleaner version of his friend. But where Michael would usually bound towards him, with an amiable smile and a hand held out in welcome, he walked uncertainly, limping slightly, with misery etched over his pale face. Lawrence jumped up and offered his hand, an oddly formal gesture, but one that allowed him to clasp Michael's hand and hold it briefly in a physical demonstration of solidarity.

"Sit down, my friend," said Lawrence. "Coffee or tea?"

"Tea, if I must."

Lawrence nodded towards the waitress, waiting patiently for her cue.

"What can I get you, sirs?" she asked brightly.

"Coffee for me and tea for Mr Farrow. And I'll have the same breakfast as yesterday?"

"The waitress smiled. "An extra serving of bacon?"

Now Michael was with him, Lawrence felt justified in abandoning restraint. "Yes, please. What will you have, Michael?"

"I'm not hungry."

"My friend will have griddled crumpets with a poached egg on top," said Lawrence, remembering Michael's breakfast orders of old.

Michael glanced up as if about to disagree but said nothing.

They sat in silence until the waitress returned with their drinks, and Lawrence waited to speak, trying not to push too hard until Michael had consumed something. He hadn't eaten for some time, and refuelling was paramount.

"Here you go," said the waitress, placing a silver tray on the table and unloading the contents. Michael stared impassively, and Lawrence stirred the teapot before pouring an insipid brew that needed more stewing time. He stirred in milk and a large sugar before passing it to Michael.

"Drink up," he said. Michael obeyed as if hypnotised and seemed to relax as he sipped the drink.

"Are you still upset about Aurora?"

Michael cast a withering look. "Upset? That doesn't come close to how I feel about abandoning the woman I love."

"I understand, but you couldn't have done much more."

"Or indeed, much less."

"You tried, Michael. And you still don't know if you actually saw Aurora?"

"How does that help? If it was Aurora, then I left her to her fate. If it wasn't, I'm in the same position as before, not knowing where she is or how she fares."

"I don't know what to say. How can I help?"

"By leaving me to my thoughts."

"But you must talk about this. It isn't healthy to keep your worries to yourself."

"I have talked. I understand my predicament better than you think. A wise counsel has given me a clear view of my situation and how I might find peace."

"Thank you," said Lawrence as the waitress placed a large plate of eggs and bacon in front of him. He tucked in, managing a few hearty forkfuls before realising that Michael had not touched his breakfast.

"Come on. Eat up," he said.

Michael cast a withering stare before scooping the egg from the crumpet and cutting a small piece, which he chewed as if it had turned to ashes in his mouth.

"Praying must help, of course," said Lawrence. "But a human perspective is no bad thing."

"I haven't been praying. That's part of the problem."

"You said you'd found a way to inner peace."

Michael ignored him and speared another small piece of crumpet.

"Who are you seeing later today?"

"My bishop. He's been visiting Lambeth Palace, and I hope he will grant me an audience."

"Why?"

"To tender my resignation."

"But you've only just returned from your retreat. I don't understand."

Michael cast a pitying glance towards him. "I took a retreat because I'd lost my faith. I thought living a Christian life on an island with no distractions might help. And for a while, it did. But when I read your letter, all my thoughts turned to Aurora. My devotion to God was nothing compared to my feelings for her. I cannot serve them both. How can I face my parishioners, knowing I would abandon them without a second thought if Aurora needed me? I am not right for the Church, and it is not right for me."

"I disagree. As an Anglican, you are free to marry. Your God accepts this."

"But I must love him unconditionally, and I don't."

"What has changed?"

"I couldn't even maintain my vows during the retreat. It's not good enough."

"You judge yourself too harshly."

"Lawrence, my life is meaningless. I cannot help Aurora, and I've turned my back on God. There is nothing left for me."

"You still have friends and family. Do they mean so little?"

"Friends? Who are my friends other than you and Violet? I live alone, rattling around a great house full of ghosts and secrets. And as for family, well. My once esteemed elder brother has lost his mind and vanished off the face of the earth."

"Actually, he hasn't."

Michael placed his cutlery on his plate and stared at Lawrence. "What do you mean?"

"Francis is alive and well and living in Mexico."

"How do you know?"

"I've seen a photograph."

"Is he happy?"

"I don't know."

"And still dabbling with that filthy cult?"

Lawrence hesitated. Michael's melancholy went well beyond anything he had experienced before. He doubted the younger man was emotionally prepared to hear further details about his brother's unwise friendship with Crowley, and he regretted mentioning Francis at all.

"Well?"

"Probably."

Michael raised an eyebrow. "Don't do that, Lawrence. I'm not a child. What have you heard?"

"I saw a photograph of your brother with Felix Crossley."

"I'm not entirely surprised. They run in the same circles."

"It's more than that. Francis and Crossley are friends."

Chapter Twenty-Nine

IN SEARCH OF A FRIEND

"He's not back yet." Lawrence was sitting in the snug for the third time that day, speaking to Violet on a telephone that might as well bear his name for the time and money he had spent on it.

"I'm worried, Lawrence. Michael's behaviour is completely out of character."

"I know."

"Did he see the bishop?"

"I don't think so. He intended to, but just before he left the dining room, he said there was no point. It would all sort itself out soon."

"What do you think he meant by that?"

"No idea. Michael is usually so measured, the calmest of all of us. Yet today, he was angry and a little dramatic."

"He's suffering, Lawrence, "and has been for longer than any of us realised. I knew Aurora was trouble the moment I met her. It's not her fault, but she's brought problems to his door, and Felix Crossley is one of them."

"At least we don't need to worry about Crossley while

I'm in London. That's an issue for another day. But if I can't find Michael, I can hardly leave for Akenham. And although it's a long shot, this ritual is our only chance if Podmore is correct."

"You'd think Michael would be more interested."

"He isn't thinking straight. And I didn't labour the point about Akenham as I didn't want to raise his hopes. I regret it now. Michael thinks his situation is hopeless, but the merest possibility of finding Aurora might change his mindset. I will make sure he understands this when I next see him."

"Whenever that may be," said Violet quietly.

"How is Daisy?"

"Missing you. But Nora is a useful distraction?"

"Hasn't she left yet?"

"No. And she'll be staying on until we return from Akenham. Who else could look after Daisy?"

"And that's another thing. When I reminded Michael about friends and family, he didn't mention Daisy. Yet, how often has he looked after her? They always seemed as thick as thieves. I'm disappointed in him."

"As you say, he's not himself. Michael adores Daisy. I'm sure of it. He's got himself into such a state that he can't see the good things for concentrating on the bad."

"He seems to think he's on the path to peace."

"Oh, good. Then he must have recovered some of his faith."

Lawrence hesitated, thoughts milling in his mind like butter in a churn. "That doesn't sound right," he exclaimed.

"What doesn't?"

"If Michael has lost his faith, then how has he suddenly found a route to peace? And now I think of it, Michael didn't say he'd been praying. I just assumed it."

"What were his exact words?"

Lawrence thought for a moment. "Something about wise counsel giving him a clearer view of things."

"That could mean anything."

"I know."

"Who can he have spoken to?"

"Practically anyone. He was up at the hospital yesterday and back in his room for a long time. And we can't rule out a telephone conversation either. The hotel is very accommodating about making and taking calls."

"Hopefully, he spoke to someone at the retreat. That might help."

"True, but unlikely, given his faith issues. I wish I knew where he was."

"What time is it? I've left my watch upstairs?"

Lawrence glanced at his silver fob. Five o'clock."

"Oh dear. You ought to look for him.

"I wouldn't know where to start?"

"Are you sure he didn't go to Lambeth Palace?"

"He was adamant that it was pointless. And I'm sure he said he had other places to be."

"Search his room, Lawrence."

"It's locked."

"That's never stopped you before."

"Right. I'll do it."

"Call me as soon as you've found him."

"I will. And Violet, I love you. I know I don't tell you enough."

"I love you too. Now, hurry."

Though tempted to do something underhand, Lawrence couldn't bring himself to trick the young girl behind the reception desk. She was barely eighteen, friendly and accommodating, and it seemed only fair to treat her honestly, which meant taking a gamble over whether she would cooperate. But with the confidence of a man well-versed in getting what he wanted, Lawrence asked her for the key while singularly failing to give a reason for it.

The girl flashed a puzzled look, but Lawrence held his hand out, palm uppermost, and she obediently handed it over.

Lawrence thanked her and quickly made his way to Michael's room before she could consider the wisdom of her actions. He wrinkled his nose as he stepped inside. The room was still musty, fuggy in the way a room gets when the occupant fails to ventilate adequately. Michael's bed was unmade, his dirty clothes strewn upon it, and a suitcase lying open and abandoned in the middle of the floor. It disturbed Lawrence's sense of order, and he tidied the room, justifying the act with an internal monologue of how much easier the search would be in an orderly room. Five minutes later, with the window wide open, he began. The wardrobe was empty, as was the dressing table. A solitary Bible lay in the top drawer of the bedside cabinet. For a moment, Lawrence felt relieved at the nod to religion before remembering that he had an identical copy in his room, presumably left by the hotel staff. Frowning, he looked around the room, unsure of what he hoped to find. Then he crouched gingerly by the suitcase, racked with guilt about what he was about to do.

Michael's mind must have been less chaotic when he packed the previous day, as he'd neatly folded his clothes, such as they were. Lawrence couldn't help but smile at the disproportionate number of books compared to the minimal clothing Michael had considered necessary for a six-month escape from the world. Apart from a Bible and a prayer book, they were all works of fiction, and the little collection helped Lawrence remember the light-hearted way his friend had been before Aurora; before all his troubles began. Lawrence unzipped a washbag to find nothing more exciting than a razor, a toothbrush and a bar of soap, then turned his attention to a small compartment at the back. Inside were a few personal papers and some documents but nothing of any note that might lead him to his friend.

Sighing, Lawrence shoved the suitcase under the bed. Even while worried, he could not bear untidiness and hung Michael's dirty clothes in the wardrobe before making the bed. He found a large wooden hanger, draped Michael's trousers over, and then reached for his jacket. Something rustled in the pocket, and Lawrence removed it to see Michael's dog collar nestling in his hand. His heart lurched at the thought of Michael abandoning this most precious mark of his profession. He'd noticed that Michael wasn't wearing the dog collar at breakfast, which wasn't unknown. But for Michael to leave the hotel without it was a further acknowledgement of his diminishing faith, a loss of hope he was no longer willing to conceal from the world. Lawrence slid the jacket onto the hanger, seeing bloodstains transferred from Michael's trousers, and wondered how his wound was holding up now the nurse had dressed it. Then, turning around, he noticed something he hadn't seen before: a slip of paper that had fallen from Michael's pocket when he removed the dog collar. Lawrence picked it up and read.

"Meet me at Richmond Park tomorrow evening. Head for Pen Ponds, seven o'clock sharp."

Lawrence stared for a moment, then grabbed the room key, locked the door and, taking the stairs two at a time, made for the reception desk.

He handed the key to a girl busily writing in the register. "Did anyone leave a note for Mr Farrow?"

"Yes. I put it under his door this morning."

"Who sent it?"

"I don't know. One minute, the counter was clear. When I next looked up, this note was waiting."

"Hand delivered then?"

"Possibly. I don't know. Why?"

"Never mind." Lawrence thought for a moment. Why would Michael need to go to Richmond Park? As far as Lawrence knew, Michael had no friends in Richmond. Then he made a terrible connection, and his heart lurched in fear. Richmond Park: scene of Sophia Hickman's death, Emily Locker's terrible act of self-destruction and the unlikely final destination of Ann's friend Maria. Could someone as grounded and sensible as Michael fall prey to the same temptation to make his troubles disappear? There must be another explanation. But even as Lawrence tore down the stairs and frantically hailed a cab, he knew there was not. Someone had got to Michael in his darkest hour. And Lawrence had ninety minutes to save him.

Chapter Thirty

DISASTER AT PEN PONDS

Lawrence failed to secure an automobile, not for want of trying. Knowing it would be quicker, he ran past the row of hansom cab drivers to the other side of Battersea Park, where he had seen a regular row of drivers touting for business. But with typical bad luck, the rank was deserted, the cabbies either working or having gone home for tea. Cursing himself at the wasted minutes, Lawrence retreated to the hotel and summoned the nearest cabbie, realising when it was too late to back out that he'd secured the services of a hackney cab driver. Lawrence hadn't used a hackney cab for years, not since the nippy two-wheeled hansoms replaced their more cumbersome predecessor. But beggars couldn't be choosers, and Lawrence did not have the luxury of time. The driver was familiar with the location of Pen Ponds and promised Lawrence as speedy a journey as he could reasonably get from anyone. But to be on the safe side, Lawrence offered double the usual fare if they arrived in good time.

The cab driver was as good as his word, and Lawrence

suffered an uncomfortable journey, sliding up and down the poorly padded seat as the cab tore through the town, taking corners at terrifying speed. With horns blaring and pedestrians diving out of their path, Lawrence wondered how wise he had been incentivising the reckless speed. But the driver slowed down as he approached Richmond Park with time to spare and trotted on at a respectable pace to a dirt track some distance from the water. Lawrence opened the window and called out to the driver. "I'll make the rest of the journey by foot."

"As you like." The cab slowed, Lawrence dismounted and patted the sweating bay cob.

"Here," he said, passing a handful of cash to the driver.

"Thank you kindly."

"Make sure you give him an extra bag of oats," Lawrence continued, ruffling the horse's mane.

"Shall I wait?"

Lawrence shrugged. "It's a tempting offer, but I don't know how long I'll be. Can I hail a cab nearby?"

"If you walk in that direction," said the cabbie, pointing ahead. "It's a bit of a trek, but there's always someone passing by."

"Good. Thank you. Now, I must go."

"Trouble?"

"I hope not."

Lawrence turned away, pulled his collar high, and shoved his hands into his pockets. They'd made reasonable time. It was a quarter before seven and still light. But the weather had taken a turn for the worse, the sky now overcast and threatening rain. A light wind chilled the temperature, making it feel more like an autumn day than the height of summer. Lawrence shivered, knowing it was as much from worry as the weather, then trudged towards the larger of the two ponds.

The expanse of water was greater than he had expected from the handwritten note. In Lawrence's experience, a pond was small, perhaps belonging to a village green, but easily navigable by foot. These large bodies of water were less like ponds than lakes, and Lawrence wondered if he'd get around them before darkness started falling. He would need to think clearly. If Michael's meeting were casual, it would likely occur in the open. But if of sinister intent, then they'd inevitably meet somewhere private. Michael was due to see his mysterious contact at seven, and time had already moved on since Lawrence left the cab. He had only twelve minutes to find and intercept Michael. But he would need to establish his location without being seen. Better secrete himself and watch from a safe distance.

Lawrence jogged ahead to a narrow strip of land bifurcating the two ponds, then took a panoramic look at his surroundings. The view was unimpeded around the lower pond with its square sides and open landscape but the larger pond was irregular and enclosed by woodland on the farthermost side. When Lawrence saw an open bank shrouded by trees, his instinct took over. It would make an excellent meeting place, and Lawrence felt sure that if Michael were anywhere, he would be on that side of the ponds. Lawrence glanced at his watch. The place he had identified was as far away from his current position as possible. He wouldn't get there in twelve minutes, not even if he ran all the way. But if he set off now and kept a steady pace, it wouldn't take much longer, and he'd have time to creep towards the trees and loiter long enough to hear what Michael was saying. Bracing himself, he strode purposefully into the headwind, quickly but without drawing undue attention to himself.

Halfway around the upper pond, he lost sight of the wooded shore as he rounded a bend. Several minutes passed before his route wended close enough to the edge to see it again. But he was closer now and noticed a fallen log in the centre of the small, grassed area surrounded by dense foliage. To his relief, he glimpsed a sudden movement in the shrubbery and Michael emerged from the undergrowth. Lawrence watched for a moment as Michael reached into his pocket for something. But whatever he was expecting to find wasn't there, and he wandered around the clearing for a few seconds before suddenly darting towards a particularly densely wooded area. Abruptly, he pulled up short, turned on his heel, and took a seat on a fallen log with his back to the place he'd been heading. Lawrence glanced at his watch. He was still a good five minutes away. But Michael was safe, settled, and waiting, and time was now on his side, which was just as well. Within moments of moving, Lawrence ran into a young lady carrying a large open basket weighed down with a book. But as he approached, tipping his hat courteously, the wind whipped up, billowing her skirts, dislodging the book, and releasing page after page of handwritten notes.

"Oh no. My manuscript," she cried, placing her basket on the ground, and covering it with her coat while futilely chasing pieces of paper around.

"I'll help you," said Lawrence, spotting a nearby weighty stone, which he dropped on top of her coat in case of further gusts. Dressed in trousers and without the need to protect his modesty from the wind, Lawrence collected the documents in no time. Red-faced with embarrassment, the girl clutched her clothes with one hand and lunged for the basket with the other. Lawrence removed her coat and held it while she shrugged into it. Then he passed her the basket complete with stone. She thanked him profusely and went on her way. The entire incident had stolen little more than five minutes of his precious time, and Lawrence rounded another bend, peering again towards the water's edge.

Michael was now upright and walking around the small, grassed area with his head lowered as if in silent anguish while making jabbing motions with his hands. "Is he talking to himself?" muttered Lawrence aloud, trying to rationalise Michael's odd behaviour as he stood alone and confused, the meeting not going to plan. After a moment of quiet contemplation, Lawrence concluded that it was a rehearsal. Perhaps Michael was planning aloud what he wanted to say to his contact before the meeting took place, and judging by the gestures, it was likely to be heated. There was only one thing for it. Lawrence must get close enough to hear their conversation. He strode around the uneven pond, losing sight of the bank again. By the time he emerged the next time, Michael was alarmingly close to the water's edge with his head lowered, looking for all the world as if he were about to jump in. Lawrence opened his mouth to shout before realising he was still too far away for Michael to hear. And he was overreacting. There was a world of difference between looking at the water and trying to get in it. Michael was old enough and wise enough to know if he was too close to the pond. But Lawrence kept a wary eye ahead as he pressed on, finally arriving at the edge of the copse surrounding Michael's location.

A loud yell tore through the tranquil evening as Lawrence reached the trees, followed seconds later by a splash. Lawrence darted through the undergrowth to see Michael flailing in the water by the side of the pond.

"Hold on," yelled Lawrence pointlessly. Michael still couldn't hear him, and it was too far for Lawrence to risk swimming over. He could only run through the woods, sprinting through shrubs packed so closely together that brambles and thorns ripped his clothes. But it did not stop him. Powering through the undergrowth, Lawrence finally arrived at the shoreline fifty yards from where Michael was still thrashing in the water. He hurled his coat and hat to the floor and dived into the slimy depths, crawling through tangled weeds, conspiring to drag him down to the murky bottom. Lawrence continued, arms slicing through the water, closing the distance by ten feet, twenty, thirty. But as he swam nearer, the weeds thickened and wrapped around his legs, causing him to stop for a moment to untangle himself. And all the time, Michael's struggles became feebler, as if something were preventing him from fighting for his life. Lawrence kicked away the weeds and set off again, invigorated by the momentary pause. He was gaining ground, almost there, when Michael's head bobbed under and didn't come back up again.

"Hold on," yelled Lawrence, making a last-ditch effort to reach the point where Michael had gone down, trying not to dwell on the air bubbles popping onto the pond's surface. He dived through murky waters and darkly menacing vegetation towards his drowning friend. Then he dragged Michael to the surface with a strength he did not know he possessed.

Lawrence kicked back through the pond, keeping Michael's head above the water as he lay pale-faced and silent in his arms. Lawrence's lungs screamed with the exertion of his efforts while strength ebbed from his limbs. But Michael hadn't drifted far from the shore, and to his immense relief, Lawrence's legs brushed the bottom of the pond, as he staggered to his feet. Dragging Michael onto the grassy patch of ground, he tilted his head while thumping his chest with the flat of his hand. A trickle of water oozed from the corner of Michael's mouth, but he didn't move. Lawrence tried again. Still nothing. Michael was still and quiet, his skin clammy, his eyes shut. Reaching into Michael's inner jacket pocket, Lawrence's hands closed over the glasses case he knew he would find. With trembling hands, he removed the spectacles and held the lens to Michael's mouth. And with a sick dread, he examined the glass to find no trace of steam nor a sign of breath. For all his efforts, Lawrence had been too late.

Chapter Thirty-One

A BETRAYAL OF TRUST

Lawrence sat in quiet despair, visions of a future conversation with Violet running through his head. He would tell her the awful news and watch her face crumple. She would reassure him that he could have done no more. But inside, her heart would break, and he would never accept that he couldn't have saved his friend.

"It can't end like this," Lawrence cried, thumping hard on Michael's chest. A trickle of pond water ran down the side of his mouth, glistening against his pale, lifeless skin.

"No, no, no," Lawrence slammed Michael's chest in time with his words. Once, twice, three times, then another two in frustrated despair. Michael's chest heaved, emitting a sound like the last gasp of a dying man, and he spluttered as a flood of dirty water spewed from his lips.

"Michael. Thank the Lord. You're alive."

"Where am I?" Michael's mouth barely moved as he opened his eyes. They settled on Lawrence, and he reached out a hand before violently shivering.

"Don't worry. You're safe."

"What happened?"

"Never mind that now. Let's concentrate on getting you away from here."

"I can't. I feel awful. Just let me lie down."

"Here. Take this." Lawrence removed his jacket and lay it over Michael.

"I'm afraid it's wet, but a double layer might keep you warmer while I fetch help."

"Don't go."

"You need medical attention."

"I don't want to be alone."

"Wait. I have an idea."

Lawrence placed an arm under each of Michael's shoulders and dragged him into a sitting position against the fallen log. Then he took both his and Michael's handkerchiefs from their top pockets, walked to the shore's edge and started signalling. In the distance, people meandered on the other side of the pond, but Lawrence couldn't be sure whether he was visible to them. He kept going, repeatedly using the semaphore he'd learned as a boy until his arms ached. Finally, he caught the attention of a gaggle of uniformed boys. They clustered together as if deep in discussion, and the tallest boy stood and semaphored a message of acknowledgement. Lawrence returned to Michael, who was sitting glassy-eyed, his breathing laboured.

"How do you feel?"

"Cold." Michael's teeth chattered, his lips turning blue. Lawrence sat beside him, placed an arm around his shoulders, and moved closer.

"Help is on the way. You'll feel better when you've warmed up."

"Will I? You should have left me."

"I'm sorry things are so bad for you that you felt you wanted to leave this world. But you have choices, Michael. Violet and I will do anything to help. You're our dear friend and Daisy's godfather. Please don't tread this awful route of self-destruction."

Michael pulled away from Lawrence and turned to face him.

"What do you mean?"

"Only that we will do whatever it takes to help you. Money, time, and distance are of no consequence. Just stay with us and be safe."

"Lawrence. I did not jump into the water. Somebody pushed me."

"What?"

"He tried to drown me. One minute I was peering into the water, and the next, I was in it."

"Who pushed you?"

"I don't know."

"Did your meeting take place as planned?"

"Why do you ask, and how do you know I was meeting someone?"

"Never mind. Tell me why you are here."

Michael exhaled. "To meet someone, as you said."

"Who?"

"I don't know."

"You came all the way here not knowing who you were seeing?" Lawrence tried not to sound too incredulous.

"Let me explain." Michael lowered his head, took a deep breath, and sighed. "This is embarrassing."

"I won't judge you, and I won't tell anyone else without your consent."

"I haven't been myself for some time. You know that, of course. I fell in love with Aurora and couldn't accept what had happened to her. My faith was already diminishing, and my brother's disloyalty was the final straw. I started feeling better about things while on retreat, but then I went to Duncryne and abandoned Aurora again."

"If it *was* Aurora."

"Be that as it may, my spirits were at their lowest ebb when Dickie drove me home yesterday. I couldn't face talking, so I sat in the back of his car and put my hand on top of an old card tucked down the back of the seat; a card advertising an organisation that helps in times of need."

"A charitable venture?"

"No. Someone to talk to. A person whose purpose is to comfort those suffering from melancholy, someone who listens without judging and advises on a suitable course of action to prevent further distress."

"Like a psychologist?"

"In a sense. Anyway, the card contained a telephone number and instructions to call between certain times during the day. I went to bed for a few hours when I returned to the hotel, and I couldn't sleep thinking about whether this might solve my problems. I am a very private man, Lawrence, as I know you are. And I don't know how to live in this joyless state of despair. In the end, curiosity got the better of me. I telephoned and left a message, and an hour later, a man called back."

"And that's why you didn't make it to Ann's?"

Michael nodded. "Yes. I didn't want anyone to know. Anyway, he listened, and the more I talked, the more I despaired about my sanity. I might never find Aurora, my faith is a distant memory, and my brother won't suddenly return to the fold as if nothing ever happened. I cannot change these things, and without them, I will never be a whole person. There was no way out except for one. But as a priest, I could not take it."

"I know what it's like to feel the weight of loss, Michael. But Violet and I can help you. I know it."

Michael weakly smiled and continued his story as if Lawrence had not spoken. "I knew I could not destroy myself, yet that fate seemed inevitable. I asked the man what I should do, and he said he would be in touch. And he was. Quite how he found me, I don't know, but a note arrived this morning, and that's why I'm here."

"But he didn't arrive?"

"Yes, he did. He would not let me see his face but remained concealed behind a bush, speaking to me through the shrubbery. His words were wise and beguiling, and I felt otherworldly, as if detached from my body. I remember walking to the edge of the pond and gazing into the water. He commanded me to enter, and I considered it. I really did. But as I gazed down, Aurora's reflection smiled up at me, one arm outstretched, the other clutching a child's hand." Michael sniffed, and a tear trickled down his cheek while Lawrence watched uncomfortably, not knowing what to say.

"I hesitated, knowing the image was nothing more than my imagination, but it gave me pause and the tiniest flicker of hope. Enough, just enough to know that I wasn't ready to face my maker yet. I waited. He coaxed. I closed my eyes and tried to conjure up the image of Aurora again. And that's when it happened. That's when he pushed me."

"Are you sure?" Lawrence regarded his friend with an expression somewhere between doubt and pity.

"Certain. I didn't jump into the water. Truly."

"I believe you. Did you recognise his voice?"

"Not really. At first, I thought so, but it was impossible to discern beneath his thick Scottish accent."

Lawrence stood and walked towards the water's edge, looking for signs of his would-be rescuers. A buzz of distant activity attracted his attention as a snake of people surged towards them. He returned to Michael and crouched in front of him, relieved that Michael's lips had returned to their usual colour and his shivering had settled.

"Did this man want to help you?" he asked.

"I thought so at first."

"And now?"

"I think he wanted to watch me die."

Lawrence shuddered. "I was afraid you would say that."

"Do you know him?"

"No, but he has killed before. Or if not killed, then been directly responsible for several more deaths. All here, all in Richmond Park."

"I've had a lucky escape."

"We must find out who it is. Can you remember anything that could help?"

"This might," said Michael, reaching into his coat pocket and retrieving a card. "I picked this up in the car."

Lawrence regarded the soggy piece of card, its printed contents still legible, and his face turned pale.

"What is it?" asked Michael.

"I know that number. I've seen it before."

"Where?"

"At Nuit Isis temple. Damn the man. I thought I could trust him."

Chapter Thirty-Two

DEEP IN THE DEN

Lawrence strode along Gray's Inn Road, his anger at boiling point. Michael, having refused to spend a night in the hospital, was safely ensconced at his sister's house in Berkeley Square, where he would spend the night safely. Their rescuers had taken Michael from the pond by stretcher, and he was recovering well when they arrived. But Michael's spirits were low, and Lawrence couldn't bear to leave him unattended. Despite his protestations and at Violet's suggestion, he'd taken him to Ann's. The call to Violet was the second of Lawrence's three phone calls that had set him on his current path to locate the perpetrator of Michael's ills and beard him in his den. A course of action that was undoubtedly unwise, but Lawrence had insufficient evidence to involve the Metropolitan police, and without it, they would do nothing. And the killings would continue.

Taking advantage of a nearby gas lamp, Lawrence glanced at his watch, noting it was a quarter to ten. He was a little early, but that was no bad thing. A few more yards and he had arrived, loitering outside the door of The

The Disappearing Doctor

Medical Association. Lawrence waited for a second, and a man emerged from the shadows, heralded by a wisp of pipe smoke.

"You came. I wasn't sure if you would."

"Of course. Anything for a good story." Lonni Carpenter extinguished his pipe and tapped it on the wall, loosening the contents onto the floor.

"A good story is all it will be if I can't get to the truth tonight."

"I'll take what I can get. And I promise you this much. I'll keep ferreting whether or not the police respond."

"Good man. There's a light on inside. He must be here."

Lawrence tried the door.

"It's unlocked," he said unnecessarily.

Lonni nodded, and they went inside, tiptoeing through the unlit office towards the stairs. A chink of light shone beneath the door of Doctor Ernest Greville's office. Lawrence opened it and went inside.

"What's this all about, Harpham?" Greville's head snapped up, and he regarded Lawrence through steely eyes glinting with hostility.

"Don't pretend you don't know."

"But I don't. I should be home in Kew relaxing after supper, not tearing around London in the dark. This had better be good."

Lonni Carpenter stepped from behind Lawrence and smiled menacingly.

"Two of you? What's going on?"

"He's alive."

Greville stared blankly. "What?"

"Michael is alive."

"Who is Michael? "This is getting very tiresome. Explain yourself, or I'm leaving."

"I wouldn't," said Lonni in a low voice.

"Are you threatening me?"

Lawrence flashed a warning glance at the reporter. Something wasn't right. Greville's lack of comprehension seemed more than just an act. He removed the now-dried card from his pocket and tossed it on Greville's desk. "Have it back," said Lawrence. "Michael has no further use for it"

Greville snatched up the card. His forehead furrowed as he examined the print. "But this is my telephone number," he said.

"Quite."

"What's it doing printed on here?"

Lawrence hesitated. Of all the scenarios he'd anticipated, Greville's ignorance of the situation had not been one of them. He'd telephoned Lonni to ensure that the story would not die away if something untoward happened and for physical support in the event of violence. But Greville wasn't in a fighting mood. He simply looked baffled.

"Do you deny that this is your card?"

"Yes. Emphatically. I've never seen it before in my life."

"Then why would someone use your telephone number?"

"You tell me. I don't know."

"Does anyone else have regular access to it?"

"The cleaner, I suppose. And Dickie, of course."

Lawrence and Lonni exchanged glances.

"When does Dickie use it?"

"Whenever I'm not here. He comes and goes as he pleases. And living above the office gives Dickie ample freedom to make or take calls."

"Where is he now?"

"In his flat, I should think."

"We must speak to him at once."

"I'll come too. I'm sure there's a perfectly reasonable explanation."

"He's not here," said Lawrence, after hammering on the flat door three times to a resounding silence.

"He ought to be. I need him up bright and early tomorrow." Doctor Greville frowned and glanced at his fob watch.

"Is there another key?"

"Well, yes. But I can't let you inside without asking Dickie first."

"He's not here to ask, and I'm perfectly willing to break the door down," said Lawrence. "I'm entering that flat whether or not you give me permission. It's your choice."

"Wait here." Greville strode smartly down the stairs and returned moments later with a chunky iron key he inserted in the lock. It turned with a creak.

"No need for you to join us if it makes you uncomfortable."

"I'm coming," snapped Greville.

Lawrence led the way down a dark corridor, which opened into a living area with a table squeezed under a window and a tiny range beside a cupboard. Lawrence advanced towards the ceiling lamp, lit the gas mantle, and adjusted the chain. Then he glanced around the room. Sparsely furnished, his eyes naturally fell upon a bookcase filled with large tomes, and he pulled one out and examined it. "Psychology," he murmured.

"Yes. That's Dickie's passion. He's entirely self-taught, you know," said Greville. "He'd love to have studied it, but his family didn't have that kind of money."

"Never mind that." Lawrence had already moved farther down the corridor to a room at the end. He lit a candle on the window ledge by the entrance to the bedroom and went inside. The unmade bed was empty, and the wardrobe hung open.

"Where are his clothes?" asked Greville.

"Gone," said Lawrence. "Apart from this." He reached inside and retrieved a waistcoat that had fallen on the floor.

"It looks like he left in a hurry," said Lonni as he joined them.

"Doesn't it? But why?"

"I think this might tell us," said Lawrence, removing a leather-bound journal stowed beneath Dickie's mattress.

"What's that?"

"Shall we see?" He opened the front page.

"Experiments on suggestibility," read Lawrence.

"Go on." Doctor Greville perched on the edge of the bed, staring at Lawrence in evident concern.

Lawrence continued.

"I have long believed a skilled operator can control the human mind to perform actions that would otherwise be abhorrent to the person concerned. But to prove it, one must necessarily enter a morally complex arena, one in which the choice must be contrary to the principles of the subject. I have resisted up to now but having the good fortune to discuss my theories with a sympathetic mind, one not bound by earthly considerations and, dare I say it, already morally bankrupt, has freed my inhibitions. 'Do what thou wilt' was his only comment on my proposal, followed by a plea to keep him informed of my progress. So, I have, and I will."

"Oh, my God. I know the man he's referring to," said

Greville, his shadow gesturing against the wall in the poorly lit room.

Lawrence raised the candle and read on.

"So, Mr Felix Crossley, I will begin. I have the means and motivation to contact those lost souls who will do my bidding. At first, I thought I would try to influence them to murder and mayhem, but that will draw undue attention to my project. I have refined my ideas further and will attempt to induce them to perform their own self-destruction instead."

"This doesn't sound like the Dickie I know." Lawrence broke away from the book, grimacing. "He is charming, boyish, and full of fun."

"I'm afraid it does," said Greville. "This is Dickie when he's trying to impress. He may be young, but Dickie is frighteningly perceptive, with a fierce intelligence that could have been harnessed for good. I blame myself for letting him fall under Crossley's influence."

"Knowing Crossley hasn't harmed you," said Lawrence.

"But I don't have much of an ego," said Greville. "I am long in the tooth and my own man. Dickie is confident yet still finding his way. He responds favourably to flattery and is ripe for moulding. I had hoped he would follow my example, but this dreadful account suggests otherwise. Put it away. I don't want to hear anymore."

"No. Read on," said Lonni. "You promised me a story. Now deliver it."

Lawrence turned a few pages.

"Trooper Smith – An experiment in tearing lovers apart. I won't read the entire account," said Lawrence. "Suffice it to say that under Dickie Connolly's influence, a poor young soldier lay his head on a set of railway tracks and died. How wicked. The soldier resisted but Dickie induced him to act.

And he openly writes that he could have stopped him and chose not to. He claims the experiment was a great success."

"Is there more?" Lonni rubbed a grimly-set jaw with clubbed fingers.

"Much more. Some familiar names: Emily Locker, oh and nearer the end, Ann Brocklehurst's friend Maria."

"It's my fault," said Greville. "I knew Crossley was a monster, but it suited me to befriend him. And now he has ruined Dickie's life."

"No," said Lawrence. "Dickie is old enough to make his own decisions. He is without conscience, and nobody can manipulate him to commit evil acts. The wickedness in Dickie's soul must have preceded his acquaintance with Crossley. Lawrence turned a few more pages. "Doctor Sophia Hickman – An experiment in subverting the Hippocratic Oath. A physician's death by suicide."

"Read on," Doctor Greville whispered. "I knew Sophia, and I can hardly bear to hear this, but read on anyway. I ought to suffer."

"One of my few failures," read Lawrence, glancing up, puzzled. "How was that a failure when she died?"

"Go on."

He began again.

"One of my few failures, Miss Hickman, seemed to fill all the criteria necessary for this most critical experiment. First and foremost, she was a doctor, often visiting our shop for supplies. I spoke with her regularly during our four-year acquaintance and found her suggestible and eager to please. Her pliancy was desirable, as my process involves a certain amount of seduction of the mind. And my proficiency is sufficiently well-honed that nobody knows I am doing it. Although we did not become friends in the traditional sense, her being of a different social standing to me, we nonetheless passed the time of day. But it wasn't until a few months ago that I decided she was worthy of experimentation and I should start preparing her accordingly. So, I provided a smile and a friendly face at every opportunity, and before long, she disclosed her concern at a new hospital appointment. The problem, she said, wasn't the work itself but the reputation of one of the other female doctors. This physician was known for her intolerance, which she readily expressed with no consideration for the consequences. Miss Hickman was rather unworldly, fearing confrontation, which she avoided at all costs. She was due to cover for another doctor at the Royal Free Hospital, which was playing on her mind. Naturally, I took full advantage, teasing out her concerns and weaving them into a series of more extensive, uglier dilemmas. Under the guise of a concerned helper, I presented her with a selection of increasingly uncomfortable scenarios and asked her to imagine dealing with them. They included coping strategies towards hostile colleagues and how she might react if she negligently killed a patient. By the time Doctor Hickman arrived at the Royal Free Hospital, she already feared the worst.

Sure enough, within a few days, one of the other doctors spoke curtly to her, not unkindly, but under pressure during a typically stressful day. Not that her tone mattered. I had ensured that Miss Hickman was so nervous by then that the merest look might cause anxiety. She regularly dropped by for supplies and arrived the next day, appearing normal on the surface, but passing her broken syringe with a trembling hand. I had already pre-empted her appearance and set some cards on the counter, knowing that Doctor Greville wouldn't arrive for an hour or two. She took one when I turned away, and I knew because I had already counted them. So, I expected the telephone call, which came later in the day. I had perfected a strong but convincing Scottish accent, which gave gravitas to my disguise as an eminent psychologist keen to help those with troubles. We talked several times on the telephone, though she never realised she was talking to me. She gave every sign of being ready to terminate her life, however much it went against her principles. And I, of course, encouraged her, enjoying more satisfaction than usual in her daily proximity. My other subjects were strangers, but not Sophia. I had known her, been within inches of her. My hands had brushed hers as I passed over equipment and supplies. The thrill was exquisite and, for obvious reasons, could never be repeated. Detection of my activities did not form part of my plan. When I'd wound Sophia up as tight as she could be, with a warning to keep calm outside and give nothing of her troubles away, I activated the final part of my plan.

Sophia came to collect another dose of morphia and thanked me profusely, smiling bravely and ignorant of my part in her downfall. I had treated her as a friend, but she lacked the courtesy to warn me we might never meet again. Sophia had invested her loyalty with my alter ego, and if I'd had any scruples about luring her towards death, her disloyalty had nixed them. I was ready to see her die.

We had always conducted our business anonymously, and Sophia was unconcerned when I told her I would be nearby in the park, watching from a safe distance and offering moral support. I arrived twenty minutes before she was due and concealed myself in a bush in the Sidmouth plantation. I'd given her directions and instructed her to find a marker I had placed a few feet from the tree. That way, I could communicate with her and influence her actions should she stray from the plan. Sophia Hickman came to the scene of her destruction like a lamb to the slaughter. She laid out her syringe, pills, and a drink precisely as I had suggested but was curiously reluctant to proceed with any vigour. It took half an hour to coax her into taking the first pill and a further twenty minutes for the second. She began questioning the wisdom of her decision and was clearly changing her mind. I tried. My God, I tried to make the experiment a success. They had all worked up to now, but the silly girl was for turning. I could have let her go, but she was too close, and although it was unlikely, there was always the possibility that she might, one day, compare me Dickie Connolly, to the charismatic psychologist who talked her through her problems. It was not worth the risk. So, I instructed her to lie on the ground, close her eyes and think good thoughts. And that if she still wanted to leave after twenty minutes, she must go ahead and make the best of her life. Sophia Hickman did as I told her, like the child-woman she was for all her intelligence. This Amazonian woman, tall, strapping and physically able to subdue me, lay there as asked, still and obedient until I jabbed the syringe into her arm and filled her full of morphia. She sat bolt upright for a moment, eyes wide and fully comprehending as the morphine snaked through her veins and did its work. But to be on the safe side, I sat on her chest, tipped back her head and filled her mouth with morphia tablets, then waited until her breathing became laboured under the weight of my body. The clearing where she had died lay hidden from view, rarely visited and difficult to enter. But I wasn't taking any chances. I pulled her corpse into the undergrowth and threw her possessions in with her. It took months for them to find Sophia, and the inquest ruled it a suicide. And though things could have been much worse, they weren't. Yet I'm ruling this failure. Next time it won't be.

Chapter Thirty-Three

A GLIMMER OF HOPE

Monday, June 20th, 1904

"A visitor, ma'am." Mrs Mahoney ushered Lawrence into the drawing room of Ann Brocklehurst's house in Berkeley Square.

"Lawrence. What happened? You look dreadful. Sit down. Mrs M, please fetch some brandy at once."

"Where's Michael?"

"Upstairs resting."

"Is he well?"

"Better than he was. Still in low spirits, though."

"I have disturbing news. Is he up to hearing it?"

"I don't know." Ann hesitated for a moment. "Michael has lost his spark. I fear it will never return."

"This news won't help. If anything, it will make things worse, but I cannot easily keep it from him."

"Keep what from whom?"

A tall man with slicked-back grey hair and a

commanding presence strolled into the room, nodded to Lawrence, and stood beside Ann.

Lawrence jumped up and offered his hand. "Good to see you, Mark."

"I wish I could say the same. You look like death warmed up. What's the matter? A bad day at the office?"

"You could say that. I've just delivered the worst kind of news."

"Well, have a drink then. It looks like you need one."

"Mrs Mahoney is fetching a brandy," said Ann.

"Just the one?"

"I'll ask for another. Wait a moment."

"Just ring the bell—" Mark started to say, but it was too late. Ann had left the room.

"My wife seems on edge tonight," said Mark, smiling ruefully at Lawrence.

"She's worried about Michael."

"And with good cause, it appears. Were you talking about Michael when I came in?"

Lawrence nodded. "I have bad news to impart, which can only lower Michael's spirits. Ann would prefer that I kept it from him."

"Well, she's wrong. Well-intentioned, but wrong. It's not up to us to make decisions for a grown man, no matter how mindful of his feelings. Agree?"

"I do," said Lawrence. "But Michael is at his lowest ebb. I'm glad he's here with his family. He won't take this well, I fear."

"I'll tell you what," said Mark. "Best get it over with before you change your mind. Why don't I pop upstairs and fetch him?"

"Would you?"

"Of course. Take a seat."

Mark Brocklehurst left the room, hastening towards the staircase; a man on a mission.

Moments later, Ann arrived with Mrs Mahoney and a tray of drinks. "Here," she said, handing Lawrence a large glass.

He took a sip and then another, the amber liquid pleasantly warming his throat as he swallowed.

"Where's Mark?"

"Gone to fetch Michael."

"Oh dear. "Would you like us to leave you alone?"

"I think not. You will read all about it in the papers soon enough, and Michael will need your support."

As Lawrence took another mouthful of brandy, he heard the firm tread of footsteps coming down the stairs.

"Here he is," said Mark Brocklehurst, manoeuvring Michael ahead of him. "Fetch another brandy, Mrs Mahoney."

She grimaced but did as asked, melting away towards the kitchen while all eyes turned to Lawrence.

"How are you feeling?" he asked as Michael sank into the nearest armchair.

"Much better, physically, but I'm dog tired, and my head hurts. I'll be alright though."

"Good. I have news."

"I thought you must. You have that look on your face."

"First," said Lawrence. "I must be candid. We spoke of confidential matters yesterday, but things have changed and are about to become a matter of public interest. Not your part in it, although that might occur in due course. But I made you a promise yesterday, Michael. I would like to speak freely, but that's up to you. We can always talk privately."

"I remember little about yesterday, promises or otherwise. But I have discussed these matters with my sister already. You may say anything you like in front of my family."

"Good. Well, you ought to know that Dickie Connolly was the man behind the bush. He tried to kill you. I'm afraid he is a wicked man, possibly one of Crossley's disciples."

Michael's face drained of colour, and for a moment, he looked as if he might pass out.

"Why did he want to kill me?"

"He has a passion for psychology and was conducting experiments which he recorded in a journal. You were not among the entries, but if Dickie were running true to form, you would have been in time. I suppose it was too soon after the event."

"Where is Connolly now?"

"Gone. He's taken his clothes and fled. He must have seen me coming for you and hadn't realised I was too late to witness his attack."

"I still don't understand."

"You don't need to right now. But I'll do my best to give you some context. Dickie has wilfully, with malice aforethought, induced innocent but troubled people to take their lives. He has justified it to himself as a scientific experiment. But this is just an excuse, something more palatable to ease whatever passes for his conscience. Dickie Connolly is evil to the core and used his position of trust to harm those most in need of comfort."

Michael put his head into his hands and expelled a deep sigh. "I can hardly bear to think about it," he said. "What will happen now?"

Lawrence walked to the window, his eyes drifting across the square, before turning to face Michael. "I have just had the painful job of explaining the details of Sophia Hickman's demise to her father. I visited Edwin Hickman at home after breakfast this morning. And as a father myself, I cannot imagine what he must be feeling."

"Was Connolly involved in her death?"

"Yes, but what he did was worse than mere encouragement. Sophia resisted, and Connolly killed her."

Michael opened his mouth to speak, but no words came.

"The poor man." Ann's eyes filled with tears. "How unbearably wicked. But Dickie... I can scarcely believe it. He was such a gentle man." Ann stopped and thought for a moment, and then her face crumpled. "Oh, no. Tell me he didn't. If he caused Sophia's death, did he do the same to Maria?"

Lawrence shook his head. "I'm sorry to be the bearer of bad news, but you are right. Dickie induced Maria to suicide."

"How do you know he didn't kill her?"

"He kept meticulous notes, watching Maria until the bitter end and recording every detail."

Ann visibly shuddered, and Mark took her arm. "Sit down, my love," he said, leaning beside her on the settee with his arm around her shoulders.

"To answer your previous question," said Lawrence. "I took a witness with me last night, a reporter I met a few nights ago. The two of us, and Doctor Ernest Greville, presented ourselves at the Metropolitan Police Headquarters last night. They have kept the journal as evidence and taken our allegations seriously. But if the police fail to apprehend Dickie, my reporter friend will ensure he holds them accountable."

"Then we must wait for justice," said Mark Brocklehurst.

"For a while."

"And what will you do?" Ann looked up, her eyes still glistening with tears.

"I must set my sights on someone else," said Lawrence. "I have it on good authority that Crossley is planning one of his rituals in Suffolk tomorrow night, and however remote the possibility, I must go. If there's any chance of finding Crossley, it might lead us to Aurora and is surely worth the risk."

"I'm coming too." Michael's head snapped up, his eyes clear and focused.

"Are you sure you're up to it?"

"Oh yes. If Sophia's father can endure what you've just told him about his daughter, I can rise above my feelings too. And if there is the smallest chance of finding Aurora, I'm all in."

"You shouldn't go," said Ann. "It might be dangerous. Can't you let the police handle it?"

"And tell them what? That a gang of deluded occultists might use a churchyard for their nefarious practices? They'd laugh me out of the station, and rightly so," said Lawrence. "No, I'll deal with it."

"We'll deal with it," said Michael firmly.

"Good man. Then let's head back to the hotel to pack. We'll be leaving first thing tomorrow."

Chapter Thirty-Four

THE DEVIL LIES DEEP

Tuesday June 21st, 1904

"It was decent of the Reverend Jones to offer a bed for the night," said Lawrence as he trudged across a bone-dry wheat field, trying to avoid damaging the crop.

Michael smiled. "It only took a telephone call. He didn't even ask me why, just offered the room at the rectory for as long as we wanted it. It's a pity he was out when we arrived."

"We can thank him tomorrow," said Lawrence. "And in the meantime, our luggage is safe. How far is this parish church?"

"Another mile or so," said Michael.

"Have you been before?"

"Never. But I hear it's very small."

"Well, the reverend's wife is a sprightly sixty, and I hope her husband is in similar health. There must come a time when the church can't reasonably expect a parish priest to walk miles across open fields from one incumbency to another."

"It's hardly miles. The heat makes it feel farther than it really is."

"That and my damned shoes. They are not made for countryside walks."

"I wonder if Crossley will turn up."

"Only time will tell. We must hope that Podmore knows what he is talking about."

"I still can't help thinking about Crossley's basement. I should have tried harder."

"Don't, Michael. You'll be no use if you can't overcome your feelings. We've been over this, and you still can't be sure it was Aurora. In any case, Crossley won't take meddling lightly. We must both be on our best form."

"If he arrives."

"When he arrives."

"You're more certain than I am."

"Not really. But we must hope for the best."

Lawrence paused for a moment, removed his handkerchief, and wiped it over his brow. "At least the weather is on our side. We'll be glad of it later."

Must we wait until nightfall?"

"Undoubtedly. These esoteric rituals usually take place under cover of darkness, which happens much later in the middle of June. We're in for the long haul, I'm afraid. But I have brought victuals with me. Not much, but we'll appreciate the bread and cheese later. And I grabbed a couple of ciders while you were freshening up."

"Good. I'm hungry already."

"That's a good sign," said Lawrence. "You seem brighter today, Michael."

"It's because I'm doing something. Who knows how I will feel tomorrow."

"Chin up."

"I say. Did you get hold of Violet?"

Lawrence frowned. "No. I telephoned, but nobody answered."

"That's odd. I thought she was coming to meet us."

"She wanted to. I tried to put her off, but she insisted. I can only hope she's seen sense and changed her mind."

"Look. That must be the church."

Michael pointed to an iron gate surrounded by trees, with a glimpse of a square tower beyond.

"Now I understand what Podmore meant."

"Sorry?"

"It is rather remote."

"You'll find the village, such as it is, down that track," said Michael, nodding to his right.

"I thought you'd never been here."

"Annie Jones gave clear instructions."

The gate creaked as Lawrence pushed it open, and they picked their way up the grass-covered track towards the little church. Lawrence tried the door and found it firmly shut.

"That's a pity," he said.

"Sorry, I should have mentioned it. Mrs Jones warned me."

"It would have been useful to have a bolthole. Never mind."

They circumnavigated the church, wandering to the rear and seeing a small, solitary grave with a carved wooden toy placed reverently against a hump of grass-clad soil.

"That's the little boy's resting place," said Lawrence. "Have you heard about him?"

Michael nodded. "The scandal rocked the clergy," he said, crossing himself. "Rest in peace, little man."

"The Reverend Drury lacked compassion," said Lawrence.

"I didn't know him. Perhaps he had his reasons."

Lawrence contemplated a reply. He was not especially religious and had little time for pastors casting judgement upon the smallest and weakest members of their congregation, but Michael was in good spirits, all things considered. Now was not the time for a philosophical debate about the church's failings.

"We must find the cracked tombstone," said Lawrence.

"It shouldn't be difficult in a churchyard this small."

"Hopefully not."

"What does it look like?"

"I don't know. But it's damaged."

"That doesn't help. Few of these stones lie intact."

"You take one side, and I'll take the other. We can pick out the most likely candidates."

Lawrence wandered back towards the gate, advancing to the left, where he scanned the stones, his frown deepening with every grave marker he passed. But after a few moments, Michael called him over.

"It's this one," he said excitedly, pointing to a large tomb in the northwest corner.

Lawrence stood over the intricately carved burial vault and examined the large circular crest in the centre. "How do you know?" he asked.

"Walk around the other side. You may need to squat down."

"Ah, I see what you mean." Lawrence brushed a few stalks of grass to one side revealing the centre point of a large cross chalked onto the side farthest from the church.

"Do you think one of Crossley's men did this?" he asked.

"I can't think of any other reason," Michael replied. "And the right-hand side is badly damaged. You can almost see inside."

"Good. We're on the right track, and it gives me more confidence that they will turn up tonight. We must plan how best to conceal ourselves."

The two men stared around the churchyard but saw no obvious hiding places.

"This could be a problem," said Michael.

Silence fell as they considered their options.

"Realistically, we must conceal ourselves over there," said Lawrence, gesturing towards the gate.

"I don't see how."

"We can squat behind the burial vault in the corner."

"It's risky. They'll see us when they come through the gates."

"Don't forget. It will be dark."

"Good point. Well, that's that then. What now?"

"Now, we wait."

Lawrence was dozing when he heard the first low chant, just audible over the fields. He had consumed a light supper and was anxiously waiting, contemplating how chilly it might get overnight after a sudden, unexpected squall caught them unawares.

"Did you hear that?" Lawrence hissed to Michael as he paced by the graveyard wall, barely visible in the failing light.

"Hear what?" he whispered.

"Listen."

The Disappearing Doctor

They fell quiet.

"Ah, yes. Now I can hear. It sounds like discordant singing."

"Wait a moment." Lawrence slunk towards the gate, his head low as he navigated past the metal bars, tiptoeing over the track and through a hedgerow before reaching open fields. In the distance, a procession of lights twinkled across the ground, the hypnotic glow lulling Lawrence into inactivity. His eyes adjusted to the dark and settled on a bat flitting past a nearby tree. By the time he refocused, the hooded cloaks of the torch-bearing column of men were clearer. And there were many, many more than Lawrence had expected. A rising panic coursed through him, and for a moment, he considered fleeing. But as his heart quickened and clammy chills settled over his skin, he made himself take stock. Crossley was only a man. He might believe in fantastic supernatural beings, but they weren't real. His rituals were only play-acting and nothing to worry about. Lawrence licked his lips, transfixed by the flames, eyeing a break halfway through the column of people who were carrying something. They moved quickly, unimpeded by the daytime temperature, which had long since plummeted. If Lawrence waited any longer, they would be upon him. He closed his eyes and concentrated, willing himself to move, then darted towards Michael, warning him in a gabble of words that made no sense.

"Say that again," whispered Michael.

"Crossley and his horde are on their way."

"How many of them?"

"Twenty or thirty."

"Good grief."

"They're carrying torches. Just lay low until they pass. We'll be safe if they don't see us on the way in."

The chanting grew louder, bringing a low murmur of strange-sounding names, their harsh consonants casting sinister tones. Inky darkness had settled over the silent graveyard, and Lawrence's heart thumped in anticipation of their arrival. The sound reached a crescendo as their feet thudded on stony earth, crunching towards them, while Michael and Lawrence cowered behind the vault, not risking a glimpse. The sky lightened as torchbearer after torchbearer filed into the tiny churchyard, muttering quietly now, their words melding into senseless, meaningless sounds that sent a shiver of fear through Lawrence.

Their movement seemed endless, one man after another marching through the gate, some with heavier footfall slowing down and panting as if carrying a heavy load. But still, Lawrence waited, casting an empathetic glance at Michael even though he knew his friend couldn't see it. Finally, the lighting dimmed, and the crowd moved closer to the church as the chanting stopped dead. Lawrence shivered and risked a peep.

A sea of men surrounded the carved burial vault, their torches held aloft in the air. Their tall, solidly built leader, shaven-headed, and wearing intricately embroidered robes, stood, arms raised high as the others watched silently for his instruction. Lawrence waited too, transfixed by the commanding presence of a man who must be Crossley, before realising with horror that another person was present in the party too. A small, slender woman barely clad in a petticoat lay spread-eagled atop the stone, her arms pinned down and a bandage over her mouth. Torchlight illuminated the contours of her body, a long neck, small breasts, and a gently rounded stomach.

And just as Lawrence saw her, Michael did too, standing

bolt upright with his mouth open, reacting instinctively, with no thought for their safety.

Lawrence jumped up, placed his hands over Michael's mouth, and yanked him back, tipping him over as they fell behind the stone. Michael elbowed him sharply in the ribs, and Lawrence shoved him to the ground before sitting on his stomach, his hand still tightly over Michael's mouth. "For God's sake, man," he hissed. "Shut up."

Michael jerked his head from side to side, but he was no match for Lawrence's weight. And after a moment, he quietened, and Lawrence cautiously moved his hand away.

"They have Aurora," said Michael hoarsely.

"I know. But you won't help her by giving our position away."

"Then how?"

"I don't know. But we are seriously outnumbered. Don't be foolish."

"Let me up."

"Only if you promise not to do anything stupid."

Michael stared mutely.

"Give me your word."

"Very well. I promise."

Lawrence heaved himself from Michael and peered towards the church. Still oblivious to their presence, the cultists carried on with their ritual, standing like soldiers with torches lowered while Crossley spoke.

"We are ready," he said. "But there is much to do before we awaken the one who sleeps. Tonight, we come together, druid and magician alike. As the Oak King falls to the Holly King, so the false gods fall to the mighty one. Tonight, we celebrate our shadows, however fearsome, and our dark side, however grim. We indulge our worldly pleasures, no matter how they might offend. For it is only offensive to those sitting in judgement. And who are they to determine what is right and what is wrong? What gives them the authority to declare moral turpitude on those of us who embrace our freedom and refuse to conform to the unjust laws of the Godly? Tonight, blood will spill."

Lawrence gripped Michael's wrist tightly as the younger man gasped.

"Look by his feet," he whispered urgently and felt Michael's arm relax as one of Crossley's acolytes grasped a chicken by the legs and laid it at the foot of the tombstone, just inches away from Aurora.

Michael turned away as Crossley drew a sharp-bladed knife over the creature. Its life ebbed away in seconds, blood pulsing over the stone, glistening in the torchlight.

"It's over," said Lawrence.

"I can't bear this. We must take Aurora and get away from these madmen."

"Not if they're carrying knives," said Lawrence. "They are deluded but armed. We cannot take our safety for granted."

"This is hellish," said Michael.

"All we can do is wait and hope that an opportunity arises."

"I'm not sure I can."

"Don't do it for me. Do it for Aurora."

Two of the party moved to either side of the stone and raised their flames high. The remaining torchbearers lowered their lights in a downward position behind their backs. The churchyard fell into darkness except for the area where Aurora lay still and unmoving, as if asleep. Crossley raised his hand again, then began chanting – a series of names, some of which Lawrence had heard in the Nuit-Isis temple in London. He stopped abruptly, leaned forward,

The Disappearing Doctor

and dipped his finger in the chicken's blood before daubing it on Aurora's forehead. Still, she remained immobile, showing no signs of fear.

Crossley passed the chicken carcass to a diminutive man standing to his left.

"Drink," he commanded.

The man tilted his head back, as blood flowed from the gaping hole in the chicken's neck before wiping the scarlet stain from his lips with the back of his hand.

Michael heaved, valiantly trying to retain the contents of his stomach but failing. He vomited silently in the grass beside him. And when he had finished, Lawrence patted his shoulder sympathetically, watching a tear trickle down his cheek, just visible by the light of the moon.

"Hang on," he whispered.

"It is time," said Crossley, gesturing to the figure on his other side, a tall, straight-backed man of military bearing.

The man nodded, strode over to the nearest torch bearer, and took the blazing wood. Then, with smaller, slower steps, he passed it ceremonially towards the smaller man, still standing proudly with blood dripping from his chin.

"Begin," said Crossley.

One by one, the men began chanting again, this time in English. *Honour us, Dark Lord, with the gift of power*, first softly, then louder and more frenziedly as the torch bearer approached the ancient wooden door. He paused, turned to face them, and spun around before sprinting around the church. Their voices dropped into a low repetitive murmur more like a drone than a spoken word; sinister, threatening, and otherworldly. Lawrence shivered. As the torch bearer circumnavigated the church for the first time, Crossley nodded to the tall man, who held up his hand. "One," he boomed in a deep, controlled voice. The bearer ran around again.

"Two." This time he did not wait for Crossley's signal.

"Why are they counting?" asked Michael.

"They are testing the legend."

"How?"

"Old folklore says the devil appears to anyone passing widdershins around the church thirteen times."

"We must stop them."

"It's nonsense, Michael. You'll see in a minute."

Michael's fingers closed around the crucifix dangling inside his shirt. "God help us," he said.

As the counter announced the fourth circuit, Crossley approached the tombstone again.

"What's he doing now?" whispered Michael, struggling to see what was happening beyond the ring of men surrounding Aurora.

"Hang on." With all the attention focused ahead, Lawrence risked a move. He ran diagonally, crouching from gravestone to gravestone until he was close enough to get a better view.

Crossley stood over Aurora with his hands hovering about a foot from her face. At a closer distance, Lawrence could see her firmly closed eyes. She was asleep, or unconscious, but not dead, and her breast rose and fell in the torchlight.

Crossley balled one hand into a fist, moved his arm, and lowered it towards Aurora's nostril. For one awful moment, Lawrence thought he was about to strike her. But as his hand reached her nose, she jerked her head, and her eyes flicked open. Crossley must have concealed smelling salts and woken Aurora with no suspicion of trickery. Lawrence had been right. Crossley was nothing more than a showman, and his shoulders sagged in relief. The ceremony, the isolated location and the bloodletting had taken their toll on Lawrence, who, for one moment, had contemplated the irrational.

Aurora released a piercing scream in sudden awareness of her situation, sitting bolt upright on the vault, the bandage over her mouth rippling as her breath came in ragged gasps.

"Lie down," Crossley commanded.

She stared at him, her eyes wide, and tried to place her hands protectively over her breasts. But they stopped a few inches from the tombstone as the bindings fixing her arms held up to the sudden movement. She wriggled her shoulders and groaned. Lawrence flashed an urgent look behind him, willing Michael to stay quiet and hidden, heart in mouth as he glimpsed Michael's mouth agape as if hypnotised.

By the time he turned around again, Crossley had placed both his hands on Aurora's nightdress. And with a sudden rip, he tore the linen in two, both pieces splaying over the side of the stone vault. As Aurora shivered, the counter continued, eight, nine, ten. Crossley raised his knife on the eleventh count, and on the twelfth, he placed it in the centre of Aurora's breast as every man stood with bated breath, waiting for the thirteenth. It never came. As Lawrence launched himself at the runner, bringing him down in a rugby tackle, Michael darted towards Aurora, knocking Crossley aside and gathering her up in his arms.

"You bloody fool," thundered Crossley, scrabbling around on the floor for the fallen weapon. He found it and advanced towards Michael, brandishing the knife with the sharp, blood-coated blade. "You've ruined my ceremony, and I'll make damned sure you pay."

Chapter Thirty-Five

THIRTEEN CIRCUITS TO HELL

Lawrence had taken the runner by surprise and brought him down hard. But the smaller man had recovered and struggled forcefully beneath Lawrence's weight.

Still, all Lawrence could think about was Michael and the proximity of Crossley's blade. The man bucked and squirmed, his mask hanging lopsidedly across his face.

"Stop, or you'll know about it," hissed Lawrence as two cultists noticed they were dealing with more than one intruder and advanced towards him.

With no time to spare, he punched the runner in the jaw, knocking his head back to the ground. The runner briefly tensed, then relaxed as he lost consciousness. Lawrence jumped to his feet just in time to evade the two men as they lunged towards him. He grabbed the runner's torch, removing it from the ground before the flame died.

"Michael," he yelled as Crossley's head whipped around in Lawrence's direction.

"Stop him," screamed Crossley as the men grabbed

their torches and surged across the churchyard towards him. But Lawrence was one step ahead and vaulted over the wall and towards the wooden notice board. He swept the torch across a pinned piece of paper which immediately caught light, transferring the spitting, crackling flame onto the dry wood. But Lawrence did not have time to watch the fire. He doubled back and headed around the church, this time on the far side of the low wall, crouching down and cloaked in darkness. He sped towards the rear, knowing that he would be a few paces ahead even if they caught him. But as he rounded the small church and climbed back over the wall, his face fell at the sight of half of the men still standing by the tombstone clustered around Michael and Aurora like voyeurs at an execution.

"Well, that was a waste of your time," said Crossley as Lawrence, resigned to the impotence of his position, approached the group with his hands out in supplication.

"And yours likewise," Lawrence replied.

"No matter. We'll conduct the ceremony again."

"Not this Litha," said Lawrence, glancing at his watch.

Crossley scowled, shadows from the flickering torch etching his moon face with dark, twisting furrows.

You've interrupted a critical event and will pay for that delay. A little unscheduled blood magic ceremony is in order."

"Is it really? Only, I know you're all show," said Lawrence with false bravado.

"I'm glad you think so." Crossley slid his thumb down the sharp blade, slicing the skin and holding it out for Lawrence to see. He squeezed a drop of blood onto the blade's edge and kissed it.

"Nice trick with the smelling salts," countered Lawrence.

Crossley glared and, with a sudden swift movement, jabbed the knife into Michael's hand, resting on the tombstone.

Michael yelled as Crossley removed the knife from the jagged flesh wound and brandished it in front, glaring at Lawrence.

"Alright. You've made your point. Put the knife away."

"You are in no position to tell me what to do," snarled Crossley. "And who are you anyway?"

"None of your business."

"Give me your name and that of your friend."

Lawrence shrugged as he watched Michael, oblivious to his pain, sitting with his arm around Aurora, now wearing his jacket and cleaning his wound with the remains of her nightdress.

"The intruder is called Harpham," said the counter. "He is an interfering busybody. Do your worst, master."

Lawrence stiffened at the familiar voice, more recognisable now that he was closer. The man moved, and he recognised the gait.

"Ah. I wondered where you'd got to, Major," he said, nodding amiably, trying to project false bravery. Lawrence's heart hammered in his chest. He had not expected Crossley to act on his threat, but he was unpredictable and dangerous. He'd made an enemy of the major and could expect no help from him, and Michael was unlikely to leave Aurora's side. Lawrence would gain more by keeping his cool than counting his regrets, and he was determined to hide his fear.

The major removed his mask. "I've lost everything, thanks to you," he said. Then turning to Crossley, "This is the reptile responsible for the children's loss."

Crossley raised an eyebrow and stared at Lawrence as if

he had crawled from beneath a stone." I can never replace them," he snarled. "You owe me."

"Let me finish him," begged the major.

"No. I will decide where and when we deal with troublemakers. Clear up here, and we'll take them back to Duncryne. It will be easier to dispose of them there once they tell who they are and what they know. Fetch me the vials. They're in the case." Crossley nodded to a slender man clutching a rock in his hand. He dropped it and turned towards a small suitcase leaning against the side of the church. When he turned back, he was carrying a syringe and a dozen glass tubes.

Lawrence only had seconds to consider his options. Michael was wounded, and though he could make good his escape, he wouldn't leave Aurora a second time. If Crossley drugged them and drove them to Duncryne, they would be at his mercy in the remote Scottish wilderness. He needed to act and act now. With one mighty yell, he headbutted Crossley, spun around, and charged through the remaining cultists, weaving towards the burning noticeboard, now spewing smoke and flames into the air. Slamming past and singeing his jacket, he sprinted from the churchyard and was almost clear when he felt a thud on the back of his neck. He pulled up, swaying, his vision cloudy, nausea rising in his gullet. Woozily, he turned around, standing immobile as the diminutive runner approached him.

"Well, Lawrence Harpham, I owe you one. And I don't mean that kindly."

Lawrence shook his head, trying to focus. The voice was gentle, almost friendly. And horribly familiar.

The man approached him and pressed his face inches from Lawrence, blood splatter glistening from the rough fabric of the mask that covered his eyes, his lips still scarlet. "Haven't you guessed yet?"

Lawrence pressed his hand against his pounding head, groggily trying to make his legs move. He needed to run. He must move now. Because the man standing in front of him wasn't a showman. He was a killer. Slowly, the runner crouched down, picked up the rock and removed his mask. "I know Crossley would rather I didn't kill you, but to hell with it. No need to write this up as an experiment. I'm doing it because I want to. Dickie Connolly leered as he lunged at Lawrence with the rock raised high above his head.

Lawrence watched passively, as if the scene was playing in slow motion, casually acknowledging that he was about to die but too remote from his conscious to do anything about it. Then a horn blared from nowhere, and a farm vehicle lumbered up the road, its headlamps glaring.

Dickie lowered the rock and raised his hand to his eyes, blinded by the light.

"What?" Lawrence blinked and shook his head, then blinked again, slowly drifting back to reality at the unexpected noise. He glanced behind the vehicle to hear men shouting and watched as a group of farmhands ran towards him, brandishing spades, rakes, and hoes; any implement they could find.

A large burly man approached him. "Lawrence Harpham?"

"Yes."

"We're here to help."

Lawrence didn't question the sudden appearance of his

guardian angel but pointed towards the churchyard. "My friends need help. They're in there. Watch out for the men in robes."

"Right you are."

The farmhands stormed past, shouting as they scrambled towards the little churchyard. Lawrence caught his breath and turned around to search for Dickie Connolly, but he had melted into the darkness. Lawrence turned towards the church, knowing he must help Michael, however unwell he felt, but as he moved, he noticed two figures walking towards him. One was a woman striding confidently forward. But right up until the moment Violet touched him, Lawrence thought he was hallucinating.

"I don't understand," he said.

"Thank Mr Lauchlan Rose of Rise Hall," she replied.

Lawrence reached out to shake Violet's companion's hand. Lauchlan Rose propped the pitchfork he was carrying against a wall and returned the gesture.

"Why?"

"I know you wanted to protect me, and I wanted to protect you, too. So, rather than join you, I approached Mr Rose yesterday and asked him to make his farm men available should there be any trouble in the churchyard. Mr Rose kindly allowed me to watch over the church from the back of the hall. We couldn't see much in the dark but noticed some activity in the churchyard. And when we saw your signal, I knew you needed help."

"My signal?"

"The flames. Something was burning."

"Ah. The church notice board. But Michael and Aurora are in trouble. I must go to them."

"They'll be safe now," said Lauchlan Rose confidently.

"I've good men at my disposal. And plenty of them. You are injured. Stay here, and I'll marshal the men."

He strode off without looking back, and Violet grasped Lawrence and pulled him towards her.

"You poor thing," she said. "I have been worried."

"Oh, Violet. I've missed you. I love you. Do you know that?"

But Violet didn't have time to reply.

"How very touching." Dickie Connolly's words dripped with sarcasm.

"Where did you come from?"

"Never you mind. Step away from your wife."

"Don't do this, Dickie," said Violet calmly, watching the knife that Dickie had acquired during his brief absence.

"Oh, do be quiet," said Connolly.

"You're outnumbered." Lawrence kept a protective arm around Violet.

"I said move." Dickie was snarling now, his lip curled and spittle flying from his lips. He twisted the knife, jabbing it in tiny motions towards Violet. Then he stepped to the right, grabbed Violet's arm, and pulled her to the floor.

Lawrence moved, but Dickie was faster, leaning over Violet with the knife aimed at her throat.

"Stop."

"No. It's over."

Dickie yanked his arm back, lining up for the killing stroke. But Lawrence had already swiped the pitchfork. As Dickie raised his hand, Lawrence did likewise. And a fraction before Dickie's knife descended, he thrust the rusty prong of the pitchfork into Connolly's spinal cord, inhibiting his movement forever. Dickie fell onto Violet, the knife dropping harmlessly to the floor.

Violet scrambled away, jumped up, and curled into Lawrence.

"Is he dead?"

"No," said Lawrence, jabbing his toe at the motionless body. It rolled to the side, propped up by the pitchfork tines, while Dickie's hands trembled. "His is a fate worse than death. But he'll never hurt anyone again."

Chapter Thirty-Six

A MORTAL ENEMY

Most of the cultists had fled by the time Lauchlan Rose summoned the Ipswich police, who busied themselves rounding up the injured from the churchyard. Lawrence gave his account to his old friend, Inspector Fernleigh, who agreed to suspend judgement until the next day when they would return to the station. But for now, Lawrence was sitting with Michael in Rise Hall's drawing room, trying to persuade him to go to the hospital. Once again, Michael refused to leave Aurora alone. And amid the chaos, Lauchlan Rose discreetly left the room to allow them some much-needed privacy.

"I can't thank you enough," said Michael, beaming at Violet, his eyes sparkling and the years falling from his face.

"So, you keep saying," Violet teased.

"But you were so resourceful."

"Any other course of action would have been foolish. Now, how are you feeling, Aurora? Are you warm enough?"

Aurora nodded and snuggled into a man-sized smoking

jacket Lauchlan Rose had provided while his housekeeper sought something more suitable.

"A little more toast?" Lawrence offered one of the plates of light dishes his hosts had provided while they recovered from their ordeal.

She shook her head.

"Lawrence. I must telephone Nora."

"At this time of night?"

"Yes. She is expecting my call. Can you join me for a moment?"

"Does it need two of us?"

Violet glared, and Lawrence understood. "Excuse us for a moment," he said.

Lawrence followed Violet up the passage towards a closed door at the end. She knocked twice and listened. Silence.

"Good. It's free," she said, walking into Lauchlan's study towards a tall, elegant telephone.

"What is it?" asked Lawrence.

"Try not to question Aurora. She won't say much."

"I'm hardly giving her the third degree."

"That's not what I mean. I misjudged the girl. She is clearly devoted to Michael. It's obvious from the way she looks at him."

"Then all is well."

"Sadly, it is not."

Lawrence glanced at Violet, wishing she would tell him what was on her mind. But she weighed her words carefully.

"Have you noticed anything different about Aurora?"

"Hardly. I mean, she's terrified and could do with a bath and a new haircut. Although it hasn't affected her appetite, fortunately."

"Exactly."

"I don't follow. What difference does it make that she's heavier than she was..." Lawrence raised a hand to his face. "Are you suggesting...?" His words trailed away.

"I'm afraid so. I helped Aurora into her robe. It's early days, a few months, perhaps, but Aurora is definitely in the family way."

"Poor Michael. Just when he's found her again. So much for that."

"Be careful. It may not be her fault. Crossley has used her for a long time. And although he kept her in tolerable conditions, Aurora was not free to leave."

"Right. I'll be careful. Have I been gone long enough?"

"I doubt she'll tell him immediately, and certainly not with people around. Go on ahead. I'll join you in five minutes."

Lawrence returned down the passageway, musing over his quandary. There was nothing worse than knowing something he shouldn't. And he didn't know how to keep the secret from Michael if Aurora took too long to tell him herself.

She was fast asleep when he entered the drawing room, her head nestling on Michael's shoulder.

"Quiet," he whispered, raising a finger to his lips.

"Has she said much?" asked Lawrence in a low voice.

"Just a little. As we thought, Aurora fled to London when she found the secret room in Netherwood. A friend introduced her to The Order of The Crescent Moon, and as an orphan with no relatives, comradeship appealed to her. Crossley took advantage."

"There are better ways," muttered Lawrence.

"Nevertheless. The Crescent Moon is a benign organisation. You've told me that. Only Crossley and his ilk gravitated towards the more extreme cult activities. But Aurora didn't know that would happen. Crossley is charismatic. He charmed her, and she thought he had feelings towards her. But when he told her she would be his scarlet woman, she left her position in London and headed for the countryside, finding work in Bury St Edmunds, where we met her. And there she would have stayed but for Francis and his infernal room."

"Did she know him?"

"Francis? No. She never met him but had heard his name. It wasn't until she saw the hidden room that she realised my lost brother Francis was the same man who had befriended Crossley. She made good her escape several times, but Crossley has always caught up with her. Last time, a cultist she thought a dear friend betrayed her, and Crossley took her to Duncryne."

"But he has a wife there."

"I know. I saw her. The wife is in on it, of course. And tolerates Crossley's proclivities."

"Aurora may be damaged, Michael."

"I don't care. I will do everything in my power to protect her."

"But—" Lawrence didn't have the chance to continue. The door slammed open, and Violet came charging in.

"We must go at once," she said.

"Go where? Why?"

"Nora took a telephone call only two minutes before I rang. From a man, breathless and angry. He threatened her."

"Who?"

"Crossley."

"Impossible. He could barely have reached a telephone, much less found our address and telephone number."

"I don't know how, but he did. Crossley told Nora that

he was coming for you. Coming for me, and worst of all, coming for Daisy. Our little girl is in danger."

Lawrence stood and took Violet in his arms. "We'll leave at once. You too, Michael. None of us is safe." He stared into the distance, face creased with worry. "I was wrong about Crossley. He is a dangerous, immoral man without a conscience. And we have his prized possession, Aurora. There are no limits to what he might do to get her back. Home now, to protect our nearest and dearest, for tonight, we have made a mortal enemy."

Afterword

For those true crime aficionados among you, I based this book on the disappearance of twenty-nine-year-old Doctor Sophia Hickman in 1903. She disappeared in October, and outlandish theories raged in the press until a group of boys found her body in Sidmouth Plantation on 19th October 1903. Apart from my fictional solution, I have mostly kept to the facts of the case as described in the newspapers of the time.

I more loosely based fraudulent medium Jane Savage on Mrs Strutt, wife of Major Charles Henry Strutt, who attempted to defraud Henry S. H. Cavendish, a renowned African explorer. Posing as a medium, Mrs Strutt introduced Cavendish to seances, in which she conveyed spiritual messages from his late mother. The Struts seized his fortune, only relinquishing control after a judgement against them in a hearing known as The Planchette Case.

Some of you may recognise Felix Crossley from The Constance Maxwell Series. Crossley comes partly from my

Afterword

imagination and partly from a famous occultist known as the Wickedest Man in the World, who owned a property on the banks of Loch Lomond.

Next in the Lawrence Harpham series

vinci-books.com/camden

In the shadowy streets of Edwardian London, a killer leaves a trail of bodies. Only one man can stop him.

Turn the page for a free preview…

The Camden Killer: Prologue

She tilted her head, exposing a smooth, pale neck. Excitement flared inside me, and I knew I would hold my resolve. Her gloved hand carelessly stroked a sinew, her life force throbbing beneath. It would soon be mine. She stood casually against the bar, glass in hand, elbow on the sticky counter, conversing in Yiddish with her moon-faced friend. I did not understand what passed between them, but the woman reached into her pocket and produced a handful of gold and silver coins. She was not penniless as she'd led me to believe, and for a moment, I wondered whether to abort my task. Why would she take a stranger home if not for the money?

I sipped from the foul-tasting liquor I'd selected on a whim from the barman and weighed the risk against the potential reward until an unwanted presence interrupted my musings.

"Care for some company?" asked a whiskered man, not waiting for my response. He slumped on the stool beside me and I cast an irritated glance his way. He returned it benignly, huffing a sigh laced with the smell of rotting teeth and alcohol.

"She's a bit of raspberry," he said.

"Who?"

The man nodded, snorting a dewdrop from his nose. It splashed onto the grimy wooden table, and he rubbed it away with a patched sleeve. My stomach churned.

"Dora. A sight more attractive than the plain Jane she's speaking to."

He nodded to the dumpy woman by her side, smirking as he eyed her broad figure, legs like tree trunks beneath an ill-fitting dress.

"If you say so."

"Both dolly mops," he continued. "But Dora is worth twice as much as the other."

"They are young ladies, not commodities."

The man drew himself up, hands on his hips. "I beg to differ."

"I'm not interested."

"Oh, but you are. You've been watching Dora since you arrived."

"Go away," I said, recoiling from the stench of his body odour as the man slid his hand inside his coat and scratched his armpit.

"You're not very friendly," he replied, sneering beneath hooded eyelids.

I reached into my pocket and felt for my lowest denomination coin. "Take this. Buy yourself a drink and leave me alone."

His bloodshot eyes glinted as he held out a scrawny hand. I dropped the coin in his palm. He raised one eyebrow then the other as if to encourage a further donation. I ignored him.

The Camden Killer: Prologue

"Whatever you say, gov. Thanks a bunch."

The man shambled off, propping himself against the bar, temporarily blocking my view of the women. I shuffled left and took another stool, staring through the smoky tavern and contemplating my next move. I would do it soon. Time was of the essence.

The man wobbled to the far end of the room, another drink now in hand. I drained my glass, gagging at the taste, and occupied the space he'd left. The woman stopped talking and stared at me, the larger one smiling as she played with her high-necked lace collar. She was flirting but I didn't want her. Too large, too pasty, and now I was closer, too much facial hair.

"Can I buy you ladies a drink?"

They exchanged glances, immediately recognising me as a good prospect. The barman poured our drinks, and I sipped mine slowly as they clinked glasses and noisily resumed their discussion in a language I did not understand. I knew Dora spoke English, but her friend did not. I realised I must separate them or I'd lose my opportunity, but how? Then nature intervened, and the larger woman pointed towards a gaudy, red-painted door. Dora nodded. I took immediate advantage of her friend's visit to the privy.

"Rotten weather," I said.

"Better than June." Her heavily accented voice was deeper than I'd expected. Polish, perhaps, undoubtedly Jewish.

"Ah, well. Anything is in an improvement on that."

She referred to storm Ulysses and a brutal battering from the worst winds in living memory. I sympathised. I'd bunkered down during the storm and barely left my lodgings. Not so easy when your job is on the streets. She would have been out in it, however uncomfortable.

The Camden Killer: Prologue

"I haven't seen you here before."
"It's not my usual drinking abode."
"What brings you to these parts?"
"Well, a man has certain needs."
"I can help you with those."

She stared straight at me with sympathetic, velvety brown eyes and for a moment, I was almost sorry that the light would soon leave them.

"Where?"
"Up to you?"
"Not outside."
"My place then. I must tell Milka."
"I'll wait." We finished our drinks silently, Dora flashing the occasional smile while the room buzzed with chatter. A man stood, drunkenly lurched forward, and fell onto a chair which crumpled beneath his weight. Silence briefly descended, and then the drinking resumed. Nobody assisted him. Nobody cared. Milka strode towards us, barely acknowledging the unconscious man.

Dora jabbered a few words in Yiddish. Milka scowled and uttered more sharp-edged consonants, a nod, then a brief shoulder touch before wandering off without looking at me.

"Ready?"

We walked out together, proceeding down the Tottenham Court Road. I raised my collar. The wind was still high, and a scattering of swirling snowflakes settled on our shoulders. We did not converse. There was nothing to say. We eventually arrived outside a red brick townhouse on Whitfield Street with a short flight of steps leading to the raised ground floor.

Dora fumbled for her key. It slipped and I heard a tinkling sound against the pathway as it fell. She scrabbled in the darkness without success. I lit a match, and she thanked me as her hand closed over the cold metal. The door opened and we entered. All was quiet, the other tenants safely in their rooms. Dora led and I trailed behind her.

"Shall I light the fire?"

"Yes."

I examined the room, noting with satisfaction the gas lamps on the wall. Good lighting was important for setting the mood.

Dora made the fire, prodding at the kindling with a rusty poker. It spluttered to life, and only then did she remove her shawl, exposing, once again, her soft, swan-like neck. I felt a stirring and reminded myself of my purpose. I must not get distracted with earthly desires.

Dora kicked off her shoes, revealing dirty stockings with holes. That wouldn't do, or would it? The contrast of her perfectly white skin against the reality of her condition created an appealing vision. But no. I preferred the idea of Dora in all her naked glory.

"Scuse the draught," she said, gesturing to a pile of glass shards beneath a hastily patched window. What had she used to fix it? The tatty rags looked like underwear.

"No matter."

"Come on then. Don't be shy."

Dora patted her blanketed bed and smiled coquettishly. I glanced at the pile of coins on her bedside table. Why was she doing this if money was no object?

My hands reached for my pocketknife but I thought the better of it. I'd already seen something I could safely leave behind. I accepted Dora's invitation and settled beside her. She placed an icy hand on my trousers and squeezed my manhood. No finesse.

The Camden Killer: Prologue

"Take your clothes off."

Dora obliged, stripping off her dress and stays until only clad in a shift. I watched her well-honed performance as the fire spat and crackled.

"How much?"

Dora named her price. Not unreasonable.

"For services rendered."

"Then get on with it."

Her momentary irritation gave me the impetus I needed.

"Lie down," I commanded before reaching for my pocket-handkerchief.

She lay there, voluptuously running her hands through her dark brown hair. Instinctively, I placed mine around her neck and pressed hard. Much too hard. She screamed, eyes bulging, and I knew I must commit to my plan. I grabbed a large glass shard with my handkerchief and set about my task.

Dora did not die easily. She screamed once, thrashed about the bed as blood welled from the wound in her neck, then fell to the floor with a bump, gasping long, drawn breaths.

I watched, intrigued. It was everything I had hoped for and more. Crimson blood pumping from her artery, spewing over a pristine white petticoat. She gurgled. I watched. She clutched her throat, those brown eyes anguished, pleading with me to help her. But I used my time to note every detail of her demise, the way her eyes fluttered, her shuddering frame, rasping breaths, bubbles of sputum glistening in the jagged wound. Her hands were around her throat now, bitten fingernails streaked with blood, trembling hands trying to staunch the flow, a futile effort to prolong her life for a few more minutes.

The Camden Killer: Prologue

Dora Kiernicke expired on the cold floorboards of her ground-floor bedroom. But that wasn't the plan. I'd steered clear of her thrashing body and my clothes were still pristine, which is how they would remain. I stripped and dropped my garments by the door, away from the blood. Then I jammed my hands into the tightly fitting gloves she'd obligingly removed and left hanging on the bedstead. Thus protected, I heaved her still-warm body onto the bed, removed her shift and took in every aspect of her now naked body. Her tongue lolled uselessly from her mouth, spoiling the magnificent sight. I tossed the glass shard to one side and fixed my handkerchief over her face, securing it with a knot. Still not right. Work to do.

I placed her hands on her breast. Save for the handkerchief and the gash in her throat, Dora looked angelic. I pushed her hands together in a semblance of prayer. They flopped back again. Not good enough. I tried once more. Still no success, so I gazed around the shabby room with its paucity of furniture, looking for inspiration. There was nothing in the wardrobe, and the drawers were almost empty. But frayed cords swayed beside the curtains. Dora must have used them as tiebacks during the day. They would do. I took one, wound it around her wrists, and set her hands together. It worked like a dream. Dora was now in prayer. Then I tidied the room, hung up her clothes, placed her boots by the bedside, dressed myself and removed the gloves. A tidy job, well done.

Dora lay there in perfect repose while I examined her body from every aspect, prowling the room like a hungry tiger seeking the right vantage point. I knew I must remember the scene and store it in my mind's eye forever. I inhaled the aroma of burning wood, the dry metallic smell of blood against Dora's pungent perfume. Flicking my tongue out, I tasted the air and gently ran a hand over the rough blanket, recoiling at the discomforting cheap, spiky fibres that made my fingers tingle. But details mattered. Then, in one last gesture of respect, I drew the blanket over her naked body and pulled it to her chin. Dora was dead, but I would never forget her. I unlatched the door and slunk into the night.

Grab your copy...
vinci-books.com/camden

About the Author

Jacqueline Beard is a writer and genealogist living in Gloucestershire, with an East Anglian ancestry going back to the 1500s. She writes Victorian murder mysteries and is currently working on books in the Lawrence Harpham and the Constance Maxwell mystery series. Jacqueline's books are a rare mix of true crime and fiction inspired by old newspaper reports. When Jacqueline is not writing or researching "dead people," as her husband so charmingly puts it, she is walking in the glorious Cotswolds with her dog. Jacqueline enjoys technology and spends far too much time on her computer. She dislikes flying, dentists and balloons – especially red ones.